REVELATIONS

Also available from Titan Books

WAR FOR THE PLANET OF THE APES
The Official Movie Novelization (July 2017)
By Greg Cox

DAWN OF THE PLANET OF THE APES: FIRESTORM
The Official Movie Prequel
By Greg Keyes

DAWN OF THE PLANET OF THE APES
The Official Movie Novelization
By Alex Irvine

WAR FOR THE PLANET OF THE APES

REVELATIONS

GREG KEYES

BASED ON THE SCREENPLAY
WRITTEN BY MARK BOMBACK AND MATT REEVES
BASED ON CHARACTERS CREATED BY RICK JAFFA & AMANDA SILVER

TITAN BOOKS

Dedicated to Renee Hunt

WAR FOR THE PLANET OF THE APES: REVELATIONS
Print edition ISBN: 9781785654725
E-book edition ISBN: 9781785654732

Published by Titan Books
A division of Titan Publishing Group Ltd
144 Southwark Street, London SE1 0UP

First edition: June 2017
1 2 3 4 5 6 7 8 9 10

A CIP catalogue record for this title is available from the British Library.

Printed and bound in the United States.

Did you enjoy this book? We love to hear from our readers.
Please email us at readerfeedback@titanemail.com or write to us at
Reader Feedback at the above address.

To receive advance information, news, competitions, and exclusive offers
online, please sign up for the Titan newsletter on our website
www.titanbooks.com

PROLOGUE

His first bullet hit a boy.

It happened a split second after Jefferson abruptly stopped telling the story about the bar on Alki Beach and the nastiest drink he had ever had; his words were cut short by the sniper's bullet knocking the wind and the life out of him. That's when McCullough saw the figure in the gray raincoat, hood shadowing his face, the black hollow of a shotgun barrel looking him not quite in the eye.

McCullough had been here before, many times. Sometimes he tried not to pull the trigger; sometimes he imagined the first round missing, so that the boy in the raincoat turned, and he got a good look at him—the wide, brown eyes, the smooth cheeks that had no use for a razor. But whatever he wished, his bullet always arrived, and the boy slumped against the concrete wall, his hood falling back to reveal a face full of surprise, amazement even. He couldn't have been more than thirteen.

The rain was between drizzle and a mist, as it had been for months; the wooly, low clouds hid the highest of Seattle's skyscrapers from sight, and overnight a core-chilling haze had crept down from the Cascades and flowed like dishwater through the streets. A hand-chalked sign advertising a daily special of soup and grilled cheese still stood in front of an empty café; once cheerful neon across the street, now dead and colorless. And just below a shop window advertising old-fashioned toys sat the boy, dying. At first he stared at the hole in his chest, but then he looked up and saw McCullough. McCullough felt his mouth open—had he been going to say something to the boy? What?

But then all hell broke loose, and McCullough heard himself instead yelling for his men to find cover as fire bombs that smelled like turpentine spattered nearby. He turned the barrel of his rifle to the man off to his two o'clock who had just missed him twice, an older guy with another shotgun and a gray stubble of beard and glasses that rendered him essentially faceless. He squeezed off two rounds and the man took two or three steps back before his legs gave out and he stumbled down into the clutter of paper and hemlock needles that covered the street.

Then another round from the unseen sniper clipped his ribs. It skipped off his body armor, but he still felt the shock go through him, like a breath he hadn't taken. He ducked back behind the brick wall. Forest was there, young, wide-eyed, staring down at Jefferson, who looked almost as if he'd lain down to watch the low clouds slide slowly by. The hole in his head proved otherwise, and McCullough noticed that it was the work of a high-power rifle, not a shotgun. The boy hadn't killed Jefferson, or the man in the spectacles.

"Forest," he grunted. "He's gone. Snap out of it. I need you to spot the shooter."

She looked up at him, saw his face, and her gaze hardened.

"Yes, sir," she said.

"He hit Jefferson the second we came around the corner," he said. "That means he must be somewhere between eleven and three. When I cross the street, he'll shoot, and you take a look."

"Sir…"

Instead of waiting for her protest, he let out his breath and sprinted past Jefferson's body, across the open ground to cover that seemed miles away, although it couldn't really be more than twenty feet.

He didn't hear the bullet hit anything, but his ears caught the now-familiar report of the high-caliber weapon. Someone else took a shot at him, too, but fortune stayed with him, and he rolled to cover behind a long-abandoned SUV. The sniper's rifle sang again.

He looked over at Forest, who was just returning to cover.

"Got him," she said. "Third-story window."

"Can you get a grenade in there?"

She squinted her eyes a little, thinking, remembering the layout and then nodded. "Yes, sir."

"Okay. I'll give you some cover."

He lifted himself up to peek through the passenger-side window, and a bullet smacked into the vehicle.

He counted three, then stood and began firing at the third floor of the apartment building. He saw a flicker of motion in one of the rooms, heard the sharp, pneumatic exhalation of Forest's grenade launcher. Orange flame belched from the window, and for a moment he saw the silhouette of a man with arms spread wide—then only smoke.

That wasn't the end of the fight, but after that it all grew hazy. There were a lot of them. If the so-called militia had been well trained, McCullough and his people wouldn't have walked out of the ambush with only two casualties— in fact, they probably wouldn't have come out of it at all.

But what he was fighting was not another army, just a bunch of people with guns. It was the difference between disciplined Roman troops and sword-waving barbarians, and in under half an hour the area was secure.

The boy wasn't dead yet, but he wasn't a danger, either. His shotgun lay ignored and his hands were clasped over the hole his soul was leaking out of.

McCullough stood there for a moment, watching his death complete.

Again. And once more, he opened his mouth to say something, as if there was something *to* say, but he couldn't find the words he was looking for. There were no words.

McCullough jerked awake, vaguely aware someone was talking, but the words were staticky, half formed, as if from a radio station far, far away.

"What?" he snapped.

"Sorry, Colonel." The static vanished; the syllables sharpened into language, and a familiar voice.

"You said to wake you before morning," she said.

It was Forest, in fatigues, her cap in her hand at her side, looking a little apologetic. She looked older than in his dream, her short, curly hair now had iron among the onyx, and wrinkles bunched at the corners of her lips and eyes. To look at her, the ten years since that day might just as easily have been twenty.

He knew the same could be said for him.

McCullough took a deep breath and smoothed his hand from his forehead back to the middle of his nearly hairless scalp. He was in his cabin on the *Daedalus*, lying on his bunk in his undershirt and fatigue pants. His dog tags jingled as he sat up.

"Anything to report?"

"Nothing important, sir. We left the Sound a few hours ago. The Captain is waiting on you for his briefing."

"Good," he said. "Tell him I'll be there in five."

"Yes, Colonel."

He took the Beretta M9 from under his pillow and holstered it, then reached for his shirt.

He had stopped counting how many times he'd had the nightmare. A decade had passed since he fired that fatal shot. It hadn't been the first time he'd killed someone—that had been years before, in a very different war, in a land so distant it now seemed like a dream itself. The circumstances had been similar—an ambush—and he had felt it, deep in his gut, the ending of that other life. But it had been necessary, and that was what soldiers did, had always done, since the first days of human civilization. What his father and his grandfather had done, and their fathers before them. Dying was part of the job description, but so was killing. That first man had had a mother and a father, probably a wife and children he loved. Yet McCullough had never lost sleep over him, never had a nightmare about him, much less one that visited him every few months like a spiteful ghost.

Not like the boy. Why? It hadn't been his decision to put a gun in the hands of a thirteen-year-old and point him at trained, hardened federal troops. And in some times and places, a boy that age was already a man. He had met such young men, in the last decade, their eyes as dead and cold as diamonds, childish ways long forgotten or never experienced, stone killers in adolescent bodies.

But maybe that was why the boy beneath the toy sign left his mark in McCullough so deeply. That was in Seattle, way back in the beginning, when the plague first began its ghastly march, when the militias first started to form and fester like pus in a wound. That kid hadn't been a soldier.

McCullough had seen that in his eyes. He was just a boy. The only prior combat he had ever known had probably been on a gaming console.

No, his death was notable because it had marked the end of something, the loss of a country and a world that had the luxury to think of children as something to be protected from the worst life had to offer. But that had always been a sort of delusion, hadn't it? A part of the weakness that had set them all up to fall so far. In that one thing, maybe the militias had been right. The human race could no longer afford childhood. Maybe one day, when it was all over, there could be such a thing as children again.

But not now. Now he was approaching the crucible where this world had been formed, ground zero for the virus that had wiped out—by some estimates—ninety percent of humanity. It had begun as an attempt to cure Alzheimer's disease by means of virus therapy. He thought he understood the theory well enough; viruses weren't living things in and of themselves, but packages of genetic information that hijacked living cells, altering them and producing more—duplicate—virus packages. By inserting their own genetic material into viruses—meant to replace or amend the faulty genes that created Alzheimer's— scientists had believed the disease could be erased from its victims' genetic code.

Apparently, it had worked on a single test subject—the inventor's father—for a short period. Then the disease had come back, worse than ever, and killed him.

But it had a different effect on the apes who were its first test subjects; it made them smarter. And then, one day, in a lab accident, the human-engineered virus got loose. The drug company—Gen-Sys—was able to cover up the accident long enough for the fast-growing infection to spread beyond the possibility of containment, and within days, hundreds were dropping dead, then thousands, then millions. The disease was brutal. It spread quickly and it killed fast, and nothing anyone did seemed to have any effect on it. That wasn't for want of trying. When medicine didn't provide any solutions, people found their own, blaming the epidemic on everything and everyone imaginable. Lynch mobs formed, determined to isolate and burn alive anyone who had the disease or who was thought to have been exposed, and shortly some of those mobs became more systematized. Survivors broke basically into two sorts of organizations; people who banded together to survive and preserve some semblance of civilization, and those who defined the problem as "us" and "them," in which "them"—whoever their chosen scapegoats happened to be—were fair game for "us" to exterminate.

There were a lot more of the latter than the former, and he'd spent a decade now fighting the more virulent of them. Some justified what they did through religion, others by means of other sorts of ideology, pseudo-science, racial or political beliefs.

Then, of course, there were those who were essentially thieves and murderers, opportunists for whom the world falling apart was just a chance to get theirs. He had met a lot of those. He realized something, as he reached for his jacket. In years past, he'd come awake from the dream with his heart pounding, his throat tight with remorse. Now and then, he'd even discovered his cheeks were damp.

But now he felt—free, somehow. Lighter. Because after all those years of fighting and killing and watching men and women die, something had finally changed. Like childhood, remorse was something the world no longer had any use for—and he, for one, was damn sure better off without it.

* * *

Blue Eyes found Ash where Koba had thrown him, on the hard, cold floor of the human building. His half-open eyes were misted and sunken in; dried blood was caked around his nostrils and congealed in a pool on the stone. Flies had settled on his lips and nose. Blue Eyes took his friend's arm and pulled on it, but it felt slack, like a rope. Then he yanked harder as something he didn't understand rushed up through him and suddenly exploded like a flash of light and heat inside of his head. He pushed Ash's face, and then hit him, hit him harder, punched him again and again until he was shrieking and striking the dead chimp with all his might. Unfeeling, uncaring, Ash took the blows, which only made Blue Eyes angrier, and he kept hitting Ash until long, strong arms wrapped around him from behind, pulling him into a thick, hairy chest. Raging, he turned his fury on his abductor, beating at him until his arms tired and he finally fell to whimpering, holding his hand up to his forehead and wiggling his middle finger in the same sign, over and over.

Why?

Eventually, the anger faded, but he didn't feel better. He felt as if something had been taken out of him, something he hadn't known was there, and which could now never be put back.

He realized it was Maurice holding him, looking down at him with concern.

"Why?" he asked the big orangutan. "Why is he dead?"

"Koba threw him from up there," Maurice said, indicating the balcony high above.

Blue Eyes stared at Maurice, wondering how such a wise old ape could be so stupid. The hair of Maurice's head was also matted with blood, where a bullet from Koba's gun had grazed him. Koba the killer, who shot Blue Eyes' father Caesar and blamed it on the humans. Koba who started the war in which so many died. Koba who killed Ash with his own hands.

"Ape not kill ape," Blue Eyes signed, angrily, snarling the word "kill" as best he could. "You taught me that."

"Koba was twisted inside. Man twisted him. You might understand, if you went through what he did. Why do you hit Ash?"

"He won't get up!"

"He's dead," Maurice signed.

"I know that! I knew when he hit the floor he was dead!"

But so much had been going on, and he had been so afraid himself. Of the guns, and the noise, the humans—and Koba. He was terrified he would share Ash's fate. He had dared not go to Ash's body then. And then after that, there hadn't been any time to think, to reflect or understand. Too much was going on.

But now, now that the fighting was done, and there was a pause, and he found Ash's body, so still, so small looking, so empty of everything that made Ash Ash...

"Why?" he asked again. "I know *how* he died. But why?"

"Koba wanted to make an example of him," Maurice replied.

"No," Blue Eyes persisted. "Why did he die? Why did any of them die? Why does it happen?"

Maurice loosened his hold a bit and leaned back, although he kept Blue Eyes cradled in his arms. Blue Eyes realized that a circle of apes was staring at him, but they soon shifted their gaze as Tinker—Ash's mother—folded down upon the corpse of her boy, wrapping him in her arms. Rocket sat nearby, his eyes like dark pits, staring at his dead son with no real expression.

"I don't know," Maurice said. "Apes die. Humans die. Everything dies."

Blue Eyes still felt Maurice didn't understand. He *knew*

that. Apes had died before. He remembered Sara, who was old, and one day stopped breathing. And one of the gorillas, Zara, had delivered a baby that had lived for less than a night. Keling, an orangutan, broke his arm and died a few days later of fever. In words—in signs—Blue Eyes knew what death was. He could *say* someone was dead. But until now, he had never truly wondered what it *meant*. What it meant was that Ash would never poke fun at him again, that they would never spear fish together, joke, wrestle, speculate about girls. Ash was gone.

"I'm mad at him," he told Maurice. "Mad because he provoked Koba. Mad that he's dead. Mad because he left me."

"I know," the orang said, then tapped his chest, where Blue Eyes had been pummeling him a few moments before.

"I'm sorry I hit you."

The big ape shrugged and raised his hand to his head wound, then lightly touched Blue Eyes' still-healing gashes, the claw marks the bear had given him what seemed like a lifetime ago.

"Pain is here, on the surface," the orangutan signed. Then he touched his head. "Pain is here, too, much deeper."

Blue Eyes looked down at Ash again, at his whimpering mother, lost in her grief, at Rocket's forlorn expression.

"Where did Ash go?" he asked.

"Away. Far, far away."

"What do we do with—that?" He nodded at Ash's body.

"Does it matter?" Maurice asked.

Somehow, Blue Eyes thought that it did.

"What have we done in the past?"

Maurice cocked his head. "It's always been up to the family. When Sara died, her children put her in a tree in the forest, with her favorite digging-stick. Pan too, with his good spear." His eyes widened. "Never thought about it," he said. "I guess a lot of the chimps do that, lay them

14

up in trees where the wolves and dogs can't get them. But that was after. Before, when we were human captives, the humans took the dead ones away. And those who were born wild—I don't know what they did before we all awoke. I doubt any of them remember."

"What do humans do?"

Maurice patted the side of his head. "I'm not sure," he said. "Ask Malcolm. Or your father might know. He knew humans in a different way than most of us."

Blue Eyes looked back at Ash. "I want to do something for him," he said.

"I know."

But he didn't do anything. Rocket and Tinker took the body away, and Blue Eyes was left feeling emptier than ever. He climbed up into the ruins of the tower. His father had decided to move the troop away from it; explosives set by the humans had rendered it unstable. He watched from a leaning girder as both humans and apes filed away from the place, going in different directions.

He heard the soft padding of another ape approaching.

"Caesar should not have let the humans go."

It was Fox, a chimp just slightly younger than Blue Eyes. Behind him were Flint and Shell, also chimpanzees.

Fox was larger than his name implied, big for a chimp his age. It was the way his eyes moved that gave him his name—furtive, quick, intelligent.

"The only thing they did wrong was to fight back against Koba," Blue Eyes said. He felt a resurgence of his earlier anger. Fox, always quick to notice such things, backed down.

Shell, however, did not.

"We will have to fight them again," he said.

"I don't think so," Blue Eyes replied.

"More humans are coming," Shell said, scratching at

his nearly white ear, from which he got his name. "We all know that."

Blue Eyes raised up a little.

"Shell," Fox said. "Stop. He's upset about Ash."

"Ash shouldn't have—" Shell began, but Fox silenced him with a sharp bark. Shell retreated to the next beam down, although he looked a little confused.

"Do you want something, Fox?" Blue Eyes asked.

"I saw you with Ash. I miss him too."

"Do you?" Blue Eyes asked. "You followed Koba."

"You did, too," Fox signed. "I never wanted anything to happen to Ash." He shifted on his perch, and then made a little sign, his hands on his chest held like wings, flapping.

"Remember?" Fox said. "When we were all young?"

Blue Eyes did remember, although he hadn't thought about it in a long time.

"The butterflies," he said.

"I remember," Shell signed, from his little exile. "Ash, he tried to catch one, and he fell backwards off a branch into the water."

Flint hooted with laughter, and Blue Eyes felt his anger melting away. He remembered the years they had all spent together, the often-boring afternoons in Maurice's school, the pranks they had played on Keling, the old orangutan, before he died.

Blue Eyes patted Fox on the shoulder.

"Back then," Blue Eyes said, "all I wanted to do was grow up, be an adult. Now I miss those days."

"Me too," Fox said.

Winter watched Luca pick up the gun, check it, and then sling the strap over his shoulder.

"I want to go," he signed to Luca.

"No," Luca said. "You stay here."

"But I want to fight the humans too."

Luca came over on all fours and then raised up. Winter slumped slightly, submitting.

"Here," Luca said.

"It's because of my fur, isn't it?" Winter said. "You're afraid they'll see me because I'm white."

"No," Luca said. "That's not it. You have a purpose already, here, with the women. Your father was one of the first in the gorilla guard. I promised him you would take his place one day."

Part of Winter wanted to keep arguing; he didn't want anyone to think he was a coward. But he had seen what happened to those killed by the human weapons.

"I don't remember my father."

"I know," Luca said. "But this is what he would want. It's what I want."

"I'm not afraid to fight," Winter said.

Luca lowered himself a bit.

"I know you aren't. If the women and children are threatened, I know you will protect them."

He touched Winter with his calloused knuckles, and then went to join Caesar and the others.

1

Ray walked his fingers across the gun again, wishing he had his spear instead. He'd made the spear himself, from the straight-grained wood of an ash sapling. He and his father had spent days searching for just the right tree. Then his father had built a small fire as Ray sharpened the end of his weapon with a flake of broken glass. Afterwards, he'd learned how to harden the point by turning it slowly above the flames. It was a good memory; his father wasn't around a lot, when he was little, but when he was it always seemed wonderful, ripe fruit in his hands, already peeled.

And yet he had complained.

"Why can't I have a blade?" he'd asked. Many of the other apes in the colony lashed sharpened bone or stone to their shafts. A few even had pieces of human metal.

"Blades break," his father had explained, patiently, in the hand language. "Bindings come undone. This is simple. When it dulls, you can reshape it in the fire again. This weapon will not fail you."

"But their spears are sharper," he had said.

"This will work," his father insisted.

Ray had grumbled a little more, and when they

returned to Ape Village, he'd felt small, inadequate with his simple weapon. Others had similar spears, but more had the fancier versions. Blue Eyes and Ash, for instance. For him, the spear his father helped him make only served to emphasize that his status was lower than theirs.

And yet his weapon survived his first hunt, as so many did not. And while the first wound he made might not have killed the elk, it certainly took most of the fight out of it.

He understood how the spear worked. How to make one. How to fix it. It was made from something alive, like him, and had always seemed warm to the touch, a part of him, of the forest and water and sky.

The gun was alien, cold, dead-feeling. He knew how to make it work, but not *how* it worked, and he was certain that if it broke he couldn't fix it. That it was a fearsome weapon, there could be no doubt. He had watched both man and ape die in the thunder and flame guns made, although he wasn't sure any bullet he had fired had hit anyone. It had all been too noisy and confusing.

What he did know was that his father had been killed by a weapon like this. A spear would have killed him, too, but somehow that would have been easier to understand. It would have made more sense.

He had offered Caesar his gun after the battle with the humans, after Koba was dead, but the leader had given it back to him.

"This is how we must fight now," he'd said.

Then Ray had been sent here, on the cliff-side overlooking the sea, to watch. He wasn't alone; apes were stretched out all along the line where land met the vast water, and on the great, creaking metal bridge that crossed the gap where water came into the land. Most, in fact, were on the bridge. Ray was glad he was not among them. Like the gun, the bridge was cold and lifeless, and he did not trust it. Better to be here, with the rocks and trees and sandy beach below.

But watching was boring, especially because there was nothing to see. The fog shrouded everything, and though he liked idle time, it seemed to him there was too much of it.

He put the gun down and sidled away from it, careful that the death-dealing hole in the end was pointed away from him. On impulse, he climbed up a nearby tree, but of course it didn't do anything to improve visibility, at least not of the ocean. But there was a breeze there, a little chilly, but nice, and he swayed for a while with his eyes closed.

The dawn came gently, waking the fog into a glowing cloud. And in it, he saw—something.

He climbed a little higher to get a better look. Whatever it was floated out on the water, and it was pretty big, although its actual shape was still concealed. At first he thought it might be a killer whale, like the ones he had seen the year before off the shore by the forest. But it was bigger, and angular, like something a human would make. It was moving, slowly. Caesar had predicted the humans would come by sea. This had to be them, didn't it? Come in human-made whales of some sort?

He was about to start down when he overheard voices. Human voices.

It had only been days since he had first heard human speech, and now he was sorry he ever had. Nothing good had come of it. Caesar seemed to trust some of them and now suddenly Blue Eyes seemed to agree with him. Maybe they were right, and some of the bare-skinned creatures were good.

But if so, Ray couldn't tell the good from the bad.

There were a lot of them, and they were getting close. And their guns were in their hands, not lying on the cliff like his. Ray gauged the distance and knew he couldn't make it back down in time if they were hostile.

Maybe they were friendly, and just going to help Caesar on the bridge.

But maybe they weren't.

His father had named him Ray. He said it was because when he first saw him, just after he was born, it was like seeing a flash of the sun. Quick, bright, hidden again. But his friends said it was a good name because of the way he made up his mind.

Quickly, in a flash.

So he dropped from the tree toward the cliff-side, which here was really more of a very steep slope. He felt weight leave him, and a great rush of air.

"Shit!" someone shouted. "That's one of them!"

As he crashed into the slanting earth, grasping for handholds in the scrubby trees, he heard the unmistakable, ear-splitting cadence of gunfire.

"Stop it!" he heard someone shout. "Don't shoot, you idiot!"

"Too late," another one said. "They sure as hell heard that. Come on, you bastards! Double time!"

Ray didn't try to sort out what they were going on about. They had tried to kill him, and that was all he needed to know. He raced along the hillside, springing from one precarious hold to another, toward the bridge, trying desperately to reach it before they did.

John looked out over water as flat and dull as iron. Dawn was lurking out there somewhere in the east, but at the moment it was no more than a faint gray promise in the dense fog that rolled over the waters and cloaked the ship in its damp folds.

Behind him, he heard the hollow tap of boots on the

deck. The rhythm of the stride was as familiar as his own heartbeat.

"Colonel," he said, turning.

"Lieutenant," the Colonel said. Then, with a little smile, "John."

John glanced around, but no one else was within earshot. Of course they weren't. It wasn't that it was a secret—everyone was aware that the Colonel was his father—but it was rare the Colonel used his given name. It felt a little wrong. And it reminded him of times he would almost rather forget, back when home and war were two different things. When his mother was still alive.

And yet now there was something in his father's expression, a light behind his eyes, like he had a secret he was bursting to tell.

But if that was so, he didn't tell it. Instead he fixed his regard out through the fog.

"Did you sleep well?" the Colonel asked.

"No, sir," John said. "I took the night watch. I wanted to be up when we arrived."

The Colonel nodded approvingly, then gestured to where the vaguest outline of land was beginning to form.

"What do you see?" he asked.

"Not much, sir. I thought they had re-established electricity, but there's not a single light burning. At least not so as one that gets through the fog. I thought they were going to set a beacon, or something."

"They did restore power," the Colonel replied. "But it's not clear how large an area they restored it to. Our communications with them were spotty and—precipitously terminated. If they set a beacon, like they said—well, it's either not strong enough for the fog, or someone turned it off."

"You think the apes did it?" he asked. "Turned the power off?"

The Colonel shrugged, and for a moment was silent. Then he cleared his throat, the way he always did when he was about to quote something.

"*Hither have fared to thee far-come men*," he murmured, "*o'er the paths of the ocean.*"

John struggled for a moment, trying to source the passage. Finally, he settled for an educated guess.

"*Beowulf*, sir?"

That got him another approving nod, this time with the slightest of grins.

"At least your education wasn't completely useless," the Colonel said. His tone was low, conversational, and John knew for certain that this was one of those infrequent moments when they were father and son, not colonel and lieutenant.

"It's pretty obvious," John said, following the bluff out. "Beowulf was way up in Geatland or wherever, and he heard about this monster, Grendel, that was giving some people a hard time—"

"Rippin' people's limbs off and drinkin' their blood?" his father interjected. "You *might* call that a hard time."

"Right," John said. "So he sailed across the ocean to Heorot and ripped off Grendel's arm."

"Yep."

John waited a moment, to see if his father had some further point to make, and decided he probably was waiting on him to speak instead.

"So," John said. "These apes. You think they're Grendel? Monsters?"

His father shrugged. "I don't know what they are," he admitted. "There was so little information about them before everything started falling apart. Stories about them breaking out of zoos and labs. About apes fighting their way across the Golden Gate Bridge. That happened—I've

24

actually seen footage of that. They say they got smart, somehow, that the plague that killed so many of us made them better. But we had so much more to worry about— until the distress call came, most everyone had assumed they were all dead, and that most of the rumors weren't true anyway. Hell, that could still be the case. It wouldn't be the first time that some group of survivors lost touch with reality."

"But you think they're real."

His father shrugged again. "Something happened. If we believe the transmissions from the locals, they had pulled things together here, created at least a little order from madness. They got a hydroelectric plant going—no small thing. They were on their way to a new start. But we got all of that as part of a distress call, and we haven't heard a peep out of them since. They said the apes were attacking them. With guns."

"Maybe it was one of the weirder militias," John suggested. "Remember those guys who painted their faces? The nuts who believed the apes were the messengers of God, sent to cleanse the Earth? They had that gross shrine in that old library?"

"Yeah," his father said. "Maybe. But this is where the apes were. If they exist, this is where they would be. We'll see. That's job number one—find out what the hell is going on down here. It might just be one of the usual situations, or it might have been some kind of hoax and we'll find them all singing 'Kumbaya' in the dark. But somehow I doubt it."

John understood something then.

"You want it to be true," he said.

For a moment, his father didn't say anything. But then he nodded, slowly.

"We've been fighting each other for too long, son," he

said. "What if, while we were distracted with killing each other—something else was quietly stepping up to take our place? Another species? What if—in our hubris—we created our own replacements?" He rubbed his head. "I'm so tired of killing men, son. A Grendel or two would be a nice change."

John felt his throat tighten.

"If these people need a Beowulf, sir, I know you're their man."

His father grinned skeptically.

"You're not suggesting the old man has delusions of grandeur, are you?"

"Not while he outranks me. Sir." But he was smiling, too.

His father clapped him on the back. Then, in a moment, his face changed, subtly, and he was the Colonel again. Thinking about something, intensely. Processing.

"You hear that?" he asked, after a moment.

"No, sir. I don't hear anything."

"That's right. No gunfire. No explosions. I'm willing to bet whatever was happening here is over, one way or the other—at least for the time being. So I think we can take our time. Ah, there's the light."

The gray sky had begun to bloom coral and now, rather abruptly, the east caught fire with orange radiance. The fog had transfigured into a deep saffron haze, and through it something immense began to emerge—an unmistakable work of man, sky-reaching beams and girders, suspended by what appeared to be spider web but must actually be cables of immense strength. John knew without asking that it was the Golden Gate Bridge. He had seen pictures of it when he was younger.

It was a moment for silence, but in a few seconds the stillness was interrupted by sharp, distant reports.

"There's your gunfire, sir," John said.

"Well, I've been wrong before," the Colonel allowed. He raised his voice.

"Everyone in positions," he said. "Lieutenant, you stay here and await my orders from the bridge."

2

Caesar barked, low in the back of his throat.

"What is it?" Rocket signed.

"I was starting to hope," Caesar replied in kind. Then he stretched his right hand toward the shape in the fog.

"That's a ship?" Rocket said. He got the "ship" sign a little wrong. It was new to him. But Caesar remembered learning it from a picture book, and then later, one time when Will, his human adoptive father, took him down to the docks, he had used it, over and over.

"Yes, ship," Caesar said, forming the sign correctly. "Six days," he said. "It was not enough."

Maurice came hulking up beside him, leaning on his palms. His head had been bandaged, but the stained cloth was in disarray, because despite instruction to the contrary from the human healer Ellie, Maurice couldn't stop fiddling with it.

The orangutan hadn't come alone. A human—Malcolm—was with him. He looked tired, but his blue eyes shone with a fierce, determined light that Caesar was becoming accustomed to.

"There's still a chance it doesn't have to come to this."

Caesar cut his eyes away. He thought back to when the man had come alone to the Ape Village, beaten, bullied, and humiliated the whole way. And yet he had still had the courage to stand his ground, place his life in the balance for what he believed his people needed. And later, he'd stood against his own kind for what he thought was right. He had been no less stubborn after the fight with Koba, when they learned that Dreyfus and his men had managed to contact other humans. Caesar had to admit, he had benefited from the man staying around. Malcolm was no warrior, but he knew more about warfare than Caesar did. They had spoken of tactics, and he had learned a little about explosives, such as those Dreyfus had used to try and destroy them.

"Will they go under the bridge?" he asked Malcolm.

"I don't know," the human admitted. "I told you it would depend upon what kind of ship they came in. What kind of draft… um, how deep in the water the bottom sits. If it has a deep bottom, they have to come into the harbor to dock. If it's some kind of amphibious assault ship, they could land on the beach—or almost anywhere."

"They came to the bridge," Caesar said.

"Right," Malcolm said. "That argues for a deep draft. Or maybe they're just checking things out. Look, this could be a good thing. You have decent command of the entrance to the harbor. They'll think those barrels you have floating down there are bombs. So with any luck, they'll stop to talk, rather than just rushing in. It would be nice if some of the radio equipment had survived so we could have talked with them already, but as it is I can still help with that."

Caesar felt suddenly a little dizzy. Rocket noticed and stepped closer, supporting him, but not too obviously. Where he had summoned the energy to fight Koba, Caesar did not know, but in the days following he had felt—weak. The bullet wound that had nearly killed him was far from healed, not to mention the fall and blows he'd taken on the tower. He needed rest, but there was no respite to be had. He had considered retreating back into the wilderness, hiding again, as they had once before. But he had come to believe that if he did not stop the humans from entering the city, he would not be able to stop them anywhere. And everyone was here now, the women, the children, the aged—including his own wife and infant son.

Above all, Caesar believed that the apes had to show strength—and retreating into the trees would only reveal the opposite.

They had weapons. They were looking down on their enemies from above. This was the place to be. From here they could win, he was sure of it. But what if more ships came, more humans? His army was already tired and had lost more lives in a handful of days than in the whole count of winters since fleeing the city. He had beaten Koba, and the rest of the troop would follow him; he knew that. And because they would follow him, he could not lead them to their doom. He had to be worthy of their trust. In the nearly ten years of peace, he had felt that burden lessen. But now it had returned, weighing on his neck more than ever.

"How could we talk to them?" he asked Malcolm.

"Caesar," Rocket grunted, a gentle remonstration. Caesar straightened, took all of his weight back on his own feet and glared at his second-in-command. Rocket's head dropped slightly in submission.

"Flags," Malcolm said. "We could hang a white sheet or something from the bridge. That would get their attention. Or I could go down to the shore and hail them—"

He was interrupted by reports in the distance.

"What's that?" Rocket asked.

"Guns," Caesar said. "Over toward the beach. Who is watching there?"

"Ray," Rocket said. "Hector's son."

Caesar thought about that. Ray was two years younger than his own eldest son, Blue Eyes. He was on the impulsive side, and had recently lost his father. Had he fired at the ship? Or was he just signaling that he had seen it?

Or was something else entirely going on?

"Rocket," he said. "Take six. Go see."

"Yes, Caesar," Rocket said.

"The ship is moving again," Malcolm said, suddenly.

Caesar looked back out to sea. Indeed, the ship seemed to be drawing closer. He could make out more detail now. It was longer than it was wide, sharp in the nose. It bent up in the middle, where he could make out windows. It was like an odd-shaped, floating building.

"I don't know much about Navy ships," Malcolm said. "But by the look of her she needs a dock." He hesitated. "And she has some big guns. There—and there. Maybe more that I don't see."

Caesar stared at the stubby projections Malcolm indicated. The human wasn't exaggerating—if those were really guns, they were the biggest Caesar had ever seen, bigger by far than those he remembered from the helicopters that had come after him years ago. What would guns that size do?

"How many humans could it carry?"

Malcolm took a moment.

"A hundred, maybe. Maybe half again that. It's just a guess."

Caesar nodded. Better. If Malcolm was right, apes outnumbered humans. Maybe there could be a peace. He began to think Malcolm's idea of a flag was a good one.

★ ★ ★

Blue Eyes was watching the ship when the first bullet whizzed by and hit the guard rail a few inches from his hand. At first he didn't know what it was; he heard something striking the metal, and looked to see if someone had cast a pebble at him, as a joke.

Then he recognized the clatter of guns.

He had been stationed near the south end of the bridge; the Golden Gate was long, very long, and in general the plan had been to cover the whole length of it, and then they could all move to wherever the ship tried to pass beneath. No one knew quite what to expect, and in typical fashion, Caesar's plans were flexible, designed to quickly cope with the unexpected.

And this was unexpected. The ship was just arriving from out at sea—but the shooting was from the end of the bridge. How had they managed that? Was there more than one ship? Maybe there were twenty, pouring humans forth all up and down the shore.

He remembered Ash's dead body, and all of the dead, both humans and apes, he'd seen. Death had come for them and now, he knew, it had come for him.

"Blue Eyes!" Shell snapped. "I told you. I told you we would have to fight them again!"

Fox was crouched just past Shell.

"Blue Eyes," Fox said. "You shoot, so the humans have to duck down. We'll move up."

Blue Eyes nodded, although he was only vaguely aware of what Fox was saying. But when the two chimps suddenly sprinted forward, it registered. He straightened up, propped his gun on the car, and aimed at the oncoming humans.

But terror gripped his every bone and muscle; a tiny part of his mind was screaming for him to move, but he couldn't. Down toward the end of the bridge he saw the hairless faces staring at him, the deadly muzzles of their weapons, and knew it was all over. He saw Fox and Shell jump back as bullets spattered right next to them. Fox shot him a glance full of anger and contempt, but for Blue Eyes, it didn't matter. Nothing did.

Then something hit him, hard, something furry and familiar, knocking him to the surface of the bridge as rounds tore through the air like angry hornets.

He found himself staring into the dark eyes of another ape.

"Ray?"

Ray was small for an orangutan, wiry, with an odd and distinctive spray of yellowish hair on the side of his head. He panted like he was out of breath.

"Keep your head down," Ray said. Then Ray raised up, screeching the predator alarm, ducking quickly as another swarm of death smacked into the car he'd dragged Blue Eyes behind.

Ray blinked at Blue Eyes.

"Your gun!" he signed. "Shoot back at them! Fox and Shell are in trouble!"

Blue Eyes nodded, trying to get his brain to work, to pull the breath in and out of his body, but all he could think about was the darkness awaiting him, the nothingness a bullet would bring with it. He tried willing himself to sit up, but nothing happened.

When Ray took his gun from him, he didn't object, but lay there, wishing for it to all go away as the weapon began its deafening roar.

Caesar heard a commotion down the bridge in the direction he'd sent Rocket. A moment later, one of the chimps Rocket had taken with him reappeared.

"Humans," he signed. "Many, with guns."

"Oh, no, no, no," Malcolm said. "Goddamn it, no!"

Caesar regarded the human. He knew who the attackers must be, just as Malcolm did.

"I spared them, as you asked me to," Caesar said. "They were supposed to leave."

"They were," Malcolm said. "Let me talk to them—" He started forward.

Gunfire suddenly erupted at the other end of the bridge, much closer than before, and many guns rather than one.

"No," Caesar barked. "You go now. Malcolm, you go."

Malcolm shook his head. "I can still—"

"Take him," Caesar signed to Luca, the big gorilla regarding all of this from a few feet away.

Luca grunted and grabbed Malcolm by the arm.

"Wait—" Malcolm protested.

Caesar ignored him. He picked up his rifle and started toward the gunfire.

He remembered the last battle on this bridge far too well—unarmed apes pitted against the guns of the humans. They had won, but at great cost. He had hoped to never fight such a battle again, much less in the same place. It was as if he could not escape the past; no matter how far he tried to push it away, it kept coming back to him. Would Koba somehow return as well? Or another like him?

Halfway to the south end, he found many of his apes crouched behind a partial barricade of wrecked cars. Blue Eyes was one of them, his eyes wild. Ray had Blue Eyes' gun, and was shooting at the humans advancing toward them, who were also using the old vehicles for cover. He couldn't be sure how many their attackers numbered.

Where had the humans gotten the guns? He had disarmed all of Dreyfus' surviving followers and had them escorted from the city. Were there further weapon storehouses to the south that he did not know about?

He dodged ahead to where Rocket took cover behind an overturned truck.

"How many?" he asked.

Rocket held up both hands three times, then shrugged.

Caesar risked a glance.

He nodded at several orangs crouched nearby.

"Swing below the bridge and get behind them," he told the orangutans. "Let's make this short."

Once on the bridge of the *Daedalus*, McCullough scanned the scene with field glasses, trying to work out what he was seeing. Part of him still had trouble believing it, although he had been mentally preparing himself for this for nearly a week.

The single unquestionable fact was that there was a firefight going on between two groups, the first of which mostly occupied—and seemed to have control of – the Golden Gate. The others—a much smaller group, from what he could see—were trying to push onto the bridge from the south.

His first impression was that the bridge defenders were soldiers in uniform and the attackers were some sort of rag-tag militia. But like one of those pictorial illusions that looked alternately like an old or a young woman, or a hare or a duck, this perception was a visual sleight-of-hand. The defenders were relatively uniform but were not *in* uniform. In fact, a moment of clear observation revealed that they were naked except for the fur that naturally grew on their bodies. Everything about them was wrong to his practiced eye—the way they stood, moved, crouched, waved their too-long arms, carried their guns. Guns! Not to mention that some of them were now swinging arm-over-arm beneath the bridge, probably to try and get behind the humans attacking them.

So this was the real thing. They really were apes. With military weapons.

"I'll be damned," he said.

"Colonel, those guys are about to get their asses handed to them. Sir."

That was Captain Hayes, a square-jawed Hoosier with sandy hair and narrow, slightly hunched shoulders. He moved with a limp from taking a shotgun pellet to the knee. There could be no doubt which side he was talking about, both in terms of who was winning and losing and who they ought to be rooting for.

"They are," McCullough said. "My guess is the apes got wind we were on the way and set up to ambush us from the bridge. These guys must be trying to clear them for us—or at least bring them to our attention."

He scratched his chin, felt the stubble there and realized to his chagrin he'd forgotten to shave.

"Captain Hayes, they are in range of our Bofors, are they not?"

"Yes, sir."

"Have the gunners fire on those brachiators."

"Sir?" Hayes said.

"The monkeys swinging underneath the bridge."

"Yes, sir." Captain Hayes paused. "Isn't that overkill, sir? We don't have more than about thirty shells for the Bofors left. If we get a little closer, we can use the fifty-calibers we mounted on the foredeck—"

"If we get closer, they'll have time to get behind the friendlies. Besides, I want to make an impression. Four rounds ought to do it."

"Yes, Colonel."

A moment later, the twin-barreled guns began to hammer away, firing four shells in quick succession. Two impacted the side of the span, erupting into satisfying blooms of flame and black smoke. A third struck the underside of the bridge, and the fourth actually hit one of the apes dead on. It was almost comical, the way it literally blew apart.

The fighting on the Golden Gate had stopped, with every pair of eyes—human or otherwise—turned toward them.

"Hello, there," he said, under his breath. "Have I got your attention now?"

His answer was gunfire, but the *Daedalus* was still laughably out-of-distance for small-arms fire. It was good to know that the apes either didn't know that or didn't have the discipline to care. Better yet, a bunch of them were crowded up to the side of the bridge to do their shooting, which meant that they were targets now.

"Give 'em six more," he said. "Spaced right along their line."

He watched as his orders were carried out, and explosions ran down the ape-occupied length of the bridge. Then he waited for the smoke to clear. He briefly considered using one or two of the Tomahawks, but in the end, he didn't want to risk damaging the bridge beyond repair. Much of the north was now either under control or depopulated. If they were to add San Francisco to the expanding sphere of rebuilt civilization, the bridge would be nice to have. So far, he wasn't that impressed by the apes, and he was in no particular hurry to enter the harbor now that he knew that at least some of the humans had survived and he knew where they were.

The smoke was beginning to thin; he didn't see any apes now, but he doubted very much that they'd gotten them all. More likely they had wised up and moved away from the edge of the bridge, where the angle hid them from his guns.

He was turning to the Captain when he caught a flash in his peripheral vision.

Before he could even swear, an explosion rocked the ship as the projectile struck the side of the bow. As the black cloud of smoke expanded, though, he found a few choice expletives.

"What was that?" the Captain shouted.

McCullough was already starting to calm down. Getting all excited was rarely productive.

"Probably something shoulder-launched," he said. "A Stinger, maybe. If we're lucky. Stupid. Me, not you. I underestimated them. Back off, and take us down the coast, south. There's a beach down there without much relief—no high ground. If the Sanfrans are smart, they'll follow us down, and we can set up a safe zone. And clear the decks. If they have one of those things, they could have a hundred. I don't want to give them any casualties."

Below he saw medics scrambling toward the fallen. How many had he lost? It was a bad beginning.

A moment later, a private rushed up.

"Damage?" he said.

"Messed up our paint job, sir," he said. "Not much more than that."

Relief felt like a cool river washing over him.

"Any casualties?"

"Brooks and Delacorte got a little shrapnel. Nothing serious, sir."

"Okay," he said. "I'll check in on them once we're clear. Tell them I said to hang in there."

3

Caesar picked himself up, casting about in the smoke and confusion, still feeling the shaking of the bridge in his legs. He saw the bodies of apes scattered near the guard rails. Some were still moving; others were clearly beyond help. He searched frantically for Blue Eyes, and to his relief found his son was lying where he had last seen him, unharmed but looking terrified beyond reason.

The rest of his army had sensibly moved to the middle of the bridge, but they seemed confused and disorganized. Shaking himself from his own half-stunned state, he began shouting and signing orders, keeping them to the center of the bridge where the ship's guns could not find them, directing the bulk of them to repel the humans coming from the south. They were the immediate danger; if he let them, they would take advantage of the confusion to overrun the bridge, despite their smaller numbers—and then all would be lost.

He led them himself, firing and moving from cover to cover. The humans were halfway up the span and still coming, and for a moment he thought they wouldn't be stopped; but then three gorillas, under cover of fire, cleared the next barricade by simply pushing it aside, sending their attackers scrambling to cover farther back. More apes arrived, and soon the humans were in full retreat, and he was forced to restrain his army from charging after them.

"Secure the end of the bridge," he told Rocket. "Set up barricades there. But let no one go any further."

Then, tentatively, he once again approached the side of the Golden Gate.

The fog had all but burned away by then, and he saw the ship had turned and was making its way south, along the edge of the strand where the city met the sea. Smoke curled up from near the vessel's nose.

"What happened?" he asked.

He didn't find out until everyone had more-or-less calmed down, when it turned out that one of the gorillas—Ajax—had decided to try the thing Malcolm had called a rocket launcher. It had apparently put the ship to flight.

They were already celebrating Ajax as a hero, and despite the fact that when they counted up their losses they found six apes had been killed, most of his army seemed to think they had won a victory.

Caesar knew better. If there had ever been a chance for peace, it was now lost. To him, the ship hardly looked damaged. Whoever was leading the humans in it hadn't retreated from fear, but from prudence. This was far from over. This war had barely begun.

Still, he had no intention of reprimanding Ajax. The humans on the ship had made their intentions clear. They hadn't come here to seek peace, but to demand submission. That was why they had fired their big guns, to dominate him.

In firing back, Ajax had shown the enemy that they had teeth, too, and that a display of force, no matter how surprising, would not be enough to make them offer their surrender.

He had to show these new humans he was prepared to meet force with force, life for life, and he had to do it quickly. But that meant setting a few things in order, first.

He called his best warriors together.

"Keep the bridge," he said. "Send two scouts to see where the ship goes, and the other humans too, if they go somewhere different."

"Grey?" Rocket asked.

Caesar hesitated only for a second.

"Not Grey," he signed near his chest, so only Rocket could see. Grey was probably their best living scout, but he had also been one of Koba's lieutenants.

"Singe, and one other he chooses."

Rocket signed that he understood, then went off to follow his orders. Caesar waited impatiently until he was sure things on the bridge were in hand, and Rocket returned.

"I must go into the city," he said to his captains. "But I'll return soon. Rocket, Luca, come with me. Luca, bring Ajax and any other gorillas you can find. And bring Blue Eyes and Ray."

As McCullough anticipated, the human fighters made their way south along the beach. When he deemed it safe, he sent one of the landing craft to pick up a few of them and bring them on board.

The leader of the human resistance in San Francisco was a fellow named Weil, a lightly built man with a burn scar on one cheek and blond hair shaved close to his skull. It didn't take long to figure out he was pretty new to the job. At first, McCullough just let him talk; he was full of talk, this fellow, and McCullough didn't see the point in wasting words on questions until he knew what to ask. The people in San Francisco had been led primarily by two men, Dreyfus and Malcolm. They had managed to create a safe zone, locate a hydroelectric power plant and put it in working order. Everything had seemed to be going fine.

But when they went into the woods to fix the power plant, they ran into the apes, and the apes weren't happy. They came riding into town on horses.

Horses.

Then Malcolm had apparently negotiated a truce.

"It was a trick," Weil said. "They never intended to let us be. They invaded the armory, took our guns, came at us without warning. Before we knew it, half of us were dead, and the rest of us were locked up."

McCullough leaned back in his chair. Weil seemed to have finally run out of energy.

"I'm confused," he finally said. "You said everybody was killed or locked up. What about you guys?"

Weil frowned. "The apes had some kind of fight among themselves," he said. "The one that came out on top let us go, but he took our weapons and turned us out of the city. *Our* city, Colonel."

"So this ape—"

"Caesar."

McCullough cocked his head.

"His name is Caesar? Did you guys name him that?"

Weil shook his head vigorously.

"That's what he calls himself, sir. He can talk—like a man."

McCullough blinked.

"Well," he said, wondering if he believed it. Did Weil have some reason to lie? Had he been part of some sort of hysteria? "That's—that's something," he finally said. "So this Caesar, he granted you your parole, basically?"

Weil shifted uncomfortably.

"Well, like I said, he let us go. But we knew you guys

were coming, so we figured we would help as much as we could—"

"Sure," McCullough said. "And I appreciate the effort. It would have been nice to sail straight into the harbor, but at least you alerted us to their presence. If you hadn't, they might have surprised us and done some real damage. As it is, we'll make do. So, Dreyfus, Malcolm—what happened to them?"

"Dreyfus is dead," Weil said. His expression grew darker. "Malcolm—he's with the apes now."

"With the apes?"

"I don't know if he was always with 'em, or if he just went their way after Caesar won. He was always going on about how we could live in peace with them."

"You think he was right?"

"They attacked *us*," Weil said. "*They* broke the peace."

"I get that," McCullough said. "I just want to be clear about something. I'm here to aid the local government. The local *human* government. Is that who I'm talking to?"

Weil wavered for an instant, but then he nodded.

"Yes, sir," he said. "With Dreyfus gone, and Malcolm with them—we're it."

"Okay," McCullough said. "Here's what we're going to do. Without a harbor, I can't dock this ship, but we can use the landing craft to move back and forth. This is a good area, and our guns can keep it covered. We'll fortify those buildings just off the beach. You bring whoever you have—combatants, non coms, children—we'll do what we can to keep them safe. Meanwhile, I need maps. Numbers. Locations. I want to know where the apes are and what they're doing. Once you and yours are safe, and I know exactly what I'm up against, then we'll give you your city back. How does that sound?"

Weil looked relieved. "It sounds good, sir. But I'm

warning you, sir. They're tough, and they're scary as shit."

"Well," McCullough said. "So am I."

Grey folded himself into the shadows of the rooftop, his dark-eyed gaze picking over the beach below. The ship was still far out in the water, but from what he had seen at the bridge, its guns could still find him if they knew where he was. They could also find the sandy beach below, where humans were as busy as ants, setting up tents and building barricades to cover various approaches to the little cluster of older buildings. Earlier, he had watched two smaller boats leave the big one and come ashore, and with them they brought guns. A lot of them. None so big as the ones on the boat, but some were bigger than any he had ever seen.

Red, restless, reached over to get his attention, albeit submissively. Red was a gorilla, on the small side for his kind, with rusty fur that gave him his name.

"Are they building a village?" the younger ape asked.

"No children," Grey signed. "This is for war only. I think their big ship cannot come to land while Caesar controls the bridge. So they come here to build their strength. Some of the humans we fought are with them, see?"

"I see," Red signed excitedly. "Caesar was wrong to let them go."

Grey glanced at Red, remembering another scouting expedition. There had been three of them, then. Himself, Stone—and, of course, their leader Koba. Of those three, he was the only one left alive. Caesar had sent them on that expedition, to seek the source of the humans who had invaded their forest. He had not chosen Grey for this one, favoring Spear and Singe instead. They were off a little further toward the beach, watching what he was watching, as unaware of Grey's presence as the humans.

"What will we do?" Red persisted.

Grey wished he knew. After Koba's death, he had returned his allegiance to Caesar, and Caesar had graciously taken back his support. Grey was grateful, on one level. He knew he had been disloyal, keeping information from Caesar because Koba told him to. Grey hadn't known that it was Koba who shot Caesar—like everyone else, he assumed it was one of the humans. Believing that, he had helped Koba start the war. If he had known...

It troubled him. He wasn't sure. He might have followed Koba anyway. Koba was strong, and saw the humans for what they were. But Caesar had given them the gift of freedom, and of the waking. It would have been a hard choice, if he had been given it.

But now it no longer mattered. Koba was defeated, and Caesar ruled.

"We will follow Caesar," he said.

"Follow Caesar?" Red signed, expressing disbelief. "We beat the humans. We won. Caesar gave our victory away, and now we must fight them again. It makes no sense. If Caesar had died, and Koba still lived, this would not be."

"The ship would still be here," Grey said. "We would still face those guns."

"Koba would have found a way to beat them," Red said. "Koba was strong."

Grey shook his head. "Koba was my friend. My leader. But he was driven by hatred, not sense. If these humans had been the only ones, yes, we could have beaten them. Now, with these men come from far away, with their weapons—maybe we cannot win."

Red became agitated, so much so that he had a hard time keeping still—he kept picking at his own hair and fluttering his thick fingers around his face. He even let out a low grunt. Grey feared he would give them away. But the younger ape finally settled down.

"If that's true, why are we still here in the city?" he asked. "Why not flee to the forest?"

"Caesar has a plan," Grey said.

"He had a plan before. Let the humans do their work, then they would go away. Didn't happen."

Grey didn't answer right away. He felt as if he was balanced on the narrowest, weakest of branches, with a fatal fall on all sides.

"We need someone else to lead us," Red said. "If we cannot fight them, let us flee. Make a new village far, far away. Grow strong."

"What leader?" Grey snorted. "You?"

"No," Red said. "You. Koba trusted you. Others know that. You know Caesar is weak."

"He beat Koba," Grey said.

"The tower shook," Red signed, dismissively. "It was bad luck for Koba. But I mean inside." He thumped his chest. "Caesar is weak because he loves humans too much. Even now he still thinks we can have peace with them. Even after they killed more of us on the bridge."

"Don't presume to know what Caesar thinks," Grey said.

"That's right," Red said. "We don't know. Caesar does not explain himself. We want a new leader."

"We?" Grey said. "Who is we?"

"I will not name them," Red said. "But there are many of us. Many who followed Koba. And you were his right hand. You could lead us."

"Lead you in what?"

"You once told me you and Koba found a place, far from here, a good place to live."

Grey shrugged. "Yes. Further north. But we thought humans were all dead, so it didn't seem worth the trip."

"You could lead us there and leave Caesar to fight here. We take the women with us."

That thought held Grey for a heartbeat. He could never confront Caesar; not after Koba's defeat, not after he went slinking back to him, begging forgiveness. Even if he could work up the nerve to challenge him, he would probably fail. If Koba couldn't beat Caesar, probably no one could. But to leave, start a troop of his own—that sounded possible.

But there were problems.

"Take the women," he scoffed. "How? Cornelia is the leader of the women. She would never allow them to betray Caesar, even if they wanted to. And they don't want to—he is Alpha. Proves it again and again. And if we tried to take them by force, the gorilla guard protects them."

"There is a way," Red said. "I have a plan."

Grey listened as Red laid out his ideas. He drew a deep breath, wishing that Red didn't make so much sense. Now he was the one having trouble keeping still. He looked away from Red, back at the beach.

"Caesar didn't send you to scout here," Red said. "He doesn't trust you anymore."

It was as if Red knew his thoughts. Grey knew Caesar no longer had reason to trust him, but it was still humiliating, to have once been so esteemed in the troop, and now…

He tried to shrug it off.

"Then why did you come anyway?" Red persisted. "You're supposed to be on the bridge."

"I wanted to see what we're facing," Grey said.

"Because you don't trust Caesar, either," Red said.

Grey kept watching the humans. He and Koba and Stone had returned to the human town, without Caesar's knowledge. Had seen them getting their weapons ready for war, even though they told Caesar they wanted peace.

Koba had been right, and Caesar had been wrong. That Caesar beat Koba in a fight didn't change that. It didn't make his judgment regarding humans any better.

Coming to this place, he and Red had passed the zoo, where Grey had lived when he was young, before Caesar came. He remembered it only a little, but what he remembered he did not like.

Grey had always been content to follow, whether Caesar or Koba. What mattered to him was apes, that they never return to the way things were, that his children and their children go on living in freedom.

Koba said Caesar had lost his way. To Grey, that seemed even more true now. They could not hope to fight these humans and their ships and their guns. Red was right. They needed a new leader. If that had to be Grey, so be it.

"Taking the women will be difficult, even with your plan," he said. "Most gorillas will follow Caesar."

"I am a gorilla," Red said. "There are others. And I have some ideas."

Red had lots of ideas, Grey reflected. Red was smarter than Grey. He accepted that. But sometimes the young gorilla got ahead of himself. Sometimes he stepped onto rotten branches.

In listening to Red, Grey knew he might be doing the same. But inside, he felt easier, now that the decision was made. And although he was dead, he thought he felt Koba's presence. It was almost as if he could see the ape telling him that he'd made the right decision.

4

Caesar glanced up at the tower, remembering his battle there with Koba. Remembering killing him.

Only Koba knew everything Koba had been through, back before he had been released from the Gen-Sys labs. His scars said a lot—his unalloyed hatred of humans said more. And although Koba had kept most of the details of his years of torture to himself Caesar knew that compared to Koba, his own early life had been—fortunate. He had been raised by good humans who loved him and almost—almost—treated him as one of their own. His own exposure to the cruelty humans were capable of came only later, when he was taken away to live with other apes. That was also when he met Rocket, who had been the Alpha in that place. Rocket had put him through a lot, but soon after Caesar took his place as the dominant male, he became—and remained—a good and trusted friend. In some ways, Rocket had almost seemed relieved to settle into the role of second-in-command.

Koba, too, had been a trusted friend. Once they were free of the humans and in the woods—just apes among apes—any worries Caesar might have had about the bonobo had melted away. In those days, Koba hadn't had any interest in taking Caesar's place as leader, or if he had, he had been careful not to show it. But when—after ten winters—Malcolm and his people happened upon Caesar's colony, things changed. Koba could not coexist with humans, and in Koba's mind that meant no ape could. Caesar had been unable or unwilling to think the consequences of that through, right up until the moment that Koba shot him.

But as much as Koba's betrayal had dismayed and enraged him, he had come to understand that it was his own blind spot that had enabled that disloyalty. Koba hated humans because he understood them, had the worst of what they were deep inside of him, festering, waiting to take over. And Koba had probably been right; Malcolm aside, most of the humans would never have been able to stand the thought of apes living so near, even if Koba had never taken charge and attacked them. They had been preparing for the worst, after all, and many humans and apes alike could only see the worst. Koba had brought the war with humans sooner than it might have happened, but it was always going to happen. Caesar saw that, now, as Koba had.

And now that war was upon them he had to consider the possibility that they—that *he*—might lose.

In the forest, he had built a city of wood and earth. But looking once again at the human city, and the things they had made—things so far beyond what he knew how to build—he felt a familiar uncertainty. He had never aspired to be human—at least, not since he was little and actually thought he was. Apes living with apes, on their own terms, in their own way, was all he had ever desired. But there was another thing he understood, after all of these years.

He and his troop had been lucky.

Lucky to have escaped the city with as few losses as

they'd had. Even once in the forest, where he thought they would be safe, they were not. Men came after them, with guns and flying machines and eventually fire bombs. He and the other apes had outwitted their human hunters for a time, survived those first hard days, but just barely, and only with the aid of humans who sympathized with them.

And then the humans stopped coming. From the treetops, he had watched fires in the city. He didn't know what had happened, and for some time he did not care. All that mattered to him was that the battle was over, and that for whatever reason the humans seemed to have forgotten them. In time, he sent out a few scouting parties, who returned with the news that the humans were dying from some malady, and that those who survived seemed to be bent on killing each other anyway.

Caesar grieved for them, but he was also grateful to be left alone, whatever the reason.

Now he knew much more, and he understood that if there had been no sickness the humans would never have stopped hunting them. In the change of a moon or less, he and his followers would have most likely been killed or recaptured to live out their lives in laboratories and internment facilities. Nothing he knew, no tool he had possessed could have stopped that from happening. It wasn't his mind or his leadership that had saved them back then. They had just been lucky.

Now, once again, apes faced annihilation at the hands of an enemy Caesar did not understand enough about. He thought he knew a thing or two about human weapons, but now he was starting to realize that what he knew was probably only the single finger of a hand, when what he really faced were ten fingers curled into a pair of fists. The big guns on the ship were terrifying. What other fatal surprises did the newcomers have in store?

So he found Malcolm again, where the gorillas had taken him. He was in a room in a building across the street from the tower where Koba had died. In an attempt to kill them all, Dreyfus had set off explosives in the basement of the tower, and it was now an untrustworthy shelter.

Malcolm looked up at him as he entered, glancing warily at Rocket and Luca, who flanked him.

"Am I your prisoner?" Malcolm asked as Caesar entered.

"Yes," Caesar said, using spoken language. "But not for long. Before the day ends, I will send you away. Far away, where you will be safe. Your son, your wife, too. Like I said days ago."

"Send them," Malcolm said. "Send Alexander and Ellie. But let me stay. I can help you. Humans have been fighting wars for thousands of years. We know a lot about it. Whoever that is on that boat out there—he might know a *whole* lot about it. Much more than you. It's not just the weapons they have, it's the centuries of accumulated knowledge about *how* to fight."

Caesar nodded. "The way you make buildings, he makes war?"

Malcolm looked a bit startled at the comparison, but then nodded, vigorously.

"Exactly," he said. "That's exactly right."

"But you know how to make buildings, not war."

"Well, yes," Malcolm admitted. "I'm not a general or anything—"

"Then you go," Caesar said. "For your son. For your wife. For me. Go make a new start, where men have good hearts. Maybe one day, we will meet again."

Malcolm held his gaze for a moment, still defiant, but then Caesar saw the change in him—a loosening of his shoulders. A shift in his stance and in his eyes. He wasn't an ape, but the way humans spoke with their bodies had much in common with them.

"You feel responsible," Caesar said. "You want to fix it. You can't. I told you—apes started war. Humans will not forgive that. And they will not forgive humans who stand with apes."

Malcolm lowered his eyes.

"Alexander has been through so much," he said. "I hoped—"

"War is not for him," Caesar said. He paused. "Or for my son. Blue Eyes will go with you. He will believe he goes to protect you. Do you understand? A favor to me." He paused, then rested a hand on Malcolm's shoulder, a gesture of trust he remembered from childhood.

"You know it's right."

Malcolm pursed his lips for a few heartbeats, and then nodded.

"I can do that," he said. "But what about the others? The young ones?"

"I will keep them safe," Caesar told him. "Gather what you need."

Malcolm nodded, but still he stayed where he was.

"There's something you should know," he said. "I went through the wreckage of the radio room. They were keeping notes. We know they contacted these guys in the north, obviously. But it looks like they may have gotten hold of someone down south, too. It's not clear where, or how much information they exchanged. But you might have to deal with—trouble—from down there, too."

Caesar regarded him for a moment.

"What is in the south?" he asked.

Malcolm shrugged. "In the old days?" he said. "More cities. Los Angeles was the biggest. Much bigger than San Francisco. We haven't heard much of anything for years. But the few rumors that did come our way weren't good."

Caesar nodded. "Thank you."

"Good luck, Caesar," Malcolm said. Then he left.

After Malcolm was gone, Rocket shifted uneasily.

"What?" Caesar asked.

"Blue Eyes will be hard to convince," Rocket said. "He will want to stay and fight."

Caesar remembered Blue Eyes on the bridge, cowering behind a car. Rocket hadn't seen that, and he wasn't about to tell him about it. But Rocket was probably right, anyway. Blue Eyes had a lot of pride. He would try to make up for the fear he had shown today, which could well get him killed all the more quickly.

"I know that," Caesar said. "That's why you're going with him—to make sure he doesn't come straight back."

Rocket raised up in protest.

"Caesar, no," he said. "I belong here, with you."

Caesar considered his old friend carefully, unwilling to say everything he was thinking. Rocket had suffered much at the hands of humans, too. Not so much as Koba, but enough. And his son had been killed, only days ago. Caesar didn't know what that felt like, and he didn't want to know. But as much as he trusted Rocket, he knew the older chimpanzee must be nearing his breaking point.

But he didn't say any of that. A wise leader was not necessarily the most truthful one, he was beginning to understand.

"You are my second, Rocket," he said instead. "If we fail here, fighting these men, the colony will need you. And they will need my son, my heir. But it's more than that. We ignored humans for too long; just hoped they had gone away. We were wrong; first the humans here found us, now some from the north. You heard Malcolm. I must know about the south. What is down there? More humans?

More forest? We don't know, and right now we must know everything we can. You will take Malcolm and his family south, yes, and Blue Eyes will go with you. Once you find a safe place for Malcolm, then you look, understand? And see. Be my eyes and ears. The world is large, and we know only a corner of it. I want to know a little more, at least about what we are up against. And Blue Eyes—I have kept him too close. He must learn to lead. Without me."

Rocket rocked back a little restlessly, his eyes cutting back and forth.

"Is this what you command?" he finally asked.

"He is my son," Caesar said. "You are the only one I trust to watch over him. To teach him how to be a leader."

"Why?" Rocket signed. "I could not even protect my own son."

For just that second, Caesar finally saw how raw Rocket's feelings were, how much damage he had suffered.

"You could not know what Koba would do," Caesar said. "Ape not kill ape. We all believed it. Koba broke the trust."

Rocket pant-hooted in anger, but then backed off immediately, his shoulders slumping, his back half-turned.

"I trust you, Rocket," Caesar said. "With my son. With my troop. Do you understand?"

Rocket was silent for another moment, then slowly reached out his hand in submission.

"I understand, Caesar," he finally said. "I will do as you say." Then he paused. "What about Rain? She has a little one in her."

"We need to move them, and quickly," Caesar said. "The humans who were with Dreyfus know where we are, and could lead the soldiers from the ship here. The city is large, very large. We will find a haven for them." He touched Luca, who had been silent throughout their conversation, on the shoulder. "The gorilla guard will take them."

Luca's heavy eyebrows arched up.

"You will remain with me, Luca," Caesar said. "Pick someone to lead the guard."

"Yes, Caesar," Luca signed, obviously relieved.

"We still control the bridge," Caesar said. "The boat cannot land on shore. We will beat them. We will beat them, and we will go on as we were before."

Blue Eyes heard his mother coming long before he saw her. She still wheezed a little from her sickness, and of course his little brother Cornelius was weighing her down. When she arrived at the top of the building, Cornelius bounded from her back and rushed over to him on all fours. Blue Eyes let Cornelius clamber up onto him, but continued to sulk.

"Are you ready?" his mother asked.

"He's just trying to get rid of me," Blue Eyes complained. "He's afraid I'll get killed, like Ash."

She came near and touched his face. "So am I," she said. "What would you say if I told you I begged him to send you away?"

"I would say you shouldn't have done that," he said, after a moment.

"Well, I didn't," she said. "But I'm glad he is. And he's not just getting rid of you. It's important we know what else might threaten us."

"Why not just send Rocket and Ray, then?" he said. "Why must I go?"

She made a little snorting sound.

"Rocket is strong, loyal, full of courage. But he isn't all that smart. You are."

"Really? I let Koba fool me."

"Koba told you what you wanted to hear," she said. "Knowing that is a different kind of smart than I'm talking

58

about. You will see things differently than Rocket. What might not attract his notice will be a red fruit to you. Where he sees only two sticks and then two more sticks, you will see four. That's why your father is sending you."

"Then why doesn't he tell me this himself?" he asked.

"He's busy, if you haven't noticed," she replied, gently.

"Busy," Blue Eyes signed.

She came closer, their foreheads touching, and he remembered clinging to her fur when he was little, like Cornelius. How safe he'd felt, how protected. He remembered firelight and smoke and the sounds of evening, when everyone returned to the village. How happy he was to see his father, when he came home—and how fleeting those moments were. There was always some conversation that needed had, some broken thing that needed fixed, someone who needed disciplined, a place his father had to go. Time alone with his Caesar was like the pale little flowers that bloomed only once a year, and then for only a single morning before they withered and were gone. That, or a perfectly ripe pear—hard to find, and harder to keep to oneself. And then—after a certain point—he could never get away from his father. But it wasn't time to themselves, father and son. It was just his father treating him like an infant, keeping him near so he would be safe. While Ash wandered the woods, Blue Eyes followed his father from one boring thing to another. When Ash led hunting parties, Blue Eyes went with his father, always the second spear, never allowed to act on his own instincts.

Of course, when he had, it hadn't turned out all that well, he thought, tracing his fingers on the marks the bear had left him.

As usual, it seemed almost as if his mother could read his mind.

"You always said he treated you like a baby," she said.

"How many times did you beg him to hunt before he let you? How many times did you ask if you could travel to the next valley to see what was there? To explore the hills with Ash? Don't you understand? He's giving you what you always asked for. Command of yourself."

He remembered the battle on the bridge, hiding while Ray fought with *his* gun. But he couldn't bear to tell his mother about that. She, above all, could not know how weak he had been.

"But I want to fight," he said, instead.

"No, you don't," she said. "It's not what you're good at. It's not what you're made for. Even as a little thing, you were always trying to see what was in the next tree, never content with where you were. Take this gift from him, Blue Eyes. Please."

"What choice do I have?" he signed.

But he knew, somewhat to his shame, that she was right. The thought of traveling, of seeing what no ape had ever seen—it excited him more than he wanted to admit. And every time he closed his eyes, he saw Ash, or what was left of Ash, and he knew that death was coming for him as surely as it had come for his friend.

He didn't understand it. He was afraid of it, and when the guns started firing on the bridge, his feelings had petrified him.

In his deeps, he knew he was not an ape worthy of the troop. Not a son worthy of Caesar. It was his secret shame that he *wanted* to go, to get as far away from this place of death as possible, to seek life instead.

5

They left early the next morning, three apes and three humans with eight horses. Blue Eyes was just checking his packs yet again when he saw someone approaching from the corner of his eye. He expected that it was Rocket or Ray, but whoever it was just stood there quietly, as if waiting to be noticed.

He finally turned, ready with a smart comment, but then he froze.

It was Lake. She was about his age, and when they were little they had played together, but at a certain point boys had mostly gone to their games of tag and pretend-spears, and girls had played mothering games with pieces of fur or their younger siblings, and he hadn't thought about Lake much at all. More recently, though, he had been thinking about girls his age a lot, and Lake in particular. Ash had kidded him about it, mercilessly.

Now she was standing so close he could smell her without even trying.

"Hi," he signed, not quite sure what to do.

She looked a little cross.

"Weren't you going to say something?" she asked.

"What?"

"What, what, what?" She repeated the sign several times, derisively.

He just blinked.

"Something like, 'goodbye,'" she said, when he failed to answer.

"Goodbye?" he replied, tentatively.

She looked a little angrier. "You really were just going to ride away, weren't you?"

"I... guess?" he said.

"You're an idiot, Blue Eyes," she said, and walked away.

He watched her go, his head spinning. He heard a little chuff of air and realized Rocket was there, laughing at his expense.

"What?" he demanded.

"What, what, what?" Rocket signed, in imitation of Lake.

"I don't understand," Blue Eyes said.

"Then she's right," Rocket said. "You are an idiot. But don't worry—you don't have to figure anything out. She already has."

Blue Eyes glanced around, embarrassed, wondering who else was there to hear. Ray hadn't arrived yet, but the humans were quietly seeing to their horses. One of them, Ellie—the nurse who had saved his mother's life with her medicine— grinned. Alexander, Malcolm's son, shook his head.

"Get a clue, man," he said.

Once they started riding, none of them talked much, except for the occasional exchange between Malcolm and Rocket on which way to go. Part of this was practical; Malcolm, Ellie and Alexander were not fluent in sign language, and the three apes struggled with spoken language. But a heaviness seemed on them too, as if the fog had acquired weight. Alexander seemed content to sketch in his book, pressing it to the saddle horn and trusting his mount to follow the others. Once or twice Blue Eyes craned his neck to try and see what the human was drawing, but could never make it out clearly. Ellie seemed to be studying their surroundings more than anything else. Ray just looked uncomfortable on his mount, and kept scooting his feet up to squat on its back rather than riding on it properly.

Blue Eyes knew Ray, but Ray had been better friends with Ash, who had been more tolerant of the younger ape hanging around them. He was a little odd, partly because he was an orangutan, but partly because he was just… a little different.

They rode along streets empty of humans or apes, but they were scarcely lifeless. Birds and squirrels they saw in great numbers, and once a doe and her fawn bolted from their path into the undergrowth between buildings. Blue Eyes found himself wondering what it had been like, when humans ruled this place, when each of the hundreds and hundred-hundreds of buildings had been inhabited. The size of the abandoned city continued to amaze him—just as he imagined they were about to reach the edge of it and enter a forest or grassland, more structures arose as if sprung from seed, like some dandelion-building had scattered its progeny to the winds. He began to wonder if perhaps the forest was the only place in the world not covered in the ruins of human habitations.

As the sun rose higher, Rocket began to act a little strangely, taking odd turns and stopping for long moments, his expression like that of someone looking far away, seeing things that Blue Eyes could not see. It was odd, because Rocket was usually the most down-to-earth of the older apes, rarely distracted by anything happening inside of his head.

They came to a slightly more open, wooded area in the hills, and Rocket finally slowed and brought his horse to a stop in front of a fence made of wire braided to look like honeycomb. At first, Blue Eyes didn't understand why Rocket had led them here; beyond the fence was just another building, angular like most human structures, but with the skeleton of some sort of dome above that still had a few panes of what appeared to be white glass here and there. But then he saw the images of apes on the side of the building; chimpanzees—a male, a female, and a baby in a tree.

Malcolm too dismounted.

"San Bruno Primate Shelter," Malcolm said. That was when Blue Eyes noticed the letters, standing on the edge of the roof. "Is this—did you live here?" Malcolm asked Rocket.

Rocket continued to stare a few moments; then he nodded his head.

"Yes," he finally croaked. "Here. Rocket here. Caesar, here. Maurice, here. Cornelia." He made an odd, sad sound. "Buck."

Blue Eyes clambered down and walked over to join Rocket, feeling a little awestruck.

"This is the place?" he signed. "Where Father began the fight?"

"Yes," Rocket said. "I almost forgot. But then I started to remember. Things looked familiar." He scratched his shoulder. "So long ago."

Blue Eyes stepped through a rent in the fence and took a few steps toward the place, unsure what he was feeling. It was like a story made real, like the glyphs Maurice wrote come to life. So much led back to here, so many stories about how it all started. Rocket had been Alpha, here, when his father first arrived. But his father had conquered first him, then the other apes, then the humans that kept them captive.

He looked back at Rocket, questioningly. "Are you going in?" he asked.

"No," Rocket said. "I will never go back in there."

Blue Eyes hesitated, but he felt he had to see it, and continued.

He had been to the house where his father grew up, raised by humans. He had seen the pictures of him and his human family, the room where he lived and played, and he had finally begun to understand his father's feelings toward the strange, nearly hairless creatures that at once so resembled chimpanzees and were so frightfully different. Malcolm and Alexander and Ellie had been there as well, helping, and that had made that understanding easier. Not all humans were bad.

But there were no such tales of this place. No ape who had been here remembered it fondly. His mother called it the "under place," and sometimes "the maggot hole," so he was surprised to find that it was above the ground. He had pictured something more like a cave.

He went on, Malcolm and the others following him, including Ray. Only Rocket remained outside, with his memories.

The door was broken, and it was dark inside. They passed through a corridor of small rooms with iron bars, and Blue Eyes began to understand his mother's names for the place. It wasn't *actually* underground, but it nevertheless felt that way.

They finally reached a large room, with the dome they had seen outside as its ceiling. It was now mostly a latticework open to the sky. There, almost as if recalling a dream, Blue Eyes saw the artificial tree his father and the others had spoken of, the walls painted to resemble the outside. But it was all smaller than he had imagined. Much smaller.

Only then did it dawn on him. He looked back at the dark corridor. On the way in, he had been assuming the little rooms they had passed were for storing food or something.

"Those were the cells," he said. "That's where they stayed."

It was beyond belief.

Malcolm may not have gotten every sign, but he must have understood some of it, because his face darkened.

"It wasn't right," he said. "The way we treated them, in those days."

"Dingy," Ray said. "And so little. Hard to believe. I would have gone crazy."

Blue Eyes went back and stared into one of the tiny, box-shaped rooms. He tried to imagine being in there, with the door closed. But even now, with the building in ruins, knowing he could walk in and walk out whenever he wanted—he still felt the walls trying to squeeze him, cut off his breath. He realized now why Maurice refused to talk about this place at all, and that he had never really understood what his father and Rocket were trying to say. He had grown up among trees that touched the sky, horizons that approached forever in every direction, the endless sea and the unlimited depths of the sky above.

To be in one of those tiny cells, cramped, unable to run, to climb, to taste the rain and feel the wind, hear the hush and murmur of leaves.

It was unthinkable. Unacceptable. No ape could live in such a place and not go crazy.

But his father had endured here, and Rocket and Maurice had lived here for much longer.

Maybe, before the change, before the wakening, apes were different.

But Blue Eyes didn't believe it. They might not have been as smart, but they were still apes, and apes were meant for the forest, not tiny boxes of shadow hidden from the sky. Not an underplace, a maggot hole.

Maybe his father, Maurice, and Rocket *had* gone

crazy. Maybe that's why they had tried the impossible—and succeeded. Maybe sane apes would have failed, and died, or wasted away their lives in the dark and in despair. Maybe to make things better, his father and the others *had* to become insane. Maybe they still were, in a way. Maybe that's what they and humans had in common, living too long in dark little boxes. All smart. All crazy.

He almost laughed, for the first time in a long time. It was worth thinking about. And it would explain a lot.

He was shocked from his thoughts by the sudden angry chatter of gunfire outside, and then again, closer. With a grunt he ran back toward the exit, unlimbering his rifle. Malcolm was ahead of him.

Bullets met them at the entrance, spattering against the black stuff human roads were built of. Malcolm fired—Blue Eyes could not see what at. From the cover of the door, he made out Rocket, crouched behind a car. He too leaned out and shot at something.

Malcolm jerked his chin toward the wooded hill. "They're up there," he said. "I'll go left, you stay here and cover me. I think I can flank them."

He spoke quickly, and Blue Eyes wasn't exactly sure what he meant, but as Malcolm started running from cover, Blue Eyes saw someone move in the trees. For a moment, he felt that same paralysis that had seized him at the bridge. But then he saw Rocket clap his hand to his shoulder as a bullet hit him. With an angry bark, he stood up and jerked the trigger. The weapon slammed painfully against his shoulder and left his ears ringing. Rocket—apparently not too badly wounded—shot again, then ran up to the cover of another car, as Malcolm did the same off to their left.

Then, for what seemed like a long time, nothing happened. Malcolm and Rocket advanced once more—

Rocket waved Blue Eyes up to the car he'd first been hiding behind. Then he and Malcolm moved into the trees from two different directions. More time passed, as Blue Eyes watched the trees.

Finally, first Malcolm and then Rocket reappeared.

"Whoever it was, they're gone now," Malcolm said. "We'd best get going while it's clear."

They mounted back up and ran the horses for a bit. Blue Eyes cast frequent glances behind him, but if anyone was following, he didn't see any sign of them.

They brought the horses down to a trot, then back to a run, alternating so as not to tire them excessively.

"What do you think?" Malcolm asked Rocket.

"I don't know," Rocket said. "Two, maybe three."

"That's what I thought, too." He glanced over at Blue Eyes. "I don't think they were locals. I think we're being followed, probably by some of the guys who attacked you on the bridge."

"Humans," Blue Eyes said.

"That's my guess," Malcolm replied. "We looked down here, last year, and it was empty. I haven't seen any sign of habitation this whole way. We must have brought them with us."

"They follow this far, maybe follow farther," Blue Eyes grated out.

"Yeah," Malcolm said.

"Why?"

Malcolm didn't say anything, but he glanced at Ellie.

"You think they're after us," she said. "Me and you and Alexander. Because we helped Caesar."

"It's a good bet," he said. "Why waste men following a few chimps walking away from the fight? They're outnumbered as it is."

"We should split up then," Ellie said.

Blue Eyes shook his head in the way that humans used to mean *no*.

"Father said to see you safe," he said. "We see you safe."

Malcolm nodded, and didn't argue any more.

The next day there was no sign of further pursuit, but they had to make a decision. The road they were following was bordered on one side by yet more abandoned human buildings, albeit mostly small ones that did not rise far from the earth. On the other lay a lake, and beyond that mountains thickly covered in scrubby-looking forest. A bridge led across the water toward them.

"The coast is that way," Malcolm said, gesturing across the water, in the direction the sun went in the evening. "East is San Jose. We sent scouts all down through here last year, and what few survivors they found came up to stay with us. There's nothing for us there. But there were a few settlements in the mountains, people who preferred to keep to themselves. Not violent. Some of them know me. I think we'd be okay there."

"Take us," Blue Eyes said.

"No offense," Malcolm said, "but I'm not sure we would still be welcome if we rode in with you. If you're headed to the coast, we can stay together another few miles. If you're headed off east or due south, I think this is where we say goodbye."

Blue Eyes looked around them. He knew he would feel more comfortable in the hills, but he was supposed to be searching for threats to the troop.

"Where should I look?" he said.

Malcolm shrugged. "Like I said, we looked and didn't find much, but we only went so far. I think you want to head toward Los Angeles. There were four million people down there back in the day—some of them must have survived. Finding out was on our to-do list after getting the lights back on." He sighed, and for a moment his mind seemed to wander. Then he rubbed his forehead.

"The Central Valley has gone pretty wild on the northern end. We heard rumors that the south was divided up between a couple of militia groups that were still duking it out; that might be worth a look. Anyone with vehicles could come up I5 in a few days if they wanted to, so they might be a problem for your people. But a lot of the valley is almost desert now, without irrigation. I have a feeling those guys have their hands full just surviving.

"If I were really looking for a credible threat, I think I would follow the coast down. They obviously still have some ships up north; there could as easily still be some down south. There are islands where survivors may have been able to isolate themselves, and if any military presence remains, I would guess it would be on the coast."

Blue Eyes looked to Rocket.

"Your choice," Rocket signed, absently fingering the graze wound on his shoulder. "You're leading now."

Blue Eyes considered his options. He knew his father was looking for news of possible threats, but Blue Eyes thought that there were other things to keep an eye out for. Like a new place to live. From here, the mountains didn't look all that promising, but in his admittedly limited experience, forests liked the coast. If there weren't any humans over there, but there were more trees—it might mean a new home.

"We'll stay with you longer," he told Malcolm. "Then go down the coast."

6

"Forest, report."

It sounded loud, but she knew a yard away no one could hear the Colonel's voice in her earphones. No human being, anyway. But what about apes? How sharp was their hearing?

She didn't know. She hadn't paid that much attention to things like that, back in the day. She remembered her dad reading her the stories about the little monkey and the man with the hat. She had loved the stories, but it was the man she had liked best. He reminded her of her dad. The monkey was always messing things up.

Like her mother, whom she almost never saw. But when she did show up, there was usually trouble, and not the fun kind. The kind of trouble that narcissistic drug addicts caused was rarely fun. It was better to hang out with the man in the hat, the guy who saw you through the bad breakups with your boyfriend, watched you walk at graduation, cheered you on when you chose to serve your country rather than take the college scholarship.

Last she'd heard of him he was still alive. Of course, that made sense—you didn't usually hear from someone who was dead. But she hadn't had any news of him dying either. Like all survivors, she was genetically immune to the Simian Flu, so maybe he had been, too. It was possible.

But no one was genetically immune to a bullet, or being set on fire, and that's what had killed a lot of people in the last ten years. She knew the odds first-hand, and they weren't good.

Still, as they said, ignorance was hope. Maybe one day, when the peace was finally won, she would see him again. It was something to look forward to.

"We're getting pretty close, according to the locals." She glanced around and located some street signs.

"Market and Eighth," she reported.

A moment's silence, and the sound of paper rustling. She had an image of the Colonel, bent over his field desk, tracing his calloused finger on one of his maps. She remembered screens, digital information, Global Positioning Devices. Hell, the satellites were still up there, as far as anyone knew, beeping, transmitting their data to a world now mostly deaf to their information.

No, down here they were back to the early twentieth century—or the nineteenth, or even earlier. The Colonel, she knew, sort of liked it that way. He preferred his paper maps and his compass, his pistol, his knife, his e-tool. Things that kept working after the world ended.

"You've still got a bit to go," the Colonel informed her. "Forest, don't do anything fancy. You know the drill."

"Yes, sir, I sure do."

But she reflected that it had already been a very long day.

She didn't question the Colonel's decision not to try to go under the Golden Gate; there was no telling what the apes might shoot or drop onto them. A few of her guys were already starting to call the apes *kongs*. Not for the giant gorilla in the movie, but in reference to an old video game in which a big monkey tossed burning barrels and such from the top of a building made of leaning girders, not unlike the way the apes had fired down upon them from the Golden Gate Bridge. She found it funny— soldiers liked naming things, especially dangerous things. It gave them the feeling that they had a measure of control. And the locals had wilder stories, about a fight between two apes, way up in a half-finished building—the one they were in fact now moving toward.

Long and short, because of the kongs and the possibility of burning barrels, they hadn't tried to get into the harbor. The spot the Colonel had chosen to come ashore was much better, nice and defensible, no girders overhead from which deadly objects might be tossed. It had the sea on one side, so the ship could cover them with its gun and missiles, lakes on two other approaches, and what remained of the human resistance in San Francisco had been able to easily join them there by following the highway along the coast, the only easy way into the camp, which was now in the process of being barricaded.

So that was all good.

But the ape headquarters, as it turned out, was completely across town—around eight miles, as the crow flew, and they weren't crows. Up north they still had a handful of functioning helicopters, but their mission hadn't rated one, for some reason.

If they *had* been able to enter the harbor, they could have docked within shooting distance of the place and rolled out their armor.

Instead, she and her team were slogging through the hilliest freaking city in the world. And she'd thought Seattle was bad.

Most of her squad were hardcore, but their scouts were locals, who didn't seem as inexperienced as she feared.

Even the younger ones appeared to have had some military training. But she hadn't seen them under pressure, and that was the real test. Her own people—Roberts, Siegel, Geary, Sasaki—she knew could handle pretty much anything. Her only worry was John. Not because he wasn't competent, but because he was the Colonel's son. The Colonel could be a cold son-of-a-bitch, as hard as gunmetal, but when it came to his son, he was softer than he knew. McCullough had once told her about the Greek guy, Achilles, whose mother had dipped him in some kind of gunk to make him invulnerable to weapons when he was a baby. But she'd been holding him by the heel, so that one spot didn't get arrow-proofed, which later on turned out to be fatal. When Forest first heard the story, she had thought it was dumb, to say the least. Why didn't his mother dip him twice, holding him in different spots? Or why didn't Achilles wear some sort of armored ankle-piece?

But eventually she'd realized that that wasn't the point of the story. The meaning was that everyone had a weak spot. And while the Colonel might not know it himself, his was John.

They'd been clipping along with relative caution, but now she took things even slower. There was still plenty of sunlight left, and they didn't have to make it all the way back to base before night. They weren't in a huge hurry.

"No dogs," Geary whispered.

"What?"

"It's just—I haven't seen any dogs since we got here."

She realized he was right. Up north dogs had been an everyday fact of life. The militias used them as alarm systems and attack animals, but most were feral, wandering in packs through the streets. They didn't usually attack a group of soldiers unless they were starving, but they were always around, making stealth difficult.

"Maybe the apes ate them," she joked.

Geary glanced ahead at the local scouts.

"I guess we could ask them," he said. "Maybe *they* ate them."

"We've come across some with less discriminating diets than that," she said.

"Oh yeah," he said. "Those guys." He looked back at the scouts, his wheat-colored eyebrows scrunched together. "We vetted these guys, right?"

"Not to worry, Geary," she said. "You're too stringy. You'd taste like shit. Tough, chewy shit."

"I've been told I'm sweet as sugar," he said.

"Sure you have," she said. "Now, let's keep our wee gobs shut from here on out, okay?"

"I love it when you talk British, Forest," he said. His eyes lit up. "Say, so you think there's still anyone across the pond? I had a girl from Leeds, once. I mean, we were just internet pals, but—"

"Gobs. Shut."

Geary nodded, looking a bit sheepish.

They began seeing signs of recent activity, mostly in the form of shell casings and fresh bloodstains. No bodies, though. Someone had cleaned up.

She noticed movement up ahead and waved everyone into position, before raising her own weapon.

But it was just one of the scouts, Vega, a young woman with a short bob of black hair and an old Giants cap.

"I think they've cleared out," Vega said.

"What, did you go up there?" Forest demanded.

"Yeah," Vega said. "I thought—"

"I gave you something to do," Forest said. "Something specific. Don't improvise."

Vega shrugged, looking unrepentant. "Anyway. I didn't see any guards. And they pulled out in a hurry. Looks like they left a bunch of supplies. Harper and Lincoln have gone to check it out."

Forest began to think she had been a little too optimistic about the Sanfrans. Probably their best had died in the fighting, and she was left with the dregs.

She tapped on her headphones.

"Colonel?" she said.

"I hear you, Forest."

"Local scouts think the troll nest is empty."

"How far away are you?"

"Four blocks," she said. "The Sanfrans went ahead. Without orders. They think there might be supplies."

There was a slight pause from the other end, then a muffled curse word.

"Forest, you get the hell out of there, now. Go to phase two."

If Forest had learned one thing in her years with the Colonel, it was that you did not second guess him.

"Fall back," she shouted. "Now!"

The words were barely out of her mouth when the streets shook from a tremendous explosion. What little glass remained in the nearby buildings blew out, and smoke and dust filled the air.

So much for Harper and Lincoln, she thought. By the sound and smell of it, it probably wasn't anything complicated, a cache of gasoline and explosives detonated by a fuse or grenade. But if her squad had been there, she wouldn't have cared how tech-sexy it was or wasn't.

Gunfire began before the echoes had ended. It sounded distant, but she knew that was only because her ears were ringing. She saw one of the apes, leaping from one building to another, its arms freakishly long.

"They're on the rooftops!" She shouted.

Of course they were. Freakin' kongs.

* * *

"Fall back to checkpoint four," McCullough said. Forest didn't acknowledge; she was probably too busy, but his order was superfluous. She knew what to do. It was time to let her do it.

"Checkpoint four," he said. "Song?"

"Yes, Colonel."

"Coming your way," he said. "Be ready."

"Yes sir."

Forest and her squad hadn't simply marched across the city, but left outposts to watch their backs. Checkpoint four was special.

On one level, the expedition really had been about finding out whether the apes were still entrenched where the locals placed them; animals were territorial, and it was possible they didn't have the sense to relocate. On the other hand, he had planned for the possibility that the apes were savvy enough to set up an ambush at their old digs. Having the Sanfrans jumping ahead and springing the trap early hadn't really been in the plan—he would have preferred not to lose anyone at all—but it was probably to his advantage. If Forest could draw them back a few hundred yards, the apes would find they had walked into a trap themselves; a crossfire involving twenty troops, two mounted M60s and four rocket launchers, all looking down on a broad boulevard with minimal cover.

He switched to the camera Forest had mounted before leaving the checkpoint. He had debated whether he should use it or not; cameras were plentiful enough, but the batteries that ran them were in short supply. No one manufactured them anymore; they had to be hand-built by the guys in tech, and HQ gave them out only sparingly.

The view point was from behind one of the M60s. He

watched the entrance to the street Forest and her squad were supposed to come in by. As they arrived, John stood out, taller than any of them. A little fringe of black hair around the band of his cap argued that he needed a haircut. He'd mention that when the lieutenant got back.

For an instant, it seemed impossible that the man down there could be the same little thing he'd held against his shoulder with one palm, the same wide-eyed boy he'd said goodbye to ten years ago—or even the rangy, muscular young fellow who had moved up through the ranks to join him at Base Lewis McChord. Two years of fighting side-by-side, and yet it seemed like the beat of a hummingbird's wing.

He frowned. John was a soldier. One of his, but one of many. He didn't need to lose focus just because they shared blood.

For McCullough, waiting was the tough part; he would have preferred to be there, not giving orders over the airwaves. But on this mission, he was in charge, and there were certain command protocols in place. He could break them, but he was just getting out of hot water with the brass concerning some of his methods. Anyway, too much personal involvement on his part would suggest to Forest, John, and the others that he didn't believe they were capable, when in fact he did.

So he waited.

"Forest, you still there?"

The radio crackled. "Yes, sir. They're following us."

"How many, do you think?"

"It's hard to tell," she said, her voice composed, despite the gunfire he could hear. "They keep moving. Always under cover."

"Just bring 'em on back to the party," he said.

A few moments later he saw Forest and the others emerge into the open. He hunkered close to the screen, watching for signs of the apes appearing. Forest and her squad made it to the barricade of cars they'd set up and got down behind it.

"Where are they?" he heard Forest say. "They were right behind us."

Then, through the eye of the camera, he saw the barrel of the M60 shift. And it began to fire.

One of the apes appeared on a rooftop, and then another, then a third and fourth. All were mostly under cover from Forest's perspective, but if she had the angle right in her head, they were all vulnerable to the M60s. Song, she figured, was waiting for more of them to commit.

But then it all sort of snapped together in her head.

There weren't a dozen or two dozen apes chasing them. The four up there was all there had ever been. By spreading out, staying under cover, and firing wildly, they had made their numbers seem greater. But there were supposed to be hundreds of these things. Where were the rest?

"It's a trap," she shouted. "Up, all of you. Haul ass."

But it was too late for Geary, who was still just looking at her in confusion when the sixty-millimeter rounds walked up his back. Sasaki didn't get much further.

She managed to get her assault rifle up and tear off a few rounds as she ran toward the nearest cover, an alley probably thirty yards away. What remained of her squad was with her, trying to also lay down cover fire, but they were now in the crossfire they had intended for the apes. Bullets fell around them like hail at a steep slant. Her squad collapsed around her.

John was still up, she saw, and a hard resolve worked its way through her. There was one more thing she could do for the Colonel.

"Lieutenant," she said. "Go."

Then she turned and began firing at anything she saw moving.

But they were everywhere. They swarmed on the buildings like black flies on garbage. A sledgehammer seemed to hit her in the chest, and everything went white. The ground didn't feel like anything when she struck it, but as her vision faded back in she saw John on the asphalt only a few feet away. She managed to get her feet under her and stumble his way, but then another round hit her in the back, and the best she could manage to do was fall over his body.

I'm sorry, Colonel, she thought.

McCullough watched, unable to tear his gaze from the screen. To her credit, Forest realized what was happening. She tried to get them out, and for a heart-stopping moment he thought she might succeed.

Then John fell, and for a moment he didn't see anything at all.

Then the blood seemed to rush back into his head.

"Damn it!" he snapped. "Goddamn it!"

"Shall I send reinforcements?" Pascal asked. His normally dark face was pale. "We can send checkpoint three up."

The moment between his last breath and the next seemed to go on for a long time. He ran it through his head, how long it would take checkpoint three to get there, their odds of prevailing, the chance that anyone in Forest's squad—*anyone*—was even now still alive.

He couldn't make it work out right.

"No," he said. "No. Bring them all back—all the checkpoints. If there is anyone to bring back."

"Yes sir," Pascal said, unable to hide his dismay, but not willing to challenge him.

A face suddenly appeared in front of the camera, and for an instant McCullough was struck still by it. It wasn't human; its nose was as recessed as the opening on a skull's; no forehead rose above the eyebrows, and its huge teeth seemed almost to grin in its chinless face. But its eyes were quick, not the eyes of an animal at all, but full of intelligence, purpose, and malice.

Then it was gone, replaced by static.

Everyone at the ambush site was dead, had probably been half a minute after he spoke to Song. He pictured the beasts, quietly surrounding Song's squad, easing down from rooftops, getting behind them with knives or spears or just their strong, inhuman hands, striking all at once.

Turning his plans against him.

He felt the sudden depth to which he had underestimated these creatures, what it had already cost him, what it was going to cost him.

At just that moment, the door banged open.

"Sir!" It was a private, Stringer.

"What is it?" he snapped.

"We're under attack, sir."

McCullough unholstered his pistol and followed the man outside.

He wasn't sure what he'd expected, but a cavalry charge hadn't been on his shortlist. They were coming in from the only direction they could, the north side of the beach, through a barrage of gun and rocket fire. He had never seen anything like it, and for a moment—amidst everything else stirring in him—he was struck by the beauty of it. He was reminded of a picture he had once seen from World War II, of mounted Cossacks charging tanks.

Whatever else they were, these things were brave sons-of-bitches.

He switched his channel to the *Daedalus*.

"Lay down some fire on those bastards, goddamn it!" he snapped. "What the hell are you out there for, anyway?"

"Yes, sir," Captain Hayes replied. "We're just now aware of the situation."

As he watched, the Bofors turned and began pumping shells at the apes charging up the beach. The first few rounds struck with horrific effect; he watched with savage satisfaction as several of the apes and their mounts were literally blown apart.

The rest rode around them, smashing through the half-finished barrier and pounding into their makeshift compound. At the same time, he heard Captain Hayes swear; out on the boat, black smoke from at least three missiles was churning around the starboard guns.

He raised his pistol, trying to figure out which one of the beasts was the leader.

Just then, someone got the mounted guns rattling behind him, and another full rank of the apes went down, and the charge finally broke, wheeling and galloping back up the beach the way they had come.

He stood there, still gripping his pistol, knuckles white, beads of sweat beginning to drip into his eyes.

"They're on the run, sir," Pascal said. "Shall we give chase?"

"No," he said. "Hell, no. Are you crazy? That's probably exactly what they want us to do."

He knew for a fact that the apes still controlled the Golden Gate Bridge. That must have been where the charge was staged from. He had considered reducing it before taking them on in the city, but he hadn't been sure what a pitched battle against these things would be like. The bridge could be like their Thermopylae, their Hot Gates—a relatively small number could hold a narrow approach against greater numbers—and frankly, he wasn't even sure his numbers were greater. The Sanfrans talked as if there were thousands of apes out there.

But now he was seeing the results of leaving them on that flank. Still, without air support or significant artillery, storming the bridge could easily cut his force in half.

Especially if they just went charging up there pell-mell, on the heel of retreating cavalry. No, that was a mistake that fell right into the "all-time classic" category.

"Plug that hole, mine the hell out of it, and double the perimeter guard," he said. "And pull everyone back here."

His headset was demanding his attention. It was Captain Hayes.

"Report, Captain," he said. "How are the guns?"

"We're not sure yet, sir," Hayes replied. "But there's a good chance the port Bofs are out of commission. We still have the starboard array, of course."

"Yeah," he said, dryly. He looked around at the carnage, the drifting smoke, the sun on the water.

"Move out to sea," he said.

"Sir?"

"They may have more rockets. Hell, they may have bigger ones. Move out of range."

Then he walked over to the dead apes, to get a better look at what he was dealing with.

One was still alive, tracking him with its eyes when he got there. By its wounds, it wouldn't be breathing for much longer, but by the same evidence, it should have died immediately.

"So strong," he murmured, absently. He knelt by the beast.

"Your leader," he said. "Is he here?"

The thing narrowed its eyes and showed its teeth.

Then it grunted. At first it just sounded like nothing. But then it did it again.

"Caesar. Kill. You," it said.

It didn't sound right. There was nothing right about it. It was like the universe itself was mocking him. John had no children, no sons. His line, his father's line, a family he could trace all the way back to the Norman Conquest and certainly went back farther than that was now at an end. And these—things—lived on.

"Yeah," he said. "Well, you won't be around to see it."

Then he shot it between the eyes.

7

Ray liked being back in the woods, even if they were lower, thicker, and drier than what he was used to. But things got better as they went along, with small stands of redwoods appearing, like miniature versions of the forest that saw his birth. They still weren't as tall or large in girth as what he was used to, but after days in the boxy, unfriendly landscape of the city, they would do. It was with genuine pleasure that he scuttled up a tree when Blue Eyes told him to have a look around, climbing to the highest part that would bear him, feeling the welcome stretch in his arms.

He couldn't see much of interest, but one could hear more above the ground than on it, and what he heard soon sent him back down to report to Blue Eyes.

"Off that way," he signed. "Humans. They sound funny."

"What do you mean?" Blue Eyes asked.

Ray wasn't sure what to tell him.

"A little like orangutans, when we do the long call," he said. "But also like birds. Maybe more like birds."

That didn't satisfy Blue Eyes, but Ray couldn't come up with anything better. After consulting with the humans, the decision was made to move on toward the strange sounds. On the ground, Ray could no longer hear them, but as they drew closer they began to filter through the understory.

"I get it," Alexander said. "I guess you've never heard anything like that, huh, Ray?"

"What is it?" Ray asked.

"They're singing," Ellie answered. "It's a hymn. I used to know it."

"Like the machine at the gas station," Blue Eyes said.

Ray hadn't been there for that, but he had heard about it. Apes and humans together had worked to fix a human building that made something called electricity. It was supposed to be like lightning, captured in metal wires. On their way back to the village they had come across an old human ruin, glowing with artificial light, the first "human" light any ape under the age of ten had ever seen. And there had been strange sounds, rhythmic like drumming, voices, but not voices talking.

Ray hadn't quite been able to imagine what Blue Eyes and the rest had been describing. Now he understood, and found it weirdly beautiful.

"Yes," Ellie said. "Like at the gas station." She smiled, but it went away quickly, and she stopped talking. Malcolm stretched over to hold her hand as they continued on.

They soon reached a ridge overlooking a meadow surrounded by redwoods. A small troop of humans was gathered there, surrounding a rectangular hole in the ground. The hole was recently dug, and its dirt was piled up right next to it. From his angle, Ray could just see something was in the hole, but not what.

"What are they doing?" Blue Eyes asked Malcolm.

Malcolm looked at him oddly, then smiled a little. Ray knew smiles conveyed happiness in humans, but this one did not seem happy, to him.

"I guess you weren't around when we buried our dead, the other day."

Blue Eyes just repeated his answer in sign.

"It's a funeral," Malcolm said. "They're burying someone. It's what we do with our dead. Some of us, anyway."

"Why?" Blue Eyes asked.

Malcolm spread his hands. "Depends on who you ask," he said. "It's complicated. But it helps us move on. That's the theory, anyway."

"How?" Blue Eyes signed.

"I dunno," Malcolm said. "I guess if we put them in the ground, it forces us to acknowledge that they're really gone. I mean, a lot of people believe that we don't really die, that there is something in us that survives after the body is gone. But even if you believe that, you still have to face the fact that you won't see that person again, or talk to them—at least not for a long time. And if you don't believe that…" he trailed off, looking over at Alexander, who was drawing furiously, sketching the people and their hole.

Ray wondered if maybe he should have put his father in a hole. He had looked so broken, so lonely when Ray found him. He had lain down with him and slept there all night. He knew his father would never get up again, but it was still hard to leave him. Hard to forget sleeping next to him when he was alive, reaching out to touch him, and his father sleepily shifting to grip his hand.

Ray wondered if the human in the hole had a son, and if his son would feel better or worse with his father in the ground. It seemed even lonelier, somehow, than lying above it, where at least people might come visit his bones.

The singing was nice, though. He noticed that Ellie was humming along with the song. He experimented with doing the same, but the results were frustrating.

After a little while, the humans stopped singing and a

few of them began filling in the hole. The others walked away, slowly. Some of them were holding hands.

He was vaguely aware that Blue Eyes was still questioning Malcolm about the funeral, and getting more frustrated as he did so. Blue Eyes was not nearly as good as Caesar with the sound-speaking, and Malcolm didn't seem to understand a lot of the signs. Ray didn't try to follow their conversation. Instead, he closed his eyes, trying to imagine what it would be like underground. Would it be terrible, not being able to move, or would it be more like being held fast and warm by your mother?

They stayed until all the humans were gone, and Ray suddenly realized that Malcolm, Ellie, and Alexander were saying goodbye.

"I recognized some of them," Malcolm said. "They're decent people. They'll treat us well as long as we pull our weight. It might not be where we end up in the long run, but it'll be as safe a place to get our bearings as any."

Malcolm offered his hand to Blue Eyes, who at first seemed confused. But after a moment, Blue Eyes took it. Ray remembered the gesture was supposed to indicate trust.

"Tell your father I'm sorry," Malcolm said. "I never wanted it to come to this. I really hoped we could find a way…"

His voice faded.

Blue Eyes still looked unsure.

Ray understood. His own feelings about Malcolm— about all of the humans—were mixed. But Malcolm and Ellie had saved Caesar's life. That meant a lot.

"Caesar understand," Blue Eyes said. Then he touched Malcolm on the shoulder, as he might another ape.

"*I* understand," he said.

When he tried to touch Ellie, she embraced him, and Alexander shook his hand. Then all of the gestures were repeated—much more awkwardly—with Rocket and Ray.

"I hope you find what you're looking for," Malcolm said. "You—your people—they deserve a chance."

"Thank you," Blue Eyes said.

A few moments later the humans were riding down toward the meadow and its fresh mound of earth, and Ray was headed toward the sunset with Blue Eyes and Rocket. It felt like more than a parting—it seemed to Ray as if something important had come to an end.

That evening they tethered the horses and slept in the trees, Ray soothed to sleep by a breeze that smelled of the sea. Rocket and Blue Eyes stayed awake, signing about something.

Sometime in the night, the tree shook. It shook so furiously that Ray tumbled from it, and hit the ground so hard he fell into it. It swallowed him up. He felt the threads of tiny roots comb through his fur as he passed through the dirt.

At first he was terrified—by the darkness, by the smell of the dirt all around him, by not being able to draw breath. He fought, and he struggled, and then he grew tired.

And that was when he heard his name, or at least the sound his father used to make when calling him. He reached toward the sound, and found that he could move, and then that he could see. The darkness was now filled with stars, and the bright moon was in the sky, larger than he had ever seen it. In the light of the moon, he detected a familiar shape.

"Father?" he asked. The shape looked like him, but it was just a shadow, with no color. It took his arm and led him along a bit, until they were just in front of a tree. At least, that's what Ray thought it was, at first. But the more he looked at it, the stranger it seemed. It had no leaves, and the branches twisted and spread, meandering like rainwater on a shallow slope.

The shadow shaped like his father climbed into the branches, and then Ray noticed that some of the stars weren't stars at all, but eyes. Two belonged to his father, but there were others, many more. He thought he saw his mother there, and Ash, and Sara, all gathered in the tree.

Then he understood that it wasn't a tree, but the roots of a tree, and that he was on the other side of the dirt, beyond the hole he had fallen into, where trees were roots and their roots the trees he knew...

And then he woke up. The tree was still shaking, and Rocket and Blue Eyes were holding on to him, both panting in alarm. Below, he heard the horses' voices raised in panic.

"What is it?" Rocket demanded, as the trembling finally subsided.

But Ray knew.

"It was my dream," he said. "My dream shook the tree."

Blue Eyes held his gaze for a moment, a skeptical frown on his face.

"Tell me," he finally said.

And so Ray told him, as the old moon rose in the arms of the new, and the Owls-That-Sound-Like-Chimps hooted somewhere in the near darkness.

"What did Ash look like?" Blue Eyes asked, when he was done. "Did he look dead?"

"No," Ray said. "Just like he usually did. Only his eyes were stars."

"Malcolm said some humans think people go someplace else when they die," Blue Eyes said. "Maybe they go to the places we go when we dream."

"Maybe," Ray said. "When I dream of someplace, it's usually like someplace I know, but different. Like the village—I dream about it, but there are places in it when I dream that aren't there when I'm awake. But it feels real. Different, but real."

"Yes," Blue Eyes said. "It's all different. So maybe there, if trees are roots and roots are trees, the dead are alive, and the living are dead."

"Could be," Ray said. "In my dream, everything was upside down. Except that there was a sky under there, too."

Rocket, who had been watching them without interrupting, suddenly made an angry noise and began climbing down.

"Stupid," he said. "Dreams are nothing. Bugs in our ears. Just bugs."

They reached the coast the next morning. Ray dismounted his horse and went bounding off as soon as they came in sight of the water. He darted across the sand and began playing tag with the waves, doing hand stands on his long, graceful arms. Blue Eyes, still in a solemn mood, perched on a rock, a little cross at the younger ape, who didn't seem to be taking their journey seriously. Rocket, sitting next to Blue Eyes, noticed his silent agitation. But instead of saying anything, the older chimp slowly clambered down and walked toward Ray. Blue Eyes realized Rocket was going to discipline the young orang, and began to call out for him not to, but he didn't. He knew his father had put him in charge of the expedition, and Rocket seemed to agree that he was the leader, but whenever he saw the older ape, he felt himself begin to submit. It felt wrong to give Rocket orders. Rocket, after all, had been Alpha before his father was. He was bigger, stronger, older, more versed in the ways of the world.

So Blue Eyes just watched, feeling a little sorry for Ray, who was having fun. And he realized that he was mostly mad at the younger ape not for the way he was acting, but because he was jealous. *He* wanted to see Ash in the dream world, talk to him again, maybe fish in the dream river and boast of their catches. Why did Ray have these dreams, and not him?

He watched as Rocket drew up to Ray, and the orangutan stopped playing, watching Rocket to see what he would do. Rocket glowered at him for a second, and Ray dropped his head a little.

Then the surf rolled up, and Rocket splashed some of it on Ray with his hand. Ray looked surprised, shrieked, and splashed him back. Then he began to run, as Rocket chased him.

Blue Eyes continued to watch in astonishment as they tumbled about in the surf, playing at wrestling. He felt a powerful urge to join them, and almost did, but something stopped him—he wasn't sure what. But watching them, he felt a little better. Rocket had lost a son, and Ray a father, but for the moment they had each other. Maybe what kept him from joining in was the feeling that he might be intruding on something private between them.

But then Ray ran up and threw wet sand in his face, and with a mock hoot-pant, Blue Eyes leapt onto the beach and joined them.

And for a little while, he did not worry about death, or dreams, or what he might or might not find in the south.

8

McCullough paused with his finger on the radio switch, trying to keep his response... within prescribed limits.

"Yes, General," he said, trying for a diplomatic rather than a sarcastic tone, not entirely sure he was succeeding. "I am aware that our resources are spread thin. And with respect, this isn't the first time I've been on the bad end of that."

"I'm still trying to wrap my head around this, son," Prescott replied.

General Prescott had a voice for radio. His articulation was almost artificially perfect; he sounded avuncular, authoritative, and intelligent. In McCullough's estimation, a good deal of what his voice suggested was illusion. Physically, Prescott didn't have much of a presence. He wore thick spectacles, had a weak chin and eyes which could charitably be described as bulging. Of the current leadership, he was the only one remaining who had been a general before the Simian Flu started making its rounds, and for some reason he seemed to think that made him better than some, although he wasn't tone deaf enough to ever say that. It was as if he believed—against all evidence—that the world in which he'd risen through the ranks had somehow produced better leaders than the crucible of the last decade.

"General," McCullough said. "The fact is that we vastly underestimated these creatures. They are strong, they are smart, and they are determined."

"*We*, Colonel?" the General said. "Or *you*? There were some who thought you were allocated far too many resources for this mission. Now you're telling me you don't have enough."

"That's right, General," McCullough said. "I need air support, for one thing. These things are too agile—not just as individuals, but as units. And they do work in units. They plan. They coordinate strikes…"

"It seems to me you set the bar too low, Colonel," Prescott said. "What I hear in your account sounds like a series of mistakes you wouldn't have made against a human enemy."

"That may be true," he said. "Certainly they surprised me."

"Despite what the locals told you."

"No," McCullough said. "Sir, what the locals described was a barely organized assault that only succeeded because there were so many of these things, and because they took the human fighters flat-footed by violating a truce. What I saw today was a multi-pronged attack carried out with a great deal of precision."

"How do you account for the difference?" Prescott asked.

"Caesar."

"You're not about to start on one of your historical asides, are you, son?" the General asked.

"No, sir. I mean they've had a change of leadership. The ape leading the earlier attack is dead, apparently killed by the monkey now in charge. A chimpanzee, I'm told. And his name is Caesar."

"So now you've got a chimp down there who is a military genius?"

"No. Not a genius. But he must be smart. And at the moment, he has a lot of advantages. He's familiar with the terrain—we aren't. His soldiers can climb straight up buildings. And I'm pretty certain they outnumber us."

The General took his time replying.

"How many did you lose today, son?"

That was a question he hadn't been looking forward to answering.

"We're still not sure," he said. "As many as twenty-eight, possibly."

"You haven't retrieved the bodies?"

"General, whatever else these creatures may know, I doubt that they are familiar with the Geneva Convention or with the concept of perfidy more generally. If I had to guess—and that is part of my job—I would imagine that they're just waiting for us to try and retrieve our fallen so they can hit us again."

"You mean to say that's what you would do if you were them."

He knew Prescott was goading him, but he was starting not to care.

"You're damn right, sir," he said. "Maybe you haven't noticed, but we're fighting for the survival of our civilization. And by that I don't mean American civilization, or Western civilization—but all human civilization. Thousands of years of learning and history stand in the balance. We must win, sir. At whatever cost."

"Yes," the General said. "I'm aware of your personal philosophy. It nearly resulted in your court martial."

Yeah, McCullough thought. *You made a big show of that, didn't you?* But he knew why they hadn't gone through with it—because despite their protestations, their lingering commitment to niceties the human race no longer had the luxury to observe—they liked his results. He won.

But there were many ways to fight a war, and just now making an issue of Prescott's hypocrisy wasn't likely to advance his cause.

"My larger point," he said, trying to sound calmer, "is that we can't expect them to play fair. I won't risk soldiers I need to recover those I no longer do."

"That's not acceptable," the General said. "We still have to recruit, if we're to expand rule of law. Soldiers and their families must be respected. Imagine if John was one of the missing—"

"As a matter of fact, General, he is," McCullough said. The words sounded like they were coming from someone else's mouth, someone far distant from this conversation. "I saw him fall myself, over the video feed."

That shut Prescott up for a moment.

"My God, son," the General said. "I'm sorry to hear that. My condolences to you. He was a good soldier."

"Thank you, sir, I appreciate that. But what I really need is reinforcements. Helicopters." He paused. "Gas."

"Gas?" Prescott's voice rose a notch. "You mean like nerve compounds? Mustard gas? Son, you know better than that."

"I know we have it," he said. "We may not have used it, sir, but I know we have it. And if there was ever a time to use it—sir, they aren't human."

"Son, stop," Prescott cautioned. "That dog won't hunt."

"Sir," he said, realizing he was breathing hard.

"I understand your frustration," the General lied. "And I'm sorry about John. He was a fine boy and I know you're distraught. He is to your everlasting credit both as a leader and a father. But the real question before us is, why should we commit our time and resources to this particular theater? As strange as the situation is, from what we know these apes haven't given anyone any trouble before. They haven't tried to expand their range."

"Except into San Francisco," he said.

"It's a parochial conflict," the General said. "And I see no overarching danger. Our resources are better spent keeping the peace we've made and trying to contact other pockets of civilization. We sent you down there to find out what was going on, and we outfitted you with the resources to mop up a decent-sized problem. If you deem that problem too big to solve with the resources you have—well, then it is within the scope of your orders to return to base."

"Are you recalling me, sir?"

"I am not," Prescott said. "I'm just asking you to use your judgment. Which would be easier—to continue fighting these animals, or to move the human survivors to a safe zone?"

McCullough, of course, knew which would be easier. He knew which would most parsimoniously discharge his responsibility. But he now understood something that Prescott and very possibly none of the upper brass would even entertain. They were so attached to the idea of peace, of maintaining the pitiful slice of civilization they had half-assed managed to salvage, that they didn't see the bigger picture. Humanity had pissed off nature one too many times, and nature had plans for them. He felt in his gut as he had never known anything before that if the apes survived, humankind would not.

But it was okay, he realized. Reinforcements would be helpful; they would make the job easier. But he would get it done, regardless.

Whatever it took.

"I'll get back to you on that, sir," he said. "It's early yet."

He let the radio lie silent for a moment, then turned to the operator, Gomez.

"You say you have a signal from down south?" he said.

"Yes, sir. There is a bit of traffic that way. Weak, but I might be able to boost the signal."

"Do it," he said.

McCullough sat with his back propped against the cinderblock wall. Around the corner, he could hear the enemy, working their way nearer. Coming for him, but with a certain amount of respect, due to the number of his bullets that had found their mark. Unfortunately, he didn't have many of those bullets left.

Tom-Ten glanced over from his position. He motioned left and held up four fingers, then right and two more.

Yeah, McCullough thought. *And maybe eight more working around to the sides.*

In the most optimistic scenario, that meant he didn't have much time to make his play. But this scenario was anything but optimistic.

They called themselves the Apostles. They had started out as a typical militia group in western Washington State, holed up on a ranch, trying to fight off the Simian Flu with rifles and shotguns. When that didn't work and they started getting sick anyway, they got religion, decided God had work for them to do—that if they helped the disease weed out the sinners, he would spare them. The fact, of course, was that they had already been spared—they had been exposed to the virus and survived, which meant they were genetically immune.

But that simple fact didn't stop them. They left a smoking trail across western Washington, picking up converts as they came along, headed, as they saw it, for the sin-center of the universe—Seattle, as laughable as that would have been in the days before the epidemic.

He and his people had moved to stop them before they crossed the Cascades, or at least that was the plan. Instead, they had been ambushed on the roadside in the ruins of Ellensburg. He still didn't know what had gone wrong, only that most of his people were dead. He had managed to lead the survivors to cover in an old industrial complex. A cold night had come and gone, leaving snow behind, but no relief had arrived, and now they were all but out of ammunition.

He leaned out and squeezed off another round. He was rewarded with a gasp of pain and shock.

With each bullet he spent, something inside of him seemed to go as well, making room to let the cold in. He began to hum, and then to sing.

Got an assignment
Gave me a job
Gonna get it done now
No time to sob.

Tom-Ten chuckled harshly, a dead man's laugh. Then he joined in.

This is my ri-fle
This is my gun.
Whatever it takes
impossible or none.

McCullough fired again at the head he saw pop up from behind a row of steel barrels. He hit a barrel, and it rang like a bell.

Now the rest of his men joined him, as outside there was a sudden stir.

Fall in, fall out
Seein' Jody, seein' red.
All on the grind now
Ain't stoppin' 'til we're dead

The first of the Apostles to come around the corner took his second-to-last bullet in the chest. Two more fell as Tom-Ten, Harris and Li let fly, and then they were in, like a tide. But by then the cold was deep in him. He saw the rifle butt slamming toward his face, and a part of him just didn't care anymore.

After that, they did things to him. His nightmares didn't do it justice. He thought that they didn't have anything to take from him, but he was wrong. He tried to focus, to remember. His wife, Maggie, his son John. He remembered leaving them at the shelter, how gray it was, wondering if he would ever see them again. But in his memory, he couldn't make out their faces. He couldn't find them through the agony, and he wondered how death could be any worse.

After a long time, it was over, and he lay shackled in the dark. The pain was still there, but it seemed very far away. The cold was all through him now, and he felt beyond remorse or fear or even anger. But with all of that gone, there was still something left, something that wouldn't let him stop. He felt the eyes of his fathers on him, of history, a purpose that pressed through time and space, the impulse Horatius had felt on the bridge, Leonidas at Thermopylae, Crockett at the Alamo. He had his orders. He had his mission.

And he began to sing again, under his breath, working the slack in his chains, ignoring the grinding pain, focusing on the work, on the breath behind his words.

Eyes peeled—forward!
Past is for the weak.
Gotta job to finish
Lookin' pretty bleak.

One hand slipped free, and then the other, quicker.

After that, his memory grew even spottier. He recalled a fight and the snap of a man's neck, and then he had a gun. He remembered running through the dark and finally seeing light in the distance. Outside there were more of them. They were surprised, and they were scared. He wasn't. He took his time, making sure each bullet counted. The last tried to run, but he put a round in his back, then shot him again before rolling him over to be sure.

Gonna get it done
No matter what the price.
Nothin' gonna block me
Victory's my vice.

As he rolled him over, the young man's dead face looked up at him, so familiar.

John.

He woke, gasping, his body slicked with sweat. He hadn't remembered falling asleep, and when he looked at his watch, he realized he'd only been out for a few minutes. He was sitting in a chair with his head down on his charts. He hadn't intended to sleep at all, but two days without a wink could creep up on you, no matter what else was happening.

He took hold of himself. It hadn't been John, that day, just a boy about his age who looked a little like him. At the time, he hadn't even blinked; unlike the first boy he'd killed, there hadn't been anything childlike left in this one. When they were captured, he'd watched him shoot Harris in the kneecaps and enjoy it.

For just that instant, he felt relief. His dream had tricked him. John wasn't dead.

But then he remembered that he was. Not at his hand, but by the filthy paws of the apes.

Forest woke broken. Beyond the fact that she wasn't dead, it was the first thing she understood. Her chest hurt like fire, and every breath burned hotter than the last, and something was wrong with one of her legs. It was dark, as dark as only a city with no fire or electricity could be. How long had she lain unconscious? Long enough for night to fall, obviously.

Clenching her teeth on the agony, she forced herself to her knees, and it was then that she realized someone was beneath her, and it all came back—the reversed ambush, falling on John to protect him as best she could.

She felt through the darkness.

John wasn't stiff but that could mean either that rigor mortis hadn't set in yet or that she had been out long enough for it to be over. But then she found his neck, and the faint pulse fluttering there.

She couldn't get him to wake, though, so she spent several long, painful minutes dragging him upright and getting him into a carry on her good shoulder, discovering in the process that her other arm was sticky with congealed blood.

By inches, then by feet and yards, she started to make progress, although she didn't know what direction she was moving in. She figured as long as she wasn't moving toward the apes, one way was as good as another.

Not long after thinking that, she heard something

move, and then a light suddenly shone on her. Behind the light she could see the faint whites of someone's eyes and not much else.

For a long moment, she stood still. The light moved over her, head-to-foot, and once it was out her eyes she could see what was holding it, the dark fur on its arm, the distorted shape of its skull.

"Please," she said. "He needs help."

The ape locked its gaze on hers for what seemed like a long time. She wanted to look away, but somehow felt that it would be the wrong move. Besides, if she was about to die, she wanted to be looking her killer in the eye when it happened.

But then the ape grunted, and gestured with the light, not the way she had been going. In the actinic glow, she made out a street sign, and suddenly knew where she was and how to get back to base.

Then the light was gone, and she was alone.

Maybe it was playing with her. Maybe in ten steps it would put a bullet in her brain. But for the moment, she would act as if everything was going to be okay.

"Come on, John," she said. "Let's get you to the Colonel."

9

The coast was wild and restless. Signs of humanity remained—a building here and there, the roads, the rusting remains of cars. But they were fewer, and at times it was easy for Ray to imagine he was in places where no ape or human had ever been.

And the sea. He had seen it before, on foraging expeditions toward the sunset. All water seemed alive, somehow—streams were like children, laughing, running here or there, throwing tantrums when the rain came too hard. Rivers were slower, steadier, givers of life, but still prone to excitability at times. Even water in a still pool had a certain quickness, except when it grew very cold, and then went to sleep, like bears and raccoons in winter. Sleeping water was as hard as rock, and you could walk on it, although it was very slick.

He had wondered at times if such sleeping water dreamed.

But the sea was like a mother, grooming her child of stone and earth and trees, caressing the beach with her touch.

On this coast, sometimes the sea was as he had known her, but at others she was wild and terrible and awesome.

She came at the land not like a gentle mother, but with fight, as if determined to batter the stones of the shore to pieces. By the look of the beach—made mostly of tiny bits of shattered stone—that had been going on for a long time.

The sea gave him dreams, some stranger than those he had had of his father and Ash and the trees that were roots. One morning he awoke, dreams still clinging to him like dew, and began to draw in the sand with a stick. He was so absorbed in what he was doing that he didn't notice Blue Eyes had come up and begun watching him until the chimp tapped him on the arm.

"What is this?" Blue Eyes asked.

"My dream," he replied.

Blue Eyes looked at his drawing. "Tell me what it is," he said.

Ray showed him the first figure, a circle with rays of heat and light coiling out from it.

"I dreamed I was the sun," he said. "I was stuck to the sky, unable to move, and the sky pulled me along. And here, I saw the sea below me, and was frightened. I knew the sea would put out my flame. So I fought, but the sky didn't care. It just kept pulling me down. And finally, I went into the sea. I felt my flame sputter, like a burning stick in a pool. My flame died, and I became an ember, and finally a coal.

"My fire went out, but I could still see, and hear, although it was very quiet. I was cold, but not too cold. Fish and jellyfish and whales watched me go by, and then everything was dark, and I knew something was in the water, something huge and awful, something that wanted to eat me. I didn't see it, but it got so close I could feel its breath. I called out for help.

"And suddenly lights appeared, and the monster stopped, and I was no longer in the water, but in the sky of night, with the eyes of the stars above me, and I was no longer afraid."

Blue Eyes didn't say anything for a while.

"The sun dies every day," he finally said. "I never thought of that."

"But it also comes back every morning," Ray said. "I didn't dream that, but it does."

Blue Eyes looked thoughtful then turned toward the sea.

"Have you noticed?" he said. "Sometimes the sea is getting closer, and sometimes farther away. You can see where it was at its highest place."

"Yes," Ray said.

Blue Eyes motioned at his scratches in the sand—the sun, the fish, the nameless monster, the stars.

"Your drawing will get washed away, in a little while," he said.

Ray considered that.

"Everything on the beach gets washed away eventually," he said. "But things get washed up, as well."

Ray settled into the journey, not worrying much about what they were going to find, instead enjoying each new turn of the coast as it came into view. Near the ruins of a large house, they found a tree with red fruit like giant rose hips; breaking them open they found them to be full of tiny seeds, glistening like red frogs' eggs. They tasted crisp and tart and sweet, and though Blue Eyes had never seen such food before, Rocket thought he remembered eating something like it long ago. In the same place, they found grapes (a bit green, but edible) and figs and bitter little fruits that didn't taste good at all. He would have been content to forage in the area for days, but Blue Eyes had other ideas. Something was pushing him along, forcing him to look for something even if he didn't know quite what it was. He was like the sky in Ray's dream, and Ray was the sun stuck to him.

The earth shook again, as it had that night when he'd had his dream of the roots, but not as strongly, or perhaps they felt it less because they were not in a tree.

A little after dawn one morning, Rocket climbed down from the high thrust of stone where he'd been standing watch.

"We're being followed," he said.

"Are you sure?" Blue Eyes asked.

"Yes. I caught a glimpse of them, up in the hills, there. I thought I saw them yesterday, but I wasn't sure. Now I am."

"Maybe it's Malcolm," Blue Eyes said. "Maybe the other humans didn't want them there, or he didn't like it. Maybe they're trying to catch up."

"No," Rocket said. "The riders aren't human. They are apes. They have guns."

Blue Eyes' jaw hung open for a moment.

"Back at the ape sanctuary—"

"Malcolm was wrong," Rocket said. "It's not humans tracking him. It's apes tracking *us*."

"Who?" Ray asked.

Rocket shrugged. "Some who followed Koba were still unhappy, I think. Maybe they follow him still. Maybe they want to kill or capture the son of Caesar."

"What should we do?" Blue Eyes asked.

Rocket scratched at the scab forming on his arm.

"Hide," he said. "Wait for them. Give them a surprise." He tapped his rifle.

"Ape not kill ape," Blue Eyes protested.

Rocket pointed at the hills with his lips.

"Tell them that, when they catch up with us. I'm sure they'll listen. They tried to kill us once already, remember?"

"I don't want to kill anyone," Blue Eyes said.

Rocket waved his hand, looking frustrated.

"Then we hide and let them pass. Lay a false trail and take another way."

"You think that will work?" Blue Eyes asked.

"Killing them would work better," Rocket said, looking a little agitated. "These apes were with Koba. Koba killed Ash."

For a moment, the two seemed to face off.

Ray looked from one to the other, thinking that he agreed with Rocket, but a little unsure who he was supposed to follow if they got into an argument. Koba hadn't personally killed Ray's father the way he had Ash, but if it hadn't been for Koba's deception, the war with humans might not have started. And if the war hadn't started, he and his father could be looking for a new sapling to make a spear from, right now.

Fortunately, he didn't have to choose. Rocket relaxed and touched his forehead to Blue Eyes'.

"Your way is Caesar's way," he said. "We will not kill unless we have to."

They camped in the hills near the sea, as they did every night. But an hour after sunset, they piled plenty of wood on their fire and then left, continuing down the human road until the moon rose. Rivers and streams flowed frequently from the mountains to join the ocean at the coast. They came to one of these rivers and found that the bridge crossing it had collapsed.

"This is good spot," Rocket said.

They forded the river on their horses and rejoined the road, traveled on it until most of the mud from their horses' hooves had come off, and then went back down into the river on the other side of the broken span, leading their mounts into the shallow waters at the edge of the stream. Rocket then dismounted and did his best to erase the tracks leading back to the water.

Then they began riding upstream, their horses wading in the river.

Ray did not like the night—few apes did. Darkness meant missed branches and hard falls. It meant cougars and wolves and other predators who could see better at night, while apes could hardly see at all. Fire made nighttime bearable, kept the hungry eyes of the forest away. But now they were without fire, relying only on the heavens wheeling above them for their light. He remembered the monster in his dream of the sun and felt it might be out there, somewhere, waiting for him.

At night, dreams intruded on waking.

They passed through the bones of human settlements, and Ray wondered more about the dead of that strange race. If something of the humans who once lived here remained, what did they do? Go about their business as if alive? He found it was hard to imagine what humans had *done* here in life. Eat and drink like apes, of course, and mate and have children. But besides that, what? What were all those buildings for? What had they done in them? You couldn't hunt or forage inside of a house. Why had they spent so much time inside? Had it rained more, in the old days?

And if there were ghosts, did they eat and drink, and if so, what? Did they sleep? Life as he knew it was mostly about food: finding food, storing food, eating food. Drinking too. Urinating and defecating, which also had to do with food and drink. Then there was play, and grooming, stories, companionship, sleep. If ghosts didn't have or need those things, what would they do? Did the dead have their own food, their own drink? Was waking for them like sleep was for the living?

Everything seemed mysterious to Ray, especially

in the dark. Blue Eyes had taken this trip to bring back information to the troop. Ray began to suspect that he, too, was meant to bring something back, but not anything to do with humans or ships or guns. Something else.

In his dream of the roots, the dead had been underground, but the stars had been there. In his dream of the sun, he passed through the sea to the other side, where the stars also were. That had all been in dream. But what if you traveled far enough and long enough—what if you reached the very edge of the world. Could you swing beneath, visit the place of the dead without dying?

He didn't know. No ape knew. But if Malcolm was to be believed, there were some humans who might.

They traveled in the river until more than half the night was gone. When Blue Eyes was finally satisfied they had gone far enough, he called a rest. The banks of the river were clear of trees, covered instead with a carpet of grasses and weeds. They found the ruins of a house and took turns sleeping against it, leaving the horses to forage.

Ray took the last watch before dawn. He observed as the stars in the east began to fade, and wondered again if his dreams were true, if the stars were the eyes of the dead. If so, which stars were his father's eyes? Was there any way to know? Was there any way to talk to the star-eyed dead?

The horses whickered nervously, which was not a good sign. Ray picked up his rifle and stood for a better view.

Beneath his feet, the earth was shaking.

At first he thought it was like the other times, but this was different. It was more like the beating of a thousand drums and it did not stop, but kept going, and in fact grew louder. And in the distance, now, he heard a strange bellowing, not from one throat, but from many.

As the sun rose, the sound like thunder grew ever nearer. The light revealed that they were in a valley, wooded mountains surrounding fields of yellowed grass and a few low bushes, the river winding its way among it all.

Beside the river, a small herd of antelope was drinking, along with a few deer and some smaller animals. They too were lifting their heads, looking nervously for the source of the sound.

But then he saw the source of the drumbeats, a wave of brown rolling toward them across the fields.

He nudged Blue Eyes, who shifted and then sat up.

"What is it?" he asked.

"Cows," Ray signed.

Blue Eyes followed his gaze.

"I don't think that's the right sign," he said. "My father says there was a different one, but he couldn't remember it."

Ray shrugged. He and his father had seen these once, and that was the sign he had learned for them. They were big, maybe the biggest animals he had ever seen, with hooves like elk rather than horses, covered in thick hair, with massive, humped backs. And of course, the horns. Not branching like those of a deer or elk, but curved and sharp, like knives sticking out of their skulls. And his father had called them cows.

Of course, when he had seen them the time before, there had only been five. Now he was looking at so many he knew he could never count them, even using Maurice's tricks with sticks and scratches on stone. Now it seemed less like an ocean wave and more like a mud-slide had come down from the mountains, covering most of the open prairie, spreading fast—but this mud could walk and eat, and kill apes who got too close with their head-knives, trample them beneath their hard, sharp hooves...

Rocket was awake now, too. He roused himself, coming quickly alert, gaze searching everywhere at once.

The cows were running toward the river at full pace,

the pounding of their feet so loud now it was hard to hear much else. The antelope and deer scattered, white tails flashing in the morning sun.

"Be still," Rocket told him, and Ray realized he had been fidgeting.

"They're running for a reason," Rocket said. "Wolves. Maybe bear."

Blue Eyes ran his fingers over the scars forming over his ribs.

"Where?" Blue Eyes asked Rocket.

"Around," Rocket said. "Behind. On the edges. Watching for the weak. The small." When he said that last, he turned his gaze right on Ray.

"We have guns," Ray said.

"Yes," Rocket signed. "Be still."

"Where are the horses?" Blue Eyes asked, suddenly.

Ray, to his chagrin, realized that he'd lost track of them. After a few frantic moments of looking around, they finally spotted them down by the river, right in the path of the oncoming cows.

"We'd better go get them," Blue Eyes said.

Rocket touched Blue Eyes' shoulder and pointed. Ray looked too.

Across the field and behind the herd of cows, the grass rustled in several places. He saw one lean gray form, then another.

Wolves.

It had been a while since Ray had seen a wolf. His father and others—like Rocket—told tales of the early years of freedom, when children were often snatched by wolves, and the apes competed with the pack carnivores for game. Over the years, though, the wolves seemed to have all but abandoned the forest, seeking easier prey elsewhere.

Well, this was elsewhere; these wolves did not know apes or have any fear of them. And now the three of them had to cover the open ground between the pack and the river to reach the horses.

"Stand tall," Rocket advised. "Go fast."

They checked their weapons. Blue Eyes and Rocket both rose, then hesitated. Then Rocket took a slight step back, and Blue Eyes started to run. Rocket was a pace behind, and Ray took up the rear.

He glanced back, wondering if the wolves were after them yet, but he didn't see anything.

The cows were close, now a wall of meat and bone that wouldn't even notice him as they crushed him into the ground. He sprinted faster. The horses were stamping now, terrified.

Rocket shouted something, which Ray at first didn't understand. But then he repeated it more clearly.

"Wolf!"

He looked back and saw what Rocket meant. At least three of them were following, spreading as they came, obviously planning on coming at them from more than one direction. They were *fast*, and Rocket was already beginning to slow down. Ray knew in his gut they weren't all going to make it. Either the cows would run over them or the wolves would pull them down.

"Ray!" Blue Eyes shouted.

Ray had stopped and turned around.

"Get the horses," he signed.

Then Blue Eyes and Rocket stopped running and instead raised their guns to threaten the carnivores bounding toward them.

Ray didn't hesitate; he leapt on through the grass, short-calling. The horses saw him coming and seemed even more confused. Behind him Ray heard Rocket and Blue Eyes, barking aggressively at the wolves. A glance back showed them raised up to their full height, waving their arms and guns at the beasts. One tried to slip by to come after Ray, but Rocket got in front of it. Not sure what it was dealing with, the wolf dropped back, only to advance again a moment later.

Panting, Ray made it to the horses, who were doing a little dance themselves. He grabbed the reins of two, and climbed up onto his own, then turned to start riding toward Blue Eyes and Rocket as the cows arrived.

He whooped, because he saw he was going to make it.

He heard the stutter of Rocket's weapon, and saw the wolf leaping for Blue Eyes twist in the air. He watched as Blue Eyes raised his own weapon...

And something slammed into him. His horse screamed and bolted; he lost hold of the leads for the other two as he fought just to hold on, and screeched in consternation as his rifle tumbled into the mud. Then his mount was running full speed.

Not because of the wolves or the gunshots, but to keep from being crushed by the cows, which had suddenly changed direction due to the sound of the guns.

They were around him on every side, eyes rolling, bellowing, froth on their lips. The dry, hairy stink of them cloyed his nostrils. One came broadside against his horse, smashing his left leg in the process, and he howled again, this time in pain. After that he was clinging for dear life to the back of his horse, like an infant to its mother's belly, and all was terror and motion. As if in a nightmare he saw one of the other horses go down, dragged beneath the hooves of the herd, and knew that a similar fate could easily be his. He had not thought of trying to control the animal; it would either survive on its own wits and him with it, or they would both be trampled to death.

Through it all, he thought he heard more shooting, although how Rocket and Blue Eyes could be keeping up, he didn't know, and it might have been his ears playing tricks on him.

The incredible din of the herd continued; now and then he and his horse were near the edge of it, but just as he thought they might get free, the beasts turned, flowing like a river of muscle and hooves, and re-engulfed them. His horse stumbled, and he patted her neck, frantically trying to soothe her; then they hit water, and she stumbled again, turning beneath him so violently that his aching arms couldn't hold on any longer. He felt the pull of the world leave him, and for a long moment he wondered if he was already floating above, with stars for eyes.

Then the wind and all sensation blew out of him.

10

McCullough kissed his son on the forehead, straightened, and studied his quiet face. He could see himself there in the shape of his son's jaw, his cheekbones. But his mother was there too, in the young man's black hair, the angled arch of his brow. And there was something in the set of John's mouth that belonged to his grandfather, something that had skipped a generation. Sometimes when John was pensive, he bit his lip, and in the right light, McCullough was reminded of his own father, dead for so many years now.

"The father does not vanish," he whispered to his son, words he had read and committed to memory long before he even had a child. "Our faces do not disappear. We are fulfilled in our sons and daughters. Our faces are seen again in them."

As quietly as he said it, John stirred at the sound. His eyes cracked open.

"Morning, soldier," McCullough said.

John tried to sit up, and his eyes widened in pain.

"What happened?" Then his gaze sharpened as he saw things no longer there. "We were at the ambush," he said. "But something went wrong. The kongs were everywhere..."

"Kongs?"

"Yes, sir," he said. "Some of the men have been calling them that. How is the rest of the squad, sir?"

"They fought well," he said.

John looked troubled; he understood the implication.

"Sir?"

There was no point in sparing him.

"You and Forest were the only survivors," he said. "She saved your ass. Carried you out of there."

He watched his son struggle with the news. He wasn't as hardened as he should be, and it was a little embarrassing, almost repugnant to see the raw emotion on John's face.

"Soldier," he said, quietly but firmly.

"Yes sir," he said. "Forest—?"

"She'll live," McCullough said. He supposed he'd better not mention they'd had to amputate her leg at the knee. John had already had some hard news—he'd need to be eased into the rest of it.

John looked over at the IV in his arm. "What about me?"

"Your body armor stopped three rounds," McCullough said. "One slipped through, but it wasn't all that bad. You'll be fit for duty soon enough."

"How long have I been down already?"

"Several days," McCullough told him. "You have a concussion as well. Not too serious."

John closed his eyes. When he opened them again he had a determined look that it did McCullough good to see.

"The sooner I'm up the better. Sir. I'm ready to get at those kongs. Or did you take care of them already?"

"No," he said. "There are plenty left for you."

"Still feel like Beowulf?"

"Maybe more like Agamemnon, at this point," McCullough said.

"Let's just hope we don't get stuck on the beach for ten years like he did," John said.

"I don't think it will be that long," McCullough said. "But we're gonna take our time. No more mistakes."

"There was no way you could have known, sir," John said, softly.

McCullough shook his head. "Not knowing *is* a mistake in and of itself. I should have remembered my Sun Tzu—victorious warriors win first and then go to war, while defeated warriors go to war first and then seek to win. If it had been a human militia up there, I would have given them more credit."

He stopped then, but he wished he hadn't said it at all. A commander could afford doubts—needed doubts, in fact—but communicating them to his soldiers was counterproductive. Even if that soldier was your own flesh and blood.

"Anyway," he continued. "I've got a lot to do. Get some rest, and in the future, why don't you try standing where the bullets aren't?"

"I'll do my best, sir. The sooner I'm up and fighting with you again, the better."

McCullough nodded, his words feeling suddenly a little stuck.

"Get a haircut while you're down," he said. "That will at least be a productive use of your time."

"Yes, sir."

He stood to go.

"Dad?" John murmured.

"Yes?"

"I love you too."

McCullough met John's gaze, and then nodded slightly. "As you were," he said.

* * *

The wolves were hard to hit, always in motion, weaving in and out of the grass. Rocket yelped as a burst from Blue Eyes' gun came perilously near him, and Blue Eyes realized that if he wasn't careful, he was more dangerous to the other chimp than the wolves were. He still wasn't used to the gun, the way it moved when you pulled the trigger, like it had a life all of its own. It scared him almost as much to fire one as to have one shot at him.

A gray form streaked into the periphery of his vision. He swung toward it, but it danced away.

It looked like the wolf was grinning, which was annoying.

Rocket barked as one came up from behind and nipped at him. He swung and fired, and this time was rewarded by a squeal from the beast. With two of their number wounded, the pack finally backed off, although they didn't go all that far.

The herd of cows—Blue Eyes was still certain that was the wrong word—had swept across the river, and Ray and the horses were no longer to be seen. He hoped that the younger ape had managed to escape in the other direction—on the other side of the herd—but he had a bad feeling about the whole situation.

Rocket gestured at his ears, made the sign for "hear" as a question.

He knew what Rocket meant. It was hard to hear anything. The guns were loud, and his ears seemed full of a storm. He shook his head.

Rocket gestured at his gun, then swept his arm in the direction the cows were now receding in.

"You hear guns?" Blue Eyes asked.

"Yes," Rocket replied. His eyes didn't stay still for long; the wolves were still out there.

Gunshots either meant there were humans around, or

their attempt to lose the apes following them had failed.

They searched by the river as the wolves recovered their courage. In the churned, muddy ground they found Ray's broken rifle and one of the horses, dead, crushed by the herd. They didn't find Ray, which gave him a little hope.

According to Rocket, the gunshots had come from the direction the herd had gone, and—if he was alive— probably Ray, too. They set out in that direction with the wolves loping behind and alongside of them, albeit at a respectful remove.

A bit later they saw crows gathering in the distance, often a good sign—crows were attracted to carrion. Hunting was fine, but sometimes it was easier to find a kill that a predator had already made. If you had the numbers, and especially fire, then you could chase them off and take the meat.

In this case, however, Blue Eyes was worried more about what the prey *was*, and more specifically, he was hoping it wasn't Ray.

It wasn't. What they found instead was what was left of one of the cows. Its intestines lay in a pile, and many of the larger bones were there, including the skull, although the horns had been cut off. Missing was the vast majority of the meat, although there was a good deal of blood. Nearby, the grass had been trampled not by cows, but by horses, and they had even left some droppings for further proof of what they were.

"Humans," Rocket said. He was pointing to several tracks, the peculiarly flat prints humans left when they were wearing shoes, which was usually. He remembered his surprise once when Malcolm took his boots off, revealing feet that looked astonishingly like those of apes, although they lacked a proper toe-thumb.

That was the thing about humans that made them

fascinating but also repellent to look upon; they were so like apes in some ways, but the differences—and for some reason, especially the small differences—were disconcerting. They seemed somehow poorly made, a mockery of real apes. He knew, for instance, that Ellie was female, and that she was Malcolm's mate, but it was impossible to imagine being attracted to her weirdly distorted body, flat face and sharp nose. Not like Lake, with her supple limbs and eyes that almost seemed to glow.

"Blue Eyes?"

He jumped, realizing Rocket was trying to say something.

"No sign of Ray," Rocket informed him. "The humans went that way."

Blue Eyes had heard his father talking to his mother once about feeling something on his shoulders that wasn't there. It hadn't made sense to him, and when he asked his father about it, he explained it was a human expression about responsibility. Since responsibility was also a concept that a younger Blue Eyes had only the most casual of relationships with, that explanation hadn't helped.

But having this decision to make made him feel tired, like he was carrying an elk on a pole, and the other apes who were supposed to be helping carry the pole had suddenly walked away from the task. His last decision—to avoid the apes following them—had led them to this disaster—their horses gone and Ray missing, probably dead. What if he chose poorly this time? His father had sent him to look for humans that might be a threat to the troop, but wasn't he also responsible for Ray? What if the orangutan lay nearby, suffering, dying unless he got help?

Yes, it did feel like something heavy on his shoulders.

What would his father do?

He thought he knew, but it was hard.

"Follow the humans," he finally said.

Hopefully, that would accomplish both of his aims.

Caesar turned his face into the wind from the sea. The sun was behind him, casting the shadow of the building he stood on toward the far horizon. There was little fog, this morning; where shadow didn't fall, the sun lay upon everything like a pall of pollen. On the sea it shone like liquid gold, rolling toward him and then pulling away, leaving faint lambent lines in the sand.

The ship was a small, gleaming shape near the horizon. At first he had taken its retreat as a sign of victory, but now he was less sure. It was farther away, out of reach of the few rocket launchers they had left—but it hadn't gone completely. And on the shore, the humans continued to build. There wouldn't be another charge down the beach; that way was now closed by a wall of wire and sheet metal, and his scouts had watched the soldiers planting things in the sand. He didn't know what they were, but there were lots of them, and he was certain they were dangerous.

Things weren't going as he'd hoped. Any chance to make peace was now certainly lost. As on the bridge, most of the apes thought their first real battle against the humans had been a victory.

Caesar didn't see it that way. On one level, his plan had worked out as expected; they had used the humans' ruse against them, while at the same time launching an attack on the two places of their strength—the beach and the ship. But his hope had been to overrun the beach and destroy the ship, to stop the invasion in one swift blow. In that he had failed. His apes did not lack courage, strength, or quickness. But watching the events unfold, he had realized something; these soldiers were not like the humans

Koba had attacked. These humans were like none he had ever seen. They did not run when they should; even when their plans fell apart they fought fiercely. And they were— *organized*—in a way that apes were not. Apes cooperated, of course—they had learned to work together, chimps and bonobos, gorillas and orangutans. They had developed strategies for hunting, some driving the prey toward others to kill, and so on. These humans had strategies like that, but more of them. They were practiced at war whereas apes were new to it.

He remembered what Malcolm said, about the thousands of years of human experience at fighting. He wondered, privately, if the apes *could* win. And if they did, what would they become? He had once believed ape would never kill ape the way humans killed humans, but he had broken that law himself.

Twice he had stood in a place and believed everything was about to change. The first was the day after escaping the city, when he and his apes were free among the trees; he felt apes had a chance to be as they should be, to become whatever they wanted to become. The possibilities had seemed infinite.

Now he stood in another place ripe with potential, but it seemed as if they had only two choices: extinction, or becoming the same sort of calculating savages they now faced. Would they have to become as humans to beat them? And if so—if that was inevitable—then what was the point?

But his apes were counting on him. He had to lead them out of this. He just wished he knew how. And he needed more time.

Which, hopefully, this day would bring them.

He heard Maurice and Luca arrive behind him.

Maurice was a better climber than any chimp, and

his late arrival was nothing more than deference, letting Caesar command the view first. Luca was just a slower climber, due to his size and weight and the simple fact that he was a gorilla, and as such preferred the solid ground or low perches to swinging among branches.

"Still there," Maurice observed, nodding toward the human fortifications.

"More than ever," Caesar replied. "More came from the ship in the little boats. And they continue to build, there—there."

"Making their camp bigger," Luca said. "Spreading out into the city."

"Yes," Caesar said.

"We should attack," Luca said. "Push them back, like last time. While these humans are in the city."

Caesar followed the gorilla's gaze to where a sizable group of armed humans were moving cautiously up a distant street. Such patrols had been rare right after the last attack, but in the last few days had become more common. Caesar had resisted confronting them, because most of the probes were far from where either his warriors or the women and children were camped.

But then it occurred to him that the humans were *waiting* for a reaction, so they would know when they were getting near the ape sanctuaries.

So he had decided to try and misdirect them. The human soldiers were about as far from either hiding place as they could get—so he had decided to ambush them again. He'd sent only a few warriors, with orders to attack and then quickly withdraw. He wasn't interested in anything resembling a face-to-face fight.

In the distance, he saw a couple of black dots moving along the side of a building—Spear and the others.

A few moments later, he heard the echoes of gunfire.

* * *

To Aaron, it sounded like popcorn popping in another room, but he knew it for what it was. One of the Colonel's fishing expeditions had finally paid off, and of course it was all the way across town. Which left him sitting here, feeling stupid.

Locals like him—the northern soldiers called them all Sanfrans, although he himself was from Sacramento—had gotten a bad reputation on their first outing with the Colonel's men. Since then, they had mostly been put on high-risk duty, which was where he was at presently—on watch near the middle of town, on the off chance that an ape might run by on its way home. He had spent more than a day carefully moving into position and taking cover. And he was basically on his own—if he did find any apes, his backup was more than half an hour away, if it came at all.

Still, he preferred this duty to marching in formation, just asking to be killed by apes on the rooftops that you never saw until one of their bullets ended you.

He sat up a little, gazing off into the distance in the hopes of seeing something of what was happening—but of course, from here, through the buildings and hills, there was nothing to see, except the ugly mess the once-beautiful city had become. Years of fighting, looting, and vandalism had taken their toll, and now nature itself seemed to conspire to erase everything man had made.

He missed Dreyfus. Dreyfus had always managed to keep hope alive, to insist that better days lay ahead.

But that was before the apes came back, before God or whatever malignant power oversaw the universe decided humanity hadn't been punished sufficiently. And now Dreyfus was dead, and they had the Colonel instead. The Colonel didn't make promises; if he had a vision for a better world, he didn't share it. But he planned to exterminate the apes, and as far as Aaron was concerned, at this point, that was all the bettering the world needed.

He was just easing back down when he heard something below his second-story perch.

At first glance he saw nothing, but then realized he was looking in the wrong direction. Something dark was unwinding from the shadowed rooftop of a building over to his left—north, rather than south, where the action seemed to be.

He hated the way they moved, almost like spiders. He was always surprised by how big they were. He remembered them on TV, when he was just a kid, how small they seemed, how cute. There was one show he'd really liked, *Monkey of the House*, although it hadn't lasted that long.

Someone—he thought it had been Ben, who was now dead, a victim of the massacre when the apes invaded the city—told him that they mostly used very young apes on TV. That made sense; puppies were cute, baby seals were cute—even baby turtles and alligators had a certain appeal the adults didn't. And yeah, baby chimps were adorable.

But grown apes were just damn ugly. They were the thing under the bed, the bogeyman, the monster that you might think was human from the corner of your eye, but never once it was in your face.

He wanted to point his gun at it and shoot until it stopped moving, but this was exactly what he'd been waiting for. It must have been up there as long as he had, or longer, doing the same thing—watching for anyone who might come this way. But it hadn't seen him, had it? They weren't human, but they weren't better than human, either. They made mistakes.

It was going somewhere, probably to report to its boss, and that was a huge break. If he was the one to locate their hidey-hole, the Colonel might start treating him with a little of the respect he deserved, maybe even promote him into the ranks.

But following it across the buildings would be a problem.

He was about to let himself down to the street when another one went by, moving much faster. This one was bigger, thicker in every dimension, reddish in color instead of black, galloping along on all fours, knuckles slamming into the pavement. It was going in the same direction as the first.

He eased down and began to follow, keeping to the long morning shadows when he could. But the apes seemed intent on their destination; they did not turn to see if they were being trailed.

Now and then, he still heard the indistinct reports of gunfire. He didn't seem to be getting any closer to it.

He stopped when he saw them enter a building through broken windows on the fourth floor. He checked the address and cross-streets, backed off two blocks, and called it in. He got Lieutenant Gomez, who took the information and then told him to hang on. A moment later, the Colonel himself came on.

"Long, is it?"

"Yes, sir."

"How sure are you about this, Long?"

"I followed two apes from my post, sir. They've gone into a building on the edge of downtown. You could hide a lot of apes in there, sir."

Aaron was finally starting to feel nervous. He checked the other rooftops for guards, but he knew thirty could be watching him from behind glass, and he would never know it.

And the Colonel was taking his time answering.

"Yeah," McCullough said, after a moment. "I see it.

The tower with the greenish glass, the two antennae on top? Two blocks from a big park?"

"Yes, sir, that's it."

"Okay," he said. "Get back to your post. Or better yet, come back to base."

The receiver clicked off, then back on.

"Long?"

"Sir?"

"Good work."

11

The fight in the south was over; Caesar could just make out Spear and his apes breaking in all directions.

"Do you think they killed any soldiers?"

Caesar shrugged.

"It doesn't matter," he said. "The city is big, and there aren't that many of them. Now they will look in the wrong place for a while."

"Eventually they will find us," Maurice pointed out. "What then?"

Caesar didn't answer that. It seemed better to stay silent than admit that he wasn't sure.

He heard a sudden, strange sound, a kind of rumbling or tearing in the air itself. Maurice and Luca heard it as well, and they began turning this way and that, searching for the cause.

Luca suddenly made an alarm call and lifted his face to point with his lips.

Caesar wasn't sure what he was seeing. A long, thin stream of white smoke had come out of the distant ship, but instead of going upward like a cloud, it bent toward the city, looking something like a crooked finger, except that it kept growing longer and longer. At its tip was what looked like a small sun.

The hairs on his neck and arms stood up. The bright light suddenly winked out, leaving the cloud behind it, but now he saw something small and dark, like a spear, falling into the city. He watched with horror, trying to figure out where it was going.

And then he knew.

"The women!" he snarled. "The children! Cornelia!"

The dark thing hit a building and turned it first into light, then streams of fire, then enough black smoke to smother the world. At first there was no sound, but then it reached them, thunder like no storm had ever made.

Blue Eyes and Rocket seemed to have lost the wolves; probably they had stayed to chase the crows from the cow carcass and pick the meat. But they were in unknown territory, following humans they did not know, perhaps still being pursued by apes who wanted to kill them, so the two chimps did not build a fire that night. Instead they climbed into a tall tree and made their bed in its branches. The sky was overcast, and without fire, the night promised to be a very, very dark one.

Rocket hadn't said a lot since they'd found the dead cow, and in fact, he had been quieter than usual the whole trip. Not that he'd ever been the most communicative of apes, but he seemed lost, somehow, in his own head. So Blue Eyes was a little surprised when the older ape started signing in the dim light.

"Maybe Ray is okay," he said. "Just lost. But Ray is smart."

"He's smart," Blue Eyes agreed.

Rocket seemed to hesitate, then started moving his hands again.

"What do you think of his dreams?"

Blue Eyes wasn't sure how to answer that, and before he could try, Rocket went on.

"I am an old ape. My dreams are mostly memories, like seeing things—before the change. Or about having to pee, and peeing, and still having to go—"

"I've had that one," Blue Eyes said.

"Ray's dreams are different."

"I think so," Blue Eyes said.

Rocket looked reluctant to go on, so Blue Eyes let him have the silence to decide.

"You think it makes sense?" Rocket eventually said. "What he dreams?"

"I don't know," Blue Eyes said. "Maybe. In winter things die or go to sleep. In spring, they come again."

"Things die," Rocket said. He made a gruff sound. "Other things are born. The things that die stay dead. The new things that are born eventually die, too."

Blue Eyes scratched his side, which was now itching like mad. Then he touched Rocket lightly, picking at his fur.

"I miss Ash, too," he said.

Rocket's head dropped, so that his eyes could no longer be seen.

"Ash," he signed. "So little when he was born. Could hold him in one hand. Like you."

When he looked up, his eyes were wet.

Blue Eyes felt his throat clutch. Some of the younger apes cried. But of the elders, only his father had ever done so.

Until now.

He took Rocket in his arms, and the older chimpanzee held him tightly as the light around them dwindled away.

Ray woke with no memory of the dream, but terror followed him out of the darkness. Each breath into his lungs hurt, and each exhale felt like his last, as if he didn't have the strength to pull the air in. He knew he was awake, but he saw nothing.

Gradually he remembered—the cows and the wolves, the wild flight on the horse in a canyon of horned beasts, the last descent into oblivion. As it all came back to him, light began to leak back into his head and feeling into his body, and all of the pain in both returned as well.

He sensed he was in motion, and a familiar sort of motion at that; he recognized the gait of a horse beneath him. Had he actually fallen off at all? Or had he merely fallen asleep in the saddle? It had happened before.

But he wasn't sitting up, was he? As his eyes adjusted, he saw dead leaves and ferns, the floor of a forest, and after a moment it was clear that he was lying belly-down *across* the horse. That meant Rocket and Blue Eyes had found him, put him back on his mount, and continued on with their quest.

That was a relief. All he had to do was let them know he was okay, and everything would be as it had been before.

But then he realized his wrists were tied together, as well as his ankles, and that a rope connecting his hands and feet was cinched tightly beneath the belly of the horse.

He tried to raise his head, but his neck hurt like the blazes, and it felt feeble. As little as it lifted, however, it increased his field of vision enough to see that there were at least four more horses than the one he was riding on. And whoever was mounted on the nearest wore boots.

"I think it's awake," someone said.

It was a human voice, sort of high in pitch.

"He," someone corrected. This voice was lower, with a bit of a chesty rasp in it that reminded Ray of a gorilla. "It's male."

"It's a monkey," the first voice said. "What does it matter?"

"It's actually not a monkey," a third person corrected.

This voice had a nice lilt to it, almost musical. "It's an ape. An orangutan. There's a difference."

"Whatever," the high-voiced one said. "I still don't see how it matters whether it's a boy or a girl. They're just gonna burn it when we get to town."

"They're not going to burn it, Feliz," the third voice said. "It's harmless."

"Yeah?" Feliz said. "Gram used to tell me the monkeys were hiding out in the dark, ready to snatch my soul."

"Your Gram had an inventive imagination, and you were a difficult child," the voice countered.

"I have to admit," Feliz said, "I was picturing something a lot scarier. He just looks like a big, hairy, really ugly baby."

"Awake, is it?" the third voice said. "Hang on. Let's see."

The horse plodded to a stop, and Ray saw booted feet land on the ground. A few heartbeats later, a face appeared. Human, of course, with brown skin and dark eyes. The long hair of its head was equal parts black and silver, and was tied back so it looked like the tail of a horse.

"Hey there, fellow," she said. "I'm Carla. Who are you?"

He tried to sign "hello," but of course he couldn't with his wrists tied together.

"You don't think he understands you?" Feliz said.

"Well, he might," Carla said. "He didn't get here from Borneo, you know. He must have escaped from a zoo, or something. Or more likely his parents did—he doesn't look that old. That means there must be a breeding population around here, someplace."

"First one I've ever seen," the heavy-voiced one said. "And I've been coming up this way to hunt for four, five years now."

"This far north?" Carla asked.

"Not quite, I guess," the other replied. "Have to go a little farther north every year." He paused. "Kid has got a point, though. Ain't these things supposed to spread the plague?"

"The plague is long gone, Jack," Carla said.

"You know that for sure?"

"Yes," Carla replied. She reached to stroke the ape's fur. Ray tried to shy away, but there was only so much he could move. Besides, it didn't feel bad.

"Well, what're we gonna do with him?" Feliz asked.

"I'm not sure," Carla said. "But you don't come across an orangutan every day, and especially not all knocked out and laid in the mud. It would have been a shame not to pick him up, for all kinds of reasons."

"Yeah," Jack said. "Probably good eatin'."

"Ah, gross," Feliz said. "He looks too much like people to eat."

"There's some that eat people," Jack said.

"Well, I'm not one of 'em," Feliz said. "Anyway, there's not much meat on him, is there?"

"That depends on how hungry you are," Carla replied.

"Get back on your horse, Carla," Jack said. "I know I heard somebody else shooting back there before the buffalo stampeded, and that horse belonged to somebody. Whoever it was, I don't fancy running into them, not with just one rifle between us."

"Okay, Jack," Carla said. She paused. "You think we should make him more comfortable?"

"He'll be fine until we get back to camp," Jack said.

They reached camp before sundown. It consisted of two old buildings and a large truck. The truck was very long, looking something like a millipede, and once had been yellow, although now it was mostly leaf-and-dirt colored. In camp, Ray was finally taken down from the horse, but they didn't cut his hands and feet loose, and they then used the rope that had held him on the horse to tie him to a post on one of the wooden houses.

At least he finally got to see his other captors. Based on his voice, Ray had pictured Jack as sort of a gorilla, but he was more like an orangutan. He didn't have much hair on his head and he had big hands and long arms and a wide mouth. Feliz was young, probably no older than Alexander. She had hair the color of chanterelle mushrooms, cut just to her ears, and she wore a funny blue outfit that covered most of her body, held onto her shoulders by straps, and a black garment underneath that left most of her arms bare. She was the one carrying the rifle. The other two had long sticks held in a curve by strings. He wasn't sure what those were supposed to do.

After they tied him to the post, they got busy. He saw that they had three extra horses besides his, and two of them were loaded down with leather bags. When they unloaded the bags, chunks of meat spilled out; big slabs of bloody flesh with some bone still in. They brought most of that to a big flat wooden table and began cutting it into smaller pieces. Some of it they put in a box of white stuff that looked a little like sand. Some of it they put on a rack over a small, smoky fire. Now and then they ate scraps of it raw, or after putting it on sticks and holding it in the fire.

Feliz put the rifle into a long bag.

"Did you get your shell casings, Feliz?" Jack asked.

"All three of 'em," she said. "I don't think I needed more than the one, but I've never shot a buffalo before, and I wanted to be sure."

"Well, you sure brought it down, eagle-eye," Jack said. "And at five hundred yards or more. Your dad would be proud of you. I never thought I would see anyone who could shoot like he could, but you're gettin' pretty damn close."

"Thanks, Uncle Jack," she said.

"It's enough, don't you think?" Carla asked, as they worked at the bloody job.

"Yeah," Jack said. "Once we've got it worked down, salted it, smoked it—it'll be about as much as we can carry."

"Good," Carla said. "I'm about ready for a real bath."

Ray strained at his ropes, hoping to loosen them. They were in the forest, surrounded by familiar redwoods. If he got free, he could vanish in seconds. He still didn't know everything about humans, but he knew they were terrible at climbing and swinging. Of course, Feliz might be able to shoot him, but she didn't have the rifle in her hands. Maybe by the time she got it out, he would be out of sight.

He froze when Feliz looked his way.

"Look at you, trying to get away," Feliz said, wiping her bloody arm across her brow. She had a huge knife in one hand. He cringed as she stepped toward him.

"You want something to eat?" she asked.

Ray did. He hadn't eaten since the day before, and his stomach was rumbling.

He nodded yes, in the human manner.

Feliz's smile vanished, and her jaw dropped open.

"Did you see that?" she said.

"See what?" Carla asked.

"He nodded. The monkey."

"Stop the presses," Jack said. "Ask him what the square root of sixteen is."

"What are presses?" Feliz asked.

Jack laughed and kept working at the meat.

Ray watched Feliz as she cut a thin, red strip from the piece she was working on and brought it toward him.

"Open up," she said.

He opened his mouth.

"Damn if he doesn't understand me!" she said.

"Don't swear," Carla told her. "I told you. Apes are smart."

She gave him the meat. It was raw, and chewy, and it tasted good. She brought another piece. He opened his mouth again, but she stopped short of giving it to him.

"Can you understand me or not?" she asked. "Blink your eyes if you understand me."

Ray thought about that for a second. If he could show her he understood, would they cut his hands free so he could sign? Maybe. But then again, humans didn't use hand talk, not the ones he'd met anyway, and these three were all speaking with their voices. He remembered now how surprised Malcolm and his people had been to hear apes talk, to see them sign. He somehow doubted they would free him, even if they knew he understood what they were saying. Maybe especially if they did. Maybe if Feliz thought he was stupid, like a raccoon or an apple, she would get careless, and he could escape and find Rocket and Blue Eyes.

So he didn't blink, or nod, or anything—he just made chewing motions with his mouth. After a few moments, Feliz made a disparaging sound and gave him the meat.

"I still don't know what we're going to do with him," she said.

Jack went over and began washing his hands.

"I remember years ago, those guys in Diablo put out the word they were looking for apes," he said. "And willing to pay."

Carla snorted. "That was almost ten years ago, when they were still looking for the cure to the Simian Flu. I doubt you'd get any takers these days."

"What if they try to kill him?" Feliz said. "Back in town? Or take him from us? You may not be afraid of monk—of apes, but a lot of people are."

"Well," Jack said, "I guess we'll see when we get there. Until then, there's no use worrying about it."

Ray, for his part, was not sure he agreed. It seemed quite reasonable to worry about the possibility of being killed.

Later, when it was dark, he worked more at his bindings, but he couldn't get them loose. He was able to claw at the post, though, and even if he soon surmised he couldn't scratch through it, he did have an idea.

12

Something invisible and incredibly violent hit Winter in the face, the chest—every inch of his skin—from all directions. His eyes blinked involuntarily, and he raised his hands to swat away whatever it was, flinching down into a squat, certain something was about to strike him harder but not what or from where. Everything around him seemed suddenly much brighter.

Then the sound found his ears, and he shrieked involuntarily, jumping back from something he still didn't see, and only then did he turn enough to catch the motion from the corner of his eye. He felt heat, and the back of his throat burned as it did when the smoke from a fire got into his nose.

The building across the street had burst open, and streamers of boiling black smoke were vomiting out in what seemed like slow motion, and now the sound and impact had passed through him, and seemed to have taken his ears and sense of touch with them. He wanted to run, but he couldn't; he just stared as fire fell onto the street. His ears popped, and glass shattered up and down the building, falling like rain through the growing cloud below.

It didn't seem real at all. He had seen fire, and smoke. He had seen his village burned. But what he was staring at was like nothing he had ever experienced or imagined. He didn't even have anything to compare it to.

As he watched, dumbfounded, part of the cloud reached down toward him, like a snake striking, a snake with a gaping mouth of fire...

He saw a flash of red, and then someone caught his arm, yanked him back and through the open door he stood in, pushing him to the side so the burning stuff smashed into the stone floor and rolled past him. As he fell, he saw others scrambling away from the door, mostly women. He saw Ajax put himself between a young chimp and the smoke, and stumble as something struck him.

Then Winter was in a confusion of limbs. When he managed to fight free, he saw it was Red who had pulled him out of harm's way. The smaller gorilla panted at him. His face was covered in dust.

Outside, the sunlight went away.

"What's going on?" he signed, fingers shaking in terror.

"Humans," Red signed back. "Some kind of weapon." He held out his hand.

"Come on," he said. "Help the women with the children."

Winter looked around. The building Caesar had moved them to was spacious enough, and in the few days they had been there, they had built sleeping areas, a hearth for the fire, a store of food—they had, in short, begun a small village. Now all was pandemonium; everyone was scrambling away, climbing the walls to the balconies that overhung the vast central space. If whatever hit the other building had come here, they would all be dead. He knew that in his bones.

And he also felt like it could still happen, at any moment.

"Come on!" Red signed, tugging on him.

But Winter couldn't move; he rolled so that his face was against the wall, and began rocking back and forth.

How long he did that, he did not know, but finally a strong hand gripped his arm and pulled him way.

It was Luca.

"Stand up!" the older gorilla roared.

Almost, Winter tried to roll against the wall again, but his shame and submission to Luca overcame him, and instead he went down on all fours.

As he did, he saw Caesar arrive.

Caesar fought his way through the chaos until he found Cornelia. She had moved to the very back of the building, along with the five females she was closest to, and they had formed a protective circle around their children. For a moment, she didn't seem to recognize him; her eyes were wildly darting about, seeking the threat, the enemy, whatever was coming for them.

Then they cleared, and she knew him, and they embraced. He held her hard, his usually orderly mind suddenly a jumble. He was dizzy from the fear that he had lost her.

"What is happening?" she croaked. "Where did the sun go?"

"Human weapon," he said. "It missed you and hit the wrong building."

"Missed?" she said, staring out at the fire in the street. "Missed?"

He had seen the building the sky-spear hit when he arrived. Every time he thought he understood the destructive power of human weapons he was surprised again. Unpleasantly so.

Someone tugged on his arm, someone small.

Cornelius.

His little son tried to push his way between them, and Caesar allowed it. Cornelius, for his part, didn't seem scared; just excited, and happy to see him.

He remembered when Blue Eyes was born, how happy he had been. The birth of his first son was part of their new world, their new life, the future in which apes were free. It had been a sign to him that all would be well, that his choices had been the right ones, despite the pain and loss.

But now they were back here; clutched together amidst smoke and fire in the very city he had fought so hard to escape, surrounded by the things of man he had foresworn.

When he had told Malcolm he was ready for war, he thought he had known what he was talking about. Now, finally, he was starting to understand what the human had been trying to tell him. His first instinct had been right; apes did not belong in the realm of humanity, not even in its ruins. Maybe it was his fight with Koba that had made him feel this place was his, territory to defend. Maybe it was seeing the house he had grown up in, and all of the memories that brought back—of Will, of this city in happier times, the illusion that he belonged here. Maybe it was merely his pride, his reluctance to submit to anyone, anywhere, for any reason.

Whatever the cause, it was time to put it aside.

"We must leave here," he said.

"Yes," Cornelia said. "Koba should never have brought us here. We should never have stayed."

"I thought I could protect you," Caesar said. "I was wrong. You will go back to the forest."

"We should all go back," she said.

"It's not that easy," Caesar said. "The soldiers will follow. We will have to run, and keep running, trying always to stay just ahead of them. We can't build a village like that. We can't raise children like that."

He stroked her head. "You and the other women will go to the forest, find a new place for our children. A hidden place the humans will not discover. My army will stay here, keep them occupied until you have done that. Until your trail is cold. Then—if we cannot beat them here—we will join you."

"No," she said. "We should all go. In the night."

"It will be as I say," he told her. He put his face against hers, touching her gently, then pulled away. Cornelius followed, trying to play now.

"Later," he told his son, hoping there would be a later. "We must hurry."

Cornelia held him fiercely for another moment. He remembered years ago, when they had first come to the forest, when all seemed lost. Then she had given him the resolve to continue, to conquer, and he felt her strength again now.

"Okay," she said, as he pulled away again. She held the protesting Cornelius to her as Caesar went to find Luca.

Luca was outside, facing down one of the streets that approached the building, his weapon in hand. Red, Ajax, and Korso, a third gorilla, stood guard with him.

Flames danced in the streets, and black smoke rose from the broken building in oily coils toward the low, gray clouds that were rolling in.

He took Luca aside.

"This wasn't coincidence," he said. "They knew where they were. They could send another one of those things at any time. I want them out of here, now."

"Where should they go, Caesar?" Luca asked.

"Take them toward the water for now, but keep out of sight. When night falls, go to the bridge and cross over to the forest. The gorilla guard will take them. Find a place to hide, far from here. Do you understand?"

Luca shifted his eyes.

"Am I to go with them?" he asked.

"Get them across the bridge," Caesar said. "Escort them into the forest. Then return to me. We must move the warriors' camp as well. We will move each day, maybe more than once a day."

"We will stay in the city?"

"For a time," Caesar said. "Until we know the women and children are safe, we must fight the humans here, stop them from advancing. Then, we too will go to join them, search for another home. Maybe if we go far enough, they will lose interest."

Grey met Red beneath the ruins of the tower where Koba had died. Even less remained of it now than before; Caesar had lured the humans to it and caused another explosion using barrels of fuel and some of the human weapons. Caesar seemed to master such human things very quickly—probably with the help of his human friends, possibly without. Caesar knew a lot about humans.

In fact, Grey had begun to waver in his conviction to betray Caesar; things had seemed to be going well against the humans. What if Caesar won?

But now, considering the smoke rising in the near distance, that seemed unlikely.

"They might have all been killed," Grey snapped at Red. "What then? With no women and children, what chance do apes have?"

Red lowered his head. "I couldn't have known they had a weapon like that," he said. "No one could have known. I thought they would send soldiers, or use the guns they fired at us on the bridge." He looked up, unrepentant despite his pretense at submission. "But my plan worked," he insisted. "Caesar is sending the women and children into the forest, just as we hoped. We have separated him from them, from the future of apes. And I will be among them, with the other gorillas in the guard. When the time is right, you will join us and take control."

Grey thought of the terrible sight of the thing from the ship, the glittering spear of light and thunder. What more did the humans have?

No, Caesar could not win. His war would end in ruin. But that no longer mattered. Leaves did not rest one way forever—eventually a wind or a footstep would turn them, and what was beneath would be revealed. Red had shown the humans where the women were, or very nearly so, close enough to make Caesar send them away. And Grey had known it would happen. He was leader, after all. Caesar would blame him. And when Caesar found out, there would be no forgiveness. No amount of deference could bring about a second reconciliation. Grey had already committed himself to swing on this branch—whether it proved sturdy or snapped from his weight, only the days ahead could know.

His eyes wandered back to the ruins where Koba's remains lay. He knew what Koba would do—that he would move forward with courage, without remorse, without flinching.

He could do no less.

Blue Eyes and Rocket found the human camp the next afternoon. They approached it with great caution, but it turned out to be empty.

It hadn't been empty for long, though. The blood on the big table was still a little wet in some spots, and fresh horse dung indicated that they'd probably left no later than mid-morning.

Rocket had developed an interest in the horse tracks. Most of those they were following looked a little odd; a horse print normally looked like an elk track in reverse, but a lot fatter, an oval with a little wedge cut out of it. The human horse signs, on the other hand, were shaped more like a rainbow, and all the animals they were following had tracks like that.

Except one. One of the horses not only had normal tracks, but Rocket insisted that it was one of their horses, one of the ones they'd brought with them. That didn't mean anything in and of itself—the humans might have found the horse wandering around, riderless. It didn't prove that Ray was with them.

They very nearly missed the evidence that did. It was on a post of one of the buildings, some claw marks. Blue Eyes noticed it, but didn't examine it closely at first, but something about the marks bothered him, and just as they were about to leave, he came back for a second look.

It seemed as if something had started trying to claw through the post, but there was something else, very small. The star with four points in a circle, the same sign scraped into the great meeting stone back home. His father's symbol.

"Ray," he said, and he hooted in excitement. "Ray is with them."

They picked up the trail, following it down a narrow valley until the sun set and they were forced to find shelter in the spreading limbs of a cottonwood tree. Blue Eyes had trouble sleeping, worrying about Ray.

"What do you think they'll do to him?" he asked Rocket.

"Put him in a cage."

Blue Eyes remembered the tiny cells back at the ape sanctuary and shuddered. There were many, many stories about the cages, none of them good. When Maurice had invented writing signs to represent the different apes— chimp, bonobo, gorilla, orangutan—he had also invented the sign for "ape in a cage."

"It's to tell our story," Maurice had explained to him and the other children. "We must never forget where we came from, so we never go back there. I made this symbol in the hopes that it will never be used to speak of the present or the future, but only of the past. And you must understand what your mothers and fathers went through, so you truly appreciate your lives here. No ape should ever again be put in a cage."

That seemed like a long time ago, and the solid branches of Maurice's teaching now felt shaky and a little rotten. Ape had killed ape, and as for cages...

"Koba put you in a cage," Blue Eyes said.

"Yes," Rocket said. "And Koba put humans in cages, too."

"Why did he do that? Koba hated cages more than anyone."

"Yes," Rocket said. He looked up at the sky, and Blue Eyes realized that Rocket seemed far older than he had only a moon before, as if the events of the last several hands of days were somehow more than the rest of the years of his life.

"When I was free," Rocket finally said, "after Caesar woke us up, after we left the sanctuary, my cage stayed with me for a while." He tapped his chest, throat, and head. "Stayed in here. Sometimes I missed it. Without walls—I felt like I was falling, especially at night. Sometimes I felt like all my fur had been shaved off. Like maybe a snail feels when you pull it out of its shell. But then I started to forget. Finally, I never thought about the cage at all." He scratched at the bark of the tree.

"Koba was too smart," Rocket went on. "He could not forget. Koba left his real cage behind, like the rest of us, but he…" Rocket stopped, looking confused, as if he didn't quite know what he wanted to say. Then his uncertainty seemed to fade a little.

"Koba became a cage," he said. "Himself a cage. And cages like to be full." He looked uncertain again. "Does that make sense?"

"Yes." Blue Eyes thought of the way Koba moved, how he often flinched as if he had just walked into something. The way he touched his scars, the strange pride he had in them. He knew Koba had loved his father, had been devoted to him. For years. And yet he had turned on him so quickly, as if part of him had been sleeping all that time, closed tight inside.

Caged.

"It makes sense," he said.

Rocket looked sad. He reached out briefly to Blue Eyes, but it wasn't clear if he needed comfort or was trying to give comfort.

"Rocket thinks too hard," Rocket sighed. "It makes my head hurt. I'm not smart, like Caesar or Koba. My head is meant for other things."

Blue Eyes felt a little ashamed. He had always admired Koba for his intelligence and courage, and he had always felt that Rocket was—less. And it was true that Rocket did not think as quickly or as cleverly as some. But in the last few days, Blue Eyes had begun to feel that being clever wasn't always the most important thing.

Maurice had once tried to explain the difference between intelligence and wisdom. As a young ape, the distinction had been lost on him.

But finally, he thought he was beginning to understand.

13

The next day Blue Eyes and Rocket came to fields where plants grew in odd, regular rows. They saw a few humans tending the plants, and kept to the trees when they could, not wanting to be seen.

Not much later they came to the top of a hill.

Below it, a town stretched out.

They had seen plenty of abandoned human dwellings on the journey so far, the empty shells and abandoned snake-skins of villages, but this one was obviously alive. It wasn't large, just a cluster of about thirty buildings arranged around a common square. Unlike the structures in San Francisco, some of these seemed more like ape-work, a little irregular, built of wood and stone and parts of older structures.

It didn't take long to spot Ray. He was indeed in a cage, built of branches and posts lashed together with wire and rope, and at any given time from a handful to three handfuls of humans were gathered around, looking at him. Now and then one of them would try to poke him through the bars with a stick, or throw a rock at him, but whenever that happened, a young human would leap out of her chair and start yelling at them. Despite her smaller size—Blue Eyes felt without knowing that the human was female—much larger humans submitted to her, dropping their sticks and backing off.

He and Rocket watched all of this for a while trying to work out how many humans lived in the town. They were hard to count, partly because many of them looked alike, and he was sometimes not sure if he was counting one of them twice. But it seemed like less than a hundred, including the children.

It seemed to him that there were a lot of children, at least compared to the human colony in San Francisco. Unlike the adults, the children didn't seem hostile to Ray, although they wanted to touch him. He seemed not to mind, or if he did, he remembered the stories about what happened in cages when an ape was "bad." Several of the older apes had in particular stressed that doing anything to human children—biting or flinging things, even hooting too loudly at them—was apt to be considered "bad."

Were these the humans who had contacted those in San Francisco? If so, Blue Eyes didn't think his father had much to worry about. The town had a fence around it, the kind of wire that caught fur and flesh if you weren't careful, and there were a couple of towers that always seemed to have someone in them on guard—but aside from that, things seemed to be relatively peaceful. The children quarreled and played rough at times, but aside from the confrontations over Ray, the adults seemed mostly at ease. Except for the guards in the towers, none of them carried guns or spears. Of course, it was possible that their warriors had already set off, heeding the call of their cousins in the north, but somehow Blue Eyes doubted it. They seemed less preoccupied with fighting and more focused on the everyday chores of life—fetching water, watching after their plants, going about their business.

"We'll wait for night," Blue Eyes decided. "We should be able to sneak in and free him."

Rocket agreed, and they bedded into the brush to wait.

The lack of sleep the night before told on Blue Eyes, and as the long day unfolded, he found himself drifting in and out of a light sleep, lulled by the insects and birdsong and even the distant chatter of humans.

He had a dream of apes with the heads of birds and humans with the heads of apes, and woke with a start, wondering what was wrong, and was relieved to discover that it was just Rocket, who had also fallen asleep and slumped against him, throwing one furry arm over Blue Eyes' face.

He gently pushed the arm off.

Most of the heavens were dark, fretted like the wet, broken slate of a mountain side, but the sunward sky was a river of orange and copper above which the single bright light of the star known as the Wandering Orangutan gleamed. He was tricky, the Orang, appearing in the evening for long periods of time, and then somehow swinging across the world to show himself instead in the morning. He was never seen for long, and never after the early morning or before late afternoon. For many days of the year, the Wandering Orang didn't appear at all. Maurice said between his time at dawn and dusk he was visiting his many wives on the other side of the world. Blue Eyes hadn't thought about that story in a while, but now he found that—in his imagination—it had merged with Ray's dreams. He pictured an orangutan with a single brightly glowing eye, crossing from sunrise to sunset by swinging through the root-branches of the underworld forest, stopping now and then to visit one of his wives, as orangutans had done in days of old. Perhaps he heard the whispers of the dead. Perhaps if one listened in the right way, he might repeat those whispers…

He was jogged from contemplation by the familiar clatter of horses. He tried to look around without moving.

He had just decided he hadn't really heard anything when something flickered down below. Blue Eyes blinked, raising his head a little. And saw the lights, the lights that were not fires, or stars, the sun or the moon or the pale glow of fireflies. No, these were the human lights, for which the people of San Francisco had fought so hard, for which many apes and humans had died. When he had first seen them, Blue Eyes had felt only wonderment. But now, they brought ugly thoughts into his head. Human lights did not come without cost.

And the people here had them.

That set his mind whirling. Everything seemed changed. If these humans had the lights, they might have other things. Weapons, like those on the ships. Radios, that spoke over vast distances and called enemies to fight against his father. Other, worse things he could scarcely imagine.

Then he heard the horse whicker again, and another, and the clopping of their hooves. Off to his left, beyond the bed in the bushes he and Rocket had made, the silhouettes of horses and riders appeared, touched with autumn color by the sunset, almost glowing against the night pulling itself down upon the world.

In that faint, rosy twilight, he saw the riders were apes, two of them, staring down at the lights of the town, struck with wonder and fear, just as he was.

One was behind the other, and he couldn't tell who that one was, but the nearest was Fox. His rifle rested across his lap.

Distracted by the lights, Fox and the other ape had yet to see Blue Eyes and Rocket, but it couldn't be a coincidence that they were on the same ridge. The two must have followed him and Rocket, just as they had tracked the humans who took Ray.

Fox? He remembered that day on the bridge, when he had been frozen with fear, the look the other chimp had sent. And even earlier, on the tower, when Fox spoke against his father's plans.

When had Fox decided that Blue Eyes must die?

Gingerly, Blue Eyes nudged Rocket, who—to his dismay—made a snuffling sound. Blue Eyes reached for his gun, but Fox was already turning in his saddle, staring at him. Blue Eyes froze, his fingers inches from his weapon. Fox hooted, low, and the ape with him moved into view. Blue Eyes recognized Stripe, one of Koba's followers.

Unlike Fox, Stripe did not hesitate. He jerked his gun up, pointed it at Blue Eyes, and pulled the trigger.

His aim was spoiled, however, by the stone that Rocket hurled. It struck Stripe high in the chest and sent him plummeting from his mount. His rifle roared, sending its deadly traces of fire up toward the middle of the sky.

Fox fired, then, but he hadn't reckoned on the way the guns recoiled. The bullets kicked up dirt and leaves a few feet from Blue Eyes, and Fox also fell from his horse with a surprised yip. He hit the lip of the hill, yelped again, and vanished from sight.

By that time Rocket had his weapon and, shaking himself out of his brief stupor, Blue Eyes continued reaching for his. Another burst of gunfire sounded from behind him, and as he picked up his weapon he saw a third ape, Aghoo, riding into view, his weapon looking Blue Eyes right in the face. Aghoo was a gorilla, a massive one, and he looked almost ridiculous on his small horse.

Rocket smacked into Blue Eyes as Aghoo's rifle sounded again. That took them beyond the edge of the hill—not over the cliff where Fox had fallen, but down a steep, rocky slope.

"Run!" Rocket grunted, as they slid to a stop.

The two of them dodged off across the rocky hillside, bullets hissing by them, striking sparks from stones and cutting the branches of the tamarisk. Rocket turned and fired back as they ducked behind a boulder. Aghoo bellowed, but with anger rather than pain. Rocket shot again, but when he pulled the trigger a third time, nothing happened.

That was bad news. Their extra ammunition was on their horses, wherever they were.

That left them however many bullets were in Blue Eyes' gun. After the fight with the wolves, that might not be many.

Blue Eyes could still make out the human village below, and it was no longer quiet. Floodlights shone from the towers, and there was a good deal of yelling. A group of humans with guns was forming up near the gate.

"We have to get out of here," Rocket signed.

Blue Eyes cast one more glance down at Ray, looking up toward them from his cage. The captive orang couldn't see them of course, looking from light into darkness. But he might have seen the flame from the gunshots. He might be hoping for rescue.

But there was no rescuing Ray tonight. And if he and Rocket died, there would be no rescue, ever.

"Yes," he sighed. "Which way?"

"This slope over here is too steep for horses," Rocket said. "If they follow without horses, we might ambush them. If not, we will get ahead."

Blue Eyes nodded assent, and together they bounded off through the brush. Gunfire exploded behind them, and this time it was answered by more distant guns in the village.

* * *

McCullough listened to the reports of his officers without much comment. When they were done, he pulled himself up from behind his chair and looked out the window.

"All right," he said. "Thank you all. Dismissed."

Once they were gone, he retrieved his half-smoked cigar and lit it, taking a few deep mouthfuls of the smoke, and then releasing it in a blue-gray cloud, watching absently as the fumes roiled into fractal patterns before thinning away to invisibility.

He remembered good cigars. The one in his mouth had a good pedigree, had been rolled and packed by a venerable manufacturer of fine smokes. The leaves had been treated with respect, and the result, really, was art.

Or had been. He didn't know if the factory where his cigar was made still existed, but if it did, they were no longer shipping to anyplace he was aware of. His current stash of smokes was more than a decade old. He'd found them, abandoned, in a humidor that had been working the day before, and had taken pains to preserve them as best he could. A fine cigar improved with age, stored properly. But ten years of campaigning had left many gaps in his ability to curate them.

So the cigar—like a lot of things—was now less than it should be. But that was fine; it was what he had. It might be that a truly great cigar would never exist again, at least not in his lifetime.

But if he did his job properly, his son might smoke one. Or his grandson.

If.

He was not the sort to beat himself up. It was a waste of energy and an impediment to moving forward. He had let his mind go in circles on this ape thing, but now things seemed to be looking up a little. They were clever at misdirection, and at first he thought he had wasted one of his precious store of Tomahawk missiles on an empty building. But he seemed to have struck a nerve of some kind—the apes were active almost all over the city, although it was far from clear what they were up to.

He looked up at a rap on his door, took another puff on the cigar.

"Come in," he said.

The door pushed open to reveal Forest, balanced on a pair of crutches. Her right leg now ended at the knee. It was still bandaged.

"Sir," she said.

"Captain. You have something to tell me? Good news, I hope?"

Her expression suggested that probably wasn't the case. Of course, it could be her discomfort showing. She was still adjusting to the loss of her leg, and the medics had wanted to send her back north, to the hospital there. At the very least, they demanded she spend another week or two in bed.

But Forest was stubborn.

"Would you like to have a seat?" he asked.

"I'm fine standing, thank you, sir."

She wasn't, he could tell, but that was what made her a good soldier. She had no place for weakness in her. He admired that, on one level—but on the other hand, you didn't get extra credit for doing what you were supposed to do.

"Let's hear it then," he said.

"Well, we've confirmed contact with the south," she said. "I still couldn't tell you exactly where they are, and they've been careful not to let on."

"How do we know it's not just some guy with an old ham radio?" he asked. "Or a militia, come to that?"

"I guess we can't be sure, sir," she said. "But the way they were talking—I felt they were military, or are pretending to be. The first guy I was talking to called himself an 'OS' and when he gave up the mic to another guy, I heard him call him Lieutenant in the background. And they asked me what my rank was, and who my commanding officer was. Like that. And the signal is in the old range. And they asked for some sort of confirmation that we are who we say we are."

He nodded. "Understandable. If I had a nickel for every yahoo who claimed to represent the U.S. government— well, I still couldn't buy anything with them, but it would be a whole lot of nickels."

"Yes, sir."

"All right," he said. "I guess I better talk to them. But in the meantime, I'm getting tired of just sitting here. I don't know what the apes are up to, but I feel like the other shoe is about to drop. I don't think we can afford to wait on hypotheticals."

"May I ask what you're planning, sir?"

He nodded. "I think we have the lay of the land now. Or at least our part of it. And we've seen an uptick in activity on the bridge. I don't know what they're up to, but I don't want to be caught flat-footed again. We seem to have gained a little momentum—let's not lose it. Let's go ahead with Hercules."

She brightened a little at that.

"Yes, sir," she said. "I would like to request a combat position, sir."

He put his stogie down.

"Explain to me how that makes sense, Captain."

"I can still handle a weapon, sir. I could take a sniper position."

"We have Tucker and Chee for that," he said. "And a good number we can take off the bench, if need be. You're a good shot, but not that good."

"Sir—"

He sighed and cocked his head. "You want to go down fighting, is that it? Don't fancy the way your future looks without the leg?"

Forest stood straighter.

"I don't fancy running a radio from here on out, if that's what you mean, sir."

"I get it," he said. "You're a warrior at heart. And if I were a Viking warlord, I would put you on the front line so you could get to Valhalla, quick time. But I'm not a chieftain, and I don't need warriors. I need soldiers, and every soldier has both her worth and her limits. Even without a leg, you're more valuable to me than anyone here. But some of your limitations have increased. I'd be a terrible C.O. if I didn't acknowledge that. And you must come to terms with it, too."

She sighed, and for just an instant he saw through what the years had brought to the young woman she had been when they first met. She was still young, by the standards of another age. By the measure of this one, she was an elder.

"Yes sir," she said. "I'll get there, sir. And thank you."

Luca woke Winter a few hours after dark. Others were already up and ready; some hadn't been to sleep at all. Winter felt like he had barely rested; dreams of falling, of smoke and fire kept waking him.

He hated the night. Most apes were not fond of darkness; ape eyes saw best in the day, while those things that might make a meal of one generally saw better in nocturnal hours. But most apes, with their dark coats, could at least crouch on a limb and hide in shadow; even the lightest-haired orang or silverback could vanish from sight by being still.

But not Winter. His hair was white, like the snow which had inspired his mother to name him. Under even the faintest of night skies, he glowed like the moon. It was impossible for him to hide in the night, and he knew that from experience, from a hundred games of hide-and-seek played after dark. He was always discovered first, and when he was the hunter, they always saw him coming. When the other youths went out in early morning or after dusk, hunting small game with their throwing sticks and rockwhirls, they never invited him, because the game noticed him too, even if he was downwind.

Luca knew how visible Winter was, too, and walked on one side of him as they crossed the long span of the bridge, with Ajax and Red also crowded near, so any humans watching wouldn't spot him, look closer, and see the long line of apes moving silently from the city, across the water, back into the forest.

Warriors at their posts watched them pass.

"Why can't I stay here?" he asked Luca. "Stay and fight? I can learn to use a gun."

"I told you," Luca said. "The women have the children to deal with, the sick, the hurt, the old. They need hunters, warriors to fend off the wolves. Strong backs to help them build shelter. Protect them. This is what the gorilla guard does."

"Why? You fight with Caesar."

"Yes," he said. "Because I am third in command of the army. Because I am on the council. My place is with Caesar. The guard is the place for you."

"I don't see why."

"It's an honor," Luca said. "Before we built the village, before we raised the walls, gorillas *were* the walls. Our example was Buck, who died that we might find refuge."

"I know the story," Winter said.

"Then you should know the rest," Luca said. "We gorillas walked around the troop, encircled it, and we did not let danger pass. We are not as swift as the other apes. We are not as agile in the trees. But nothing that walks on the land can get past a gorilla."

"Except a human with a gun," Winter said.

"Now we have guns too. I will show you how to use one. Our village is burned, its walls are gone, and we must find a new place for our people. Once again, the gorillas will be the walls of the village. And you must be part of the wall, and you must be strong. For when an enemy comes at a village, it seeks the lowest and weakest part of the wall to attack. That will not be you, do you understand?"

"And it will not matter that I have no color?" Winter asked. "That an enemy can see me from across the forest?"

"One thing about a wall," Luca said. "Simply knowing it is there sends many enemies scurrying the other direction. A wall is not meant to be invisible. It is meant to be a display of strength and readiness."

By then, they had reached the far side of the bridge. Winter wasn't sure what he felt; he wanted to please Luca. He did not want to disappoint him. And yet he knew he already had.

"I was afraid," Winter signed, in the moonlight. "Back in the city, when everything shook, when the building exploded. I was so afraid. I fear I will make a poor part of the wall. I fear I will be weak."

"Fear is not weakness," Luca said. "Some say only the stones are not afraid, but I think even they worry about the ice that cracks them in winter. Everything has something to fear. Fear tells us what our limits are. It whispers them inside, where only we can hear. And we should know our limits, so fear can help us. But the thing to remember about fear is that it is not honest about those things. It lies to you, the way a mother lies to protect her child."

Luca put his arm around him.

"You will be strong when your moment comes," he said. "I know you will."

14

Ray was sleeping when the cage door opened. He had been awake most of the night; the gunfire outside of the town, he figured, might be Rocket and Blue Eyes creating some sort of distraction, so he needed to be ready to escape. He was further heartened when Jack and about twenty more humans armed themselves and rushed out of the village.

But the hoped-for rescue didn't come, and eventually he tired and closed his eyes. As he opened them again, he realized he was no longer alone in the cage. Someone else had just been shoved in with him.

But even in the dim, strange light he saw it was neither Rocket nor Blue Eyes.

It was Fox.

Fox was a few winters older than he, and a little older than Blue Eyes. He had been in his mother's belly when they crossed the bridge, and had been born only weeks after the great liberation. He was strong, smart, and something of a bully. No one knew his father, but growing up, Fox had sometimes claimed that his father was Koba. Ray had once mentioned that to his own father, who said it couldn't be true, that Fox's mother and Koba had not known each other before she became swollen with him; they were from different cages in different places.

Nevertheless, Fox acted like Koba was his father, although Koba never reciprocated. Instead, Koba had treated Blue Eyes more like a son, or at least like a sister's son, which Ray knew made Fox hate Blue Eyes. But Fox was also smart enough not to let that hatred show, at least not often.

So he wasn't surprised that Fox was one of the apes following them, trying to kill them. But the bit of empathy he had for the chimp did nothing to assuage the anger he now felt for him.

Ray poked Fox, who stirred a bit but did not wake. He thought about strangling Fox in his sleep; Fox was bigger, stronger, a better fighter. If he let Fox wake up, he might be dooming himself. But it was more than that, more than just the practical considerations of who would win a fair fight. Ray was almost surprised at how deep his hatred ran, at how much anger at Koba and his followers was living inside of him, how he really just wanted to choke the life out of the other ape.

But deeper than that anger were the words of his father, of Maurice, of Caesar.

Ape should not kill ape.

It had happened, because it had to, because Koba had to be stopped. But it did not have to happen again, no matter what he felt.

So instead Ray waited. As he did so, the cold glare of the human lights vanished, and the sun rose in the morning haze like a water lily blooming on mist-shrouded waters.

He heard someone coming and saw it was Feliz.

"Two of you now, huh?" she said. "Can't be coincidence. Do you know him? Is he your brother or something?" She cocked her head. "He kind of looks different, though.

Maybe you aren't the same kind of monkey."

He thought about trying to sign to her, but Ray had decided that it was best to let the humans believe what most of them did anyway—that he was like a raccoon or a wolf, without speech. Only Feliz acted as if she thought he might know what she was saying, and then only sometimes.

"They say there are four more out there, at least," she went on. "And some people on horses, chasing them. Were they coming here to rescue you? Were you already being hunted by someone else?"

Ray glanced back at the silent figure of Fox, puzzled. They had known apes were following them. But humans, too? How long a tail was Blue Eyes dragging behind him?

He looked again at Feliz, meeting her earnest gaze. Had he made the wrong decision? Should he try to talk to her?

"I'm sorry about all of this," she whispered. "If I had known it was going to happen—"

"Feliz!"

She jumped a bit at her name. Ray saw Jack was striding up.

"Yeah?" she said.

"We need you in the east tower," he said. "Everybody else worth a damn is out there."

"I should be too," she said.

"Well, that's not your decision," he said. "Not yet."

"Yeah," Feliz replied. "Fine." She left, but not without casting a backward glance toward him.

Maybe when she returned, he decided, he would put his toe in the water, at least. Rocket and Blue Eyes seemed to be in trouble, maybe more than he was. If there was any chance he could convince her to let him go, he probably ought to try it.

When Ray sat back down, he saw that Fox's eyes were open. His eyes widened when he saw Ray, and then he winced and touched a hand to the bloody spot on his head.

"Where are we?" Fox asked him.

"We're in a cage," Ray answered. "Why, Fox? Why did you try to kill us?"

Fox didn't answer, but sat up too, rubbing his head.

"I fell off my horse," he said. "Hit my head."

"I can see that," Ray said, impatiently. "You've been following us. Shooting at us. Why?"

Fox's nostrils flared.

"We won!" he said. "We beat the humans. You were with us, Ray. You and your father—"

Ray cut him off with a harsh throat-click.

"My father is dead because of Koba," he said. "Because of Koba's lie. Because Koba tried to kill Caesar."

"Caesar is weak," Fox said. "Stupid. He puts humans above apes. He let the humans go, even after they tried to kill us. Now they come back to kill us again. Caesar should not rule apes. He will not."

Fox stopped, then, as if realizing he'd gone too far.

"Koba is dead," Ray said. "Who is your leader? Not you. Or do you even know?"

"I know," Fox said, defiantly. "It doesn't matter. Blue Eyes will die. You will die. Real apes will live."

"You won't," Ray snarled.

He moved without thinking, smashing the knuckles of his right hand into Fox's face. Fox came at him like a bent sapling released, arms gripping his, feet kicking into his belly. Ray twisted, and they slammed into the side of the cage so hard its corners lifted from the ground. Ray howled as Fox bit his arm; he smelled blood, and then everything seemed to go away but his anger, and the universe contracted to muscle and bone colliding.

The next thing he knew, he couldn't breathe. Something was cinched around his throat, and he was dragged from

Fox. Everything went black, and then he saw red spots and finally, after many tight, labored breaths, he was sensible again, back in the cage. Fox was about a stone's throw away, tied hand-and-foot to a wooden post.

He was still panting when Feliz came back. She sized him up, and then began dabbing his cuts and bites with something that smelled bad and stung worse.

"Guess he's not your brother after all," she said. "Or at least, not a very good one."

Blue Eyes crouched in the shallows of the river, each breath feeling like a tear in the middle of his body. He and Rocket had managed to lose the mounted apes in the dark; it was dangerous riding at night, when a horse's hoof could find an unseen hole or fallen tree-trunk and send you falling to a rendezvous with a broken arm or neck. He and Rocket were no longer running from Stripe and Aghoo, but from the humans, who carried light with them. Some of them were mounted, too, but most were not. They traveled better and faster on two legs than apes did, and it was only the moonlight and the trees that had saved them from death or capture. Once among the branches, they could move without leaving a trace. By dawn they were in unknown territory.

"I think the humans have given up," Rocket said.

"Maybe," Blue Eyes said.

Rocket started to sign something, but then he didn't, instead picking the sticks from his fur.

Blue Eyes knew what Rocket was avoiding saying.

"You think we should return to my father and tell him what we have learned."

"Yes," the older ape said. "He should know about the humans with lights. He should know that Koba still has followers plotting against him."

"I agree. That's why you're going to return and tell him."

"The two of us will return," Rocket said, either feigning he didn't understand what Blue Eyes was getting at or perhaps really not seeing.

"I'm not going to leave Ray," Blue Eyes said. "You will return to Caesar. Only you."

"You'll never free Ray now," Rocket said. "The humans will be on watch for you."

"Maybe," Blue Eyes said. "Maybe not. But I have to try."

"Then Rocket will help."

"No. You have to warn my father."

Rocket considered that for a moment.

"You will return to Caesar," he said. "I will free Ray."

"My father said I was to lead," Blue Eyes said. "This is my decision. You will go. I will return to free Ray."

Rocket looked stubborn.

"Caesar will not be happy with me if I return without his son," he finally said.

"I know," Blue Eyes said. "It can't be helped." He handed their remaining gun toward Rocket.

"No," Rocket said.

"Look," Blue Eyes said. "I'll stay hidden. I won't try to help Ray unless I think I can do it easily. After you tell my father, come back here, with help, and horses."

"What about Stripe and Aghoo?"

"We were careless," Blue Eyes said. "I was careless. They must have heard our guns when we were fighting the wolves. It brought them to that place and they found our trail. I'll be more careful, this time."

Rocket avoided his gaze for a moment; Blue Eyes saw the struggle in him.

"Stay hidden," Rocket said, at last. "Keep the gun. I will return."

Then he turned and went off downstream, without a backward glance.

Blue Eyes took his time returning to the village, careful not to leave a trail. It was noon the next day before he reached it again, working his way along a different overlook, this one on the sunrise side. He found a good spot where he could both hide and see what was going on below.

He could make out Ray's cage well enough, but after a few moments of observation, he realized that something was wrong.

The cage was empty.

He heard the slightest of sounds behind him. He turned to find the end of a rifle in his face, with a human standing behind it.

"Well," the human said. "I guess I had it right."

Blue Eyes thought the human was the small female he'd seen guarding Ray's cage, although he couldn't be certain.

"I sure hope you can understand me," she said, "because if you don't put that gun down right now, I'm going to shoot you. I don't want to, but I will."

She held the rifle with authority; she could have killed him before he had even known she was there, if had she wanted to.

Reluctantly, he put the gun aside.

"Holy crap," she said. "You really do understand me, don't you?"

Blue Eyes felt a little stupid. The first humans he'd met had shown a great deal of surprise that apes understood language. Why should these be any different? He'd assumed she and Ray had had some sort of conversation, but now he was starting to realize that for whatever reason, Ray had played dumb.

He could still try the same thing. But what would be the point? He no longer knew where Ray was. Even if he somehow managed to overcome the girl and escape, what would he do then?

"I understand you," he signed.

Her eyes narrowed. "Is that supposed to mean something?"

So she didn't know the hand language.

"Understand," he said, aloud.

She jumped back as if something had stung her, and her mouth opened comically wide.

"Holy crap!" she said again. "I mean, holy cow. I'm not supposed to swear." She licked her lips. "I thought something was fishy," she said. "The other guy, the one we found with the buffalo. You're looking for him, right?"

Was "buffalo" the right word for those cows? That seemed familiar. "Yes," Blue Eyes managed. "Friend."

"Who's your friend? The one we had first, or the one that came falling down the hill?"

He realized she must be talking about Fox. He thought about it a moment, then brushed back the soil of the ridge.

He made three fingerprints in the dirt.

"Blue Eyes," he said, pointing to the first mark, and then at himself. "Rocket. Ray." After touching the dot that represented Ray, he motioned back the way they'd come.

"Lost Ray with… buffalo."

"So Ray is the fellow we found," she said. "The orangutan."

"Yes," Blue Eyes said.

"This is so freaking weird," she said. "Keep going."

Haltingly he explained that they had been on a journey, and that Fox, Aghoo, and Stripe had followed them, intent on killing them.

"Wait," she said. "Hold up. The guys Jack and everybody have been chasing—the ones on horses—those are apes too?"

Blue Eyes nodded.

"Don't that beat all to hell. I mean heck," she said. "They think they're chasing people."

Blue Eyes tapped his chest. "People," he said.

"Yeah, right, didn't mean to give offense—you know what I mean. I've never dealt with talking monkeys before. So you came to get Ray, but not the other one?"

"Yes," Blue Eyes said.

"Problem is," she said, "they're both gone. Diablo came and got 'em. Paid us good, too." She frowned. "I was against it, even with the money. But you can't piss off Diablo—I mean, you can't tee them off—because then they might cut the power. And if they cut the power, everybody gets mad. You understand?"

She spoke too quickly, but Blue Eyes thought he understood most of it.

"Where take him?" he asked.

"Diablo," she said. She fidgeted. "Sure as hell—as heck—you don't want to follow him there. I mean…" she trailed off.

"Ray is my friend," he said. "Please."

Her mouth pinched shut and her brows lowered. "I ought to turn you in, too," she said. "We can always use the bounty. And at least you'd be together."

She reached over and picked up his gun and slung it over her shoulder.

"Come on," she said.

15

Ray glared at Fox as the truck bumped along the road. They were sharing a cage again, this one made of heavy gauge wire, but they were also bound at their hands and feet and to the cage, so they couldn't reach each other. Their bondage also made it difficult for them to communicate, and rather than resort to the parlance of sound, they settled for expressing themselves with facial expressions. Besides, what was left to say once someone admitted they intended to kill you?

The new humans had arrived in four trucks, twenty of them, all wearing similar orange suits that covered them head-to-boot, and they had cloths tied over their faces, reminding Ray of the masks the midwives back home wore when someone was sick or giving birth. They talked to the humans in the village, but didn't make any attempt to speak to either him or Fox. He remembered Feliz telling him goodbye, and then the new people put a tarp over the cage, so he and Fox couldn't see. He didn't know how long they had been traveling, but it felt like forever, and he also felt a little sick, like he was going to throw up. It got worse, toward the end, as the ride grew progressively rougher.

When the motion of the truck finally halted, Ray still couldn't see where they were, because the tarp wasn't removed. Some humans picked up the cage and carried it. Ray could hear birds singing, the soughing of the wind, the burr of insects.

And he could smell the sea, the faint grassy scent of kelp, and taste the salt on his tongue. It made him feel a little better to know at least that much about where he was. The water must be nearby. He even thought he could hear the rush of waves upon sand and stone, and he certainly heard the calls of shore birds.

After about twenty steps the sounds and scents of the outdoors abruptly faded, replaced by a sort of hollow echo not quite like anything he'd ever heard before. It seemed as if he was inside of a sea-shell or an empty can. The light leaking through the tarp didn't look right at all; it was too white, maybe even a little bit blue, like the inside of a lightning flash.

When the tarp finally came off, he and Fox were in a windowless room with light gray walls and a white ceiling. A human came near and stuck something in his arm. He screeched because it hurt, first like the deep prick of a thorn, then more like the sting of a bee as the ache spread through his muscle. Then a more fundamental fear gripped him, as he understood what the thing they'd put in his arm *was*. Maurice had made a story-glyph of such a thing, and drawn an ape around it, and together they meant *injected ape*.

The cage meant many things. All of the apes who escaped during the awakening had been in cages—if not all the time, at least some of the time. Some apes in cages had been fed and cared for. Humans came to stare at them, they were sometimes handled a little roughly, but in general the only complaint those apes had of their captivity was the lack of freedom. A few even looked back at those cages wistfully—they spoke fondly of food which appeared without need for work, of soft, sweet fruits not tasted in so many years they were almost forgotten. For some, their cages had been almost a refuge from the horrors they experienced when humans took them out to do their tricks.

But for others, the cages were places where very, very bad things happened. Koba had been in such a cage, and had the scars to show for it.

Lab apes, they were called. Injected apes. That was what he and Fox were now. The humans were torturing him, just as they had so many apes in the days before his birth.

The pain from the injection didn't last, but nothing else did, either. First he felt a little sleepy, then terribly so. His limbs stopped doing what he wanted them to, and then he seemed to fall, tearing once again through the floor of the world, plunging into another place. But it was not the underplace he had been dreaming about. Here there were no stars or sky-reaching roots, no world-beneath-a-world. Here was pain, and cold, and dust in his mouth. He knew who he was, but remembered very little of who he had been. Everything in his past seemed like a sight seen from the corner of his eye; he couldn't focus or turn his head to perceive it clearly. He knew he had once had a name, and struggled to recall it, but to no avail. Nameless, without a past, he plunged into the void.

The darkness was total, at first, but eventually a pale, insipid light seemed to filter in around him; but it was not a welcoming, warm radiance, not fire or sunrise or sunset, but something more akin to the reflection from the eye of a dead fish. Still, in it he could see something lay next to him, a horizon of sorts. At first he thought it was a hill, the contours of a landscape, but then he understood the scale was all wrong—he was looking at something smaller, closer, more familiar than any topography.

It was the outline of another ape, lying on its back, held down by leather straps. Long metal needles like the injector had been thrust into its body, its neck, its eyes and tongue. And beyond he saw another ape, similarly strapped to a table, and another. His gaze seemed to float somehow up and above, so he was looking down; he saw himself, and Fox, and a hundred other apes—chimps, bonobos, gorillas, orangutans—all on their backs, their bodies cut open, stabbed, pierced, mangled. Yet they were all still alive, their eyes quick with the terrible knowledge of what was being done to them, their expressions showing their utter lack of hope for anything but a swift death.

The nearest ape—a chimp—turned its head, slowly, to look at him. Although both eyes had needles in them, one looked normal and the other was a milky scar, and his mouth was drawn up in a contemptuous sneer.

Koba.

Ray screamed and tried to tear himself free of the table, but the bands held him so tightly he could not breathe; darkness rose to blot his vision, but as it subsided, the whole awful chain of images started again—the light, the tables, apes half-eviscerated, their guts hanging out, still-living eyes rolling in awful comprehension—Koba, staring at him in raw accusation.

Now you know, Koba seemed to say.

Ray still wasn't sure it was over, but finally something changed—the nightmare cycle broke, replaced by flashes of faces, moments, feelings. His father, praising the first spear he made, tumbling in the dirt of the village with Blue Eyes and Lake when he was very little, touching a stream for the first time, noticing that underneath its quicksilver surface lay another world, where crawfish walked on their many legs, and fish darted swiftly like little slivers of the sky. He remembered his father holding him after he fell from a tree and hurt his knee; at the time, he could imagine no greater pain. But his father told him that no matter how much it hurt, it would eventually feel better.

These visions felt like that, like an elder reminding him that there were still good things in the world, that everything wasn't pain and darkness.

When real consciousness returned, he was in a small chamber, not much larger than the cage he and Fox had shared on the truck. At first he thought it was just a sort of metal frame, without walls at all, but when he reached to touch it, something solid stopped his fingers. He knew what it was, a sort of clear stuff called glass. Growing up, he'd found fragments of it, especially around old human things but sometimes just lying in the woods; it made good tools for carving wood. But he had never imagined until he went to the human city that whole walls of it could exist. There he saw huge buildings that seemed made mostly of glass, and others with dozens and hundreds of square eyes made of the stuff. Many had been shattered, but some remained entire.

There were other strange things in the room, most of which Ray did not recognize. In the main they were shiny, metal and glass and the smooth stuff that resembled shell so many human things were made from.

Two humans in the orange suits went about some unknown business in the room, mostly ignoring him.

He hurt. Examining his body, he found sore spots, bruises with stings in the center, a place on his head where the hair had been shaved and the flesh was raw. He felt groggy, and even sicker than he had on the truck.

Fox was in a chamber much like his, but across the room. He seemed to still be lost to the awful sleep, but Fox was deceptive. He might be pretending.

Not that it mattered right now.

After a little while, the humans left. That was good news, because Ray knew something about glass; it was easily broken. Certainly, the humans knew that, but maybe they didn't know *he* knew it. Their mistake.

So when they had been gone for a bit, he made a fist and punched the wall of his cage, hard, just in the center.

But it didn't break. Instead it shuddered, and made a low, wobbly back-and-forth kind of sound. Puzzled, he hit it again.

A few tries later, his knuckles were bloody, and he had decided that this glass was different than what he was used to. It was disappointing, but in the end, not all that surprising, and it explained why the humans weren't worried about keeping him and Fox in cages made of the stuff.

After a few moments, two humans entered the room. He thought one was female; she wore clothing the color of a clear evening sky that left her hairless legs bare from the knees down. The clothes were fastened with pretty metal buttons. She wore glasses over her eyes, as he had seen humans in San Francisco do, and a cloth on her face like the men who had put him on the truck. The other he guessed to be male; he was taller, and had hair redder than that of an orangutan. His clothes resembled Malcolm's; a shapeless shirt that covered him to the wrists and waist over wrinkled blue leg-coverings.

"This one's awake," the man said. "You don't need the mask, by the way."

"Very well," said the woman, pulling the cloth down so Ray could see her lips. Something about their body language, alien as it was, suggested that she was the dominant of the two. Her tone only confirmed it.

"Tell me about them."

"Well," he said, gesturing at Ray, "this one is an orangutan. The other is a chimpanzee. In terms of size and weight, the orang is pretty small.. Probably adult, but very young. The chimp falls in the average range for a young adult. Some of the labs aren't back, and what I really would like is an MRI—"

"And they're plague-free?" she interrupted, another signal that she was in charge.

"No," he replied. "They have the virus in their systems. But so do we. So does everyone still alive."

"It's identical to what we carry?" she said.

"Well, it's very close," he said. "It has some archaic traits."

Her too-shallow brow lowered in a frown.

"What the hell does that mean?" she demanded. "Archaic traits?"

"Nothing, really," he said. "At least nothing to worry about. Anything with genetic information in it—your cells, my cells, a virus—mutates a little with each generation. The mutations, for the most part, aren't meaningful; they just become random bits of code stuck in the genome. But say your great-grandfather had such a mutation. It doesn't help him or hurt him, evolutionarily speaking, so it stays in his DNA by default. He passes it on to his kids and grandkids, and one of them to you. We could use that marker to trace you back to him, even if we didn't know he was your grandfather. And we could identify your cousins the same way, while eliminating prospective cousins who aren't descended from your great-grandfather. If we knew where your grandfather lived, we could also trace the movements and migrations of his descendants. The same is true of the virus. Random mutations can tell us if we're dealing with a strain that picked up a mutation in Hong Kong, or Mexico City, or wherever. These markers allow

us to make an educated guess as to where these guys—
these apes—come from. Their version of the virus has
features common only to the original strain, the one that
originated in the Gen-Sys labs ten years ago. From that we
can deduce that these guys are descended from the original
population of infected apes."

"And their strain isn't dangerous," she said.

"Not to anyone living," he told her. "The part of its
code that had fatal effects on humans is the same as what
you and I are already immune to. The mutations that serve
as markers don't actually have any outcome on how the
virus presents itself as an infection."

"I see," she said. "But you are telling me these two are
from the same group our... ah, friends... up north in San
Francisco are dealing with."

"They must be," he said. "I could be more certain
if I had an ape on hand I knew for certain was from up
there, but the evidence is reasonably certain. It makes
sense geographically, as well. There are no topographic
boundaries that would prevent apes from that region from
coming down here."

"But they never have before," she said.

"That we know of," he said. "And maybe they never
had reason to travel before. Maybe they no longer feel safe
with a warship sitting off shore."

She lifted her shoulders and let them drop again, then
focused her brown eyes on Ray, as if searching for something.

"Then they're smart?" she said.

He shrugged. "You insisted we do the labs first. We
haven't gotten around to testing their intelligence. I always
thought the reports of their behavior were probably
hyperbole—the result of hysteria coupled with the human
tendency to anthropomorphize. And, of course, I assumed
they were all dead by now."

"Why would you assume that?" she asked.

"Well, chimps are from equatorial Africa. So are gorillas. Orangutans are from the tropics of Southeast Asia. Northern California isn't the right environment for them. It gets too cold, for one thing, and there aren't a lot of tropical fruits growing wild. So the very fact that they're still alive suggests they adapted, and very quickly, to a strange environment. Far too quickly for physical evolution to be involved. They would have had to do what humans do—modify their environments."

"In what way?"

"Build dwellings, make tools, use fire maybe, for heat and to cook their food. Orangs, for instance, live almost entirely on fruit. They only eat meat in crisis situations, and wouldn't be able to subsist for long on raw meat. Cooked meat, on the other hand, might provide them greater nutrition, as would cooked roots or what-have-you. It's what our ancestors did, you know. They used tools and fire to make a lot of things that were basically inedible to their primate systems, and used technology to increase the amount and variety of food available to them. That allowed them to move out of the tropics and settle everywhere, including the Arctic."

"Were these two apes found with any tools? Or seen using fire?"

"Not that I know of," he admitted.

"But you aren't an expert in the field?" she said.

"No," he said. "I didn't claim to be. I'm an epidemiologist by training. I did get a minor in anthropology, and if you have someone better to put on this, please do."

Her lips curved up slightly. "Primatologists are in short supply these days," she said. "I remember the one at the San Diego Zoo was hanged."

"For trying to protect the apes there," he said. "I

remember the hysteria. The irony, of course, was that those apes wouldn't have been carrying the virus at all—not unless they caught it from humans."

"Our friends say the apes up north are organized and dangerous," the female said. "I want to know just how smart they are."

"I assume you've told them about our captives?"

She quirked her mouth and shook her head.

"No," she replied. "All indications are that they really are out of Base McChord and that they represent some remainder of the legitimate government. They seem to be who they say they are, but what if they aren't? We've achieved something here. Even if they have some legitimate claim to being what's left of the U.S. military, what does that mean to us? We have our own government here, a certain level of security, of comfort, even. Until a few days ago, we didn't know these guys from Seattle existed any more than they were aware of us. There are a lot of things they don't know about us yet. That we have a working nuclear reactor, for instance. Or how extensive our arsenal is."

"I see your point," the man replied. "Do we intend to help them at all?"

"With their ape problem? I had my doubts they were telling the truth. It seemed more likely they were dealing with another militia group of some sort and didn't want to complicate their request with—let us say, questions of ethics. Now—well, their story begins to check out."

"What are they asking for?" he asked.

She hesitated.

"You know I have clearance," he said.

"Gas," she said. "They don't want to merely beat the apes. They want to exterminate them."

"Oh," he said. "I—I thought the council decided

against ever using that stuff again."

"Sure," she said. "But we didn't get rid of it either, did we? Why do you imagine that is?"

The man looked down at the floor, dominated.

"Yeah," he said. "I know."

She shrugged. "We haven't admitted having it, of course. But an alliance with these people could be fruitful. A war with them could prove devastating, destroy everything we've been working for. We must proceed with caution but leave all options open. I want to know more before we commit any resources or take sides. A lot more."

16

Briefly dizzy, John put his hand against the wall to steady himself.

"Are you okay, Lieutenant?" Forest asked, moving forward through the rubble on her crutches.

"I'm fine," he said.

"Yeah. The medics told me they wanted you in bed for another week."

"That would be too late," John said. "Besides, you're a fine one to talk."

"Well, I didn't have internal injuries."

"Right," John said, glancing at her missing leg. "Just a flesh wound. You really know how to set the bar, Captain."

She smiled slightly at that.

"You know the Colonel," she said.

"Yeah," he replied. "There isn't much gray area between strong and weak in his mind. Only slackers lay around healing and stuff."

"Did he say something to you?" she asked.

"No," he said. "Or to you, either, I'm sure. But if you had stayed down too long, what do you think would happen?"

"He'd have shipped me off," she said.

"Exactly," he said. "So we're both on the same page."

"Not exactly," Forest said. "Whether you're fit for combat right now is debatable. But in a few weeks, you will be. I'm pretty much done with that, y'know? Why not take a little time?"

John took a moment to decide if he really wanted to answer that.

"I know you two are close," he said.

"Hey. Not like that."

"No," he said. "I know you guys aren't—you know. But there isn't anyone in the unit he has more admiration for. And you go way back."

"That we do," she said.

"So if I speak freely, Captain, it has to stay between us."

"That depends on what you say," she replied. "If there's anything that could compromise the mission—"

"No. Nothing like that. No, it's just—where would I go? My mom has been dead for years. I don't have any other living relatives that I know of. Anybody I might consider a friend is—here. And the Colonel—I've already spent way more time without him than with him. I want to be here."

"Well," she said. "Then we *are* on the same page. Except given the whole pinky-swear to silence you just asked me to take, I figure there's something else."

"Yeah."

He looked around uneasily. They were on the remains of the highway above the beach, supervising the installation of a checkpoint. Off to their east lay the remains of the San Francisco Zoo, which kind of gave him the willies. Even though it had been cleared a few days ago—and even if it hadn't been, there was little reason to think the apes would have any interest in hanging out in what had essentially been a kong prison—it still felt weird.

But he wasn't looking for apes—rather, other soldiers within earshot. There weren't any. But he was still reluctant to say anything.

Forest saved him the trouble.

"You say you don't have much outside of all this," Forest said. "Well, neither do I. But your father—that's a whole other story. This is everything to him. With or without the plague, the military would have been his whole life."

"I know. I remember."

"He's the most dedicated man I've ever known," she went on. "He's on a mission, and he won't let anyone or anything stand in the way of his completing it. The only problem is—his mission—his vision—isn't necessarily the same as that of the higher-ups. And over the years that divide has been growing. There have been a couple of times he was in real danger of being removed. I was worried for him myself. But then you showed up. Since then, he's been on a more even keel."

"Okay," John said. Now that he saw she was zeroing in on the mark, he wasn't sure he wanted to finish the conversation.

But it was too late for that, now.

"Don't okay me," Forest said. "People talk. When he thought you were dead, things were starting to get a little—dangerous, let's say. He tried to get backup from Base McChord, and when that failed—well, some thought he was becoming erratic. And it takes a lot to think that, if you're one of his people. There's not a person here who wouldn't follow him into hell. But there are a few who would ask some questions about it on the way."

"I think it's better if I'm around," John said. "I know how that sounds. But my father—the Colonel. You know, my grandfather was special forces. His father was career military, too. There was a picture at our house—a painting—of, like, my six-times great-grandfather who was an officer in the continental army. We had some ancestor at Waterloo and another at Hastings. He's like the tip of a really long spear, and for him that's important. So I'm important. I'm part of something bigger because he is."

"And you?" Forest said. "Are you ready to be the tip of that spear?"

"I'm ready to be whatever he needs me to be," John said.

"See," she said. "That's not the same thing."

"Not yet," he said. "But I'm a work in progress, right?"

"We all are, kid."

He looked north along the old highway.

"Tomorrow, huh?" he said.

"It should be quite a day," she replied. "And I'll be watching it all from an armchair."

"You have an actual armchair?" he said.

She shook her head. "Probably against regulations," she said.

"Captain," he said, searching for words. "I can't ever—"

"Don't," she said. "Just don't. I like you, John. But I didn't do it for you. You know that."

"Yeah," he said. "I know. But thanks anyway."

McCullough had just finished a set of pushups when the rattle of gunfire brought him to his feet. He checked his pistol and stepped outside.

There wasn't much to see. They had extended their occupation of the beach northward, using the zoo and then the various buildings bordering the highway as cover. Predictably, the apes had begun to push back, but never in the concerted manner he was hoping for.

At first, of course, he had feared another charge down the beach, but gradually he began to understand the apes hadn't known just how close they'd come to shutting him down. Now he was in a far stronger position; the best approaches for a charge were now so heavily mined it wouldn't matter if they had tanks instead of horses. While they were short of rockets and large shells, they had plenty of mines and could always make more. They had fueled and converted a few local vehicles, outfitted them with some improvised armor, large-caliber guns, and rocket launchers.

He wasn't trying to surprise the apes; he was driving toward the bridge, slowly, a hundred meters at a time. While the main command post was still back where they had originally landed, he was now in the forward post, set up—ironically, perhaps—in one of the old zoo buildings.

By the time he got outside, the M60 on the roof of the building was chattering, on and off. He didn't see any apes, at least not at first. But then he saw a pair dodge between two buildings, then vanish. But they reappeared a few moments later, each taking a different route—one across the rooftops, the other on the ground.

A few more rounds were exchanged, with no obvious casualties on either side. Then everything was quiet for a while.

He called over the lieutenant in charge.

"Put snipers there, there, there," he said. "I don't think they'll try a full-out assault, but now that they've figured out what we're doing, I think we can expect some harassment from now on. And have those guys stay sharp—remember these things probably still have some rocket launchers. Watch the taller buildings."

"Yes, sir," the Captain said.

He stayed outside, considering the landscape. This leader of theirs, Caesar, might not be the most sophisticated general in history, but he did have a sense of the feint, of showing you a vulnerability here to pull you in, while getting ready to clobber you *there*, where you weren't expecting it. But a lot of his advantage came from being able to go around the norms of troop movement; his soldiers could swing and climb better than even the best trained and best equipped special forces units. Once you started to think of the situation in those terms—in three dimensions—it became a little easier to plan.

Still, if the apes were taking potshots at them from the east—if that was what Caesar was showing him—where was the other hand?

But he didn't get an answer, at least not in the next few hours.

That afternoon, John joined him for a patrol, under cover of the guns they had moved up on the trucks and the snipers in their various positions. They were looking to move the forward command post up another few hundred meters, while keeping everything behind them more-or-less secure. It worried him a little that they might stretch a little too thin, but as long as his manpower stayed about the same—if he didn't suffer significant losses—they probably had the troops they needed to get in position for an assault on the bridge. What he *didn't* want was to begin the assault only to find apes coming up behind him and swarming over from the city. It was exactly the sort of tactic he had come to expect from Caesar. Inching up his position wasn't sexy, but he hadn't lost a man since their initial assault on the city, and they had been able to manage their dwindling resources pretty well.

They found a suitable location, and the scouts set about determining visibility while he and John looked over the building itself.

"Greek again," he heard John murmur.

"What's that?" he asked, but then he saw. Someone

had done a bit of graffiti on the side of the building. It didn't look new; layers of smoke pollution and mold had covered a good portion of it. But the images were still easy to make out, if a little disjointed. Perhaps they hadn't all been made at the same time.

There were several depictions of apes, although the artists seemed to have only a vague notion of the characteristics of what they were trying to portray. Humans were also pictured, many of them gathered together and some apparently in flames. Oddly, the human figures were much more abstract than those of the apes, but some of them were labeled, "homo," "apostate," "misseginut"— which he took to be a misspelling of *miscegenate*—and so forth. These people were all shown being burned alive. Below all of this, painted large and in red, were the Greek letters A and Ω.

"Oh, yeah," McCullough said. "You recognize them?"

"Well, Alpha is easy," John said. "That second one is, what, Omega?"

"That's right. The first and last letters of the Greek alphabet." He traced his fingers along the marks.

"What's that about?" John asked.

"I am the Alpha and the Omega, the First and the Last, the Beginning and the End," McCullough quoted. "It's from the Bible, from the book of Revelations. Scary book, or at least I used to think so. All about the Apocalypse, the end of the world. Very popular book about ten years ago."

"I guess," John said. "But what does it mean?"

"Depends on who you ask," McCullough said. "Back before the actual end of the world, it was taken to mean that God is eternal—he was here before the world and will be here after it's all over. But during plague, it got freighted with all sorts of meanings. Some, for instance, thought it applied to humanity."

"You mean, like 'the human race will go on'?"

"The interpretation that sticks with me substitutes 'humanity' for 'God.' In essence, we created ourselves. Of all animals on Earth that evolved in four billion years, we were the ones who stood up, made fire, turned the energy inside of the very atoms that make up the universe to our wills. Before us, the universe existed, but it didn't matter, because there was nothing and no one to know about it or appreciate it."

"That sounds like what I just said. The human race is sort of eternal."

"Not the whole race," McCullough corrected. "Just the survivors. Me and you. We were genetically predestined to survive. It was written in our very DNA. In that way of thinking, the plague came along to separate the truly immortal from those destined for the dust. Some took it on themselves to help the plague out, a bit. They set fire to isolation wards and quarantines, murdered doctors and nurses who were trying to treat the sick. That kind of thing. Hell on Earth stuff."

"Oh," John said. "They were crazy."

"Crazy? When almost nine in ten of everyone you know dies, it becomes a little difficult to work out what exactly crazy is."

"Really?" John said. "Are you saying Mom deserved to die, because she wasn't 'predestined,' whatever the hell that means?"

"Don't put words in my mouth," McCullough snapped. He realized he was angry, but wasn't sure why, which made him angrier still. "I've fought against that kind of nonsense. So have you."

"Yeah," John said. "But you sound almost sympathetic."

"I can see their point of view," McCullough said. "That's not the same thing as agreeing with it. Not by a long shot."

John looked a little angry, too. The Colonel was almost glad. John had plenty to be angry about, but he almost never showed it.

"So if you're playing Devil's advocate," John said, "how do the apes figure in?"

"They're just another face of the plague. The beginning *and* the end, right? We made ourselves, we made the plague that purified the race, and we made the enemy that seeks to take our throne, so to speak. The plague we've dealt with. The apes remain. That's what is still in front of us."

John frowned and turned his attention back to the graffiti.

"They burned up sick people. Doctors. Nurses."

"Yeah," McCullough said. "Most of those that did those things are dead now, too." He sighed and put his hand on his son's shoulder.

"During World War II, some Pacific Islanders saw Westerners for the first time. It was like being visited by aliens. They brought all sort of stuff with them that seemed magical—flashlights, canned goods, chocolate. After the war was over, some of them built wooden models of airplanes and did mumbo-jumbo, trying to bring that stuff back using sympathetic magic. It made sense to them that it might work. Just because I can understand something doesn't mean I believe it, John."

"But the apes—"

"Leave all of the rest of it aside," McCullough said. "The Greek letters, the Bible, the self-importance some people bloat themselves with. When modern human beings walked out of Africa eighty thousand years ago, there were other human species all over the place. Neanderthals, for instance. But within a few thousand years, there was only one species, one race—the human race. What does that suggest to you?"

"I guess we did better than those other ones."

"That's a passive-aggressive way of saying we survived and they didn't. What it tells me is that there is room for one—and only one—intelligent, tool-using, problem-solving race. The question at this point is—is it going to be them, or is it going to be us?" He realized his breathing had quickened a little, and willed himself to calm down. "I don't mind saying, I'm rooting for us."

"Well," John said. "I guess when you put it that way."

"Is there any other way to put it?"

"I suppose not," John said.

"No, I don't either," his father replied. He paused. "How are you feeling?"

"Stronger every day."

"Good," he said. "If you're up to it, I have an assignment for you."

"Oh, I'm up to it, sir," he replied. "What's going on?"

"The apes have a good record of surprising us, so far. This time, I have a little surprise planned for them."

17

Ray had grown up with the sun and moon and stars. Each of these measured out time in a different way. The sun counted days and the stars the nights. The moon was more complicated, because it did not rise and set with days and nights, but per its own time. Maurice and some of the older orangutans—who tended to be more interested in these sorts of things than chimps or gorillas—had worked out that the moon completed its start-to-finish in the same time it took day and night to cycle around thirty times. The Wandering Orangutan was more complicated still with his long trip from dawn to dusk, as were the other mystery stars, those which did not move from night to night as most stars did, but followed their own weird, wonderful paths.

In the cage, without the sky and its children, time was different. The lights were usually lit when humans were in the room and off when they were not. They were on far more often than they were off, so that it usually felt like the longest of summer days. Without the world to tell time for him, he was left only with the rhythms of his heart, when he was hungry, when he must urinate or defecate. So, in a short time, he became confused as to how long he had been imprisoned. It might have been days or a full change of the moon. He did not know.

Fox kept to himself at first, and Ray had little desire to talk with him, but as time went on, and he began to despair of ever seeing the sky, he found he was lonely. So one day, when Fox signed to him, he sat up to give him his attention.

"Understand now?" Fox asked him.

"Understand what?" Ray asked.

"Why Koba was right."

Ray had been giving that some thought.

"I think I understand him *better*," Ray said. "I believe I understand all of the elders better. Listening to the stories is one thing. This is another." He cocked his head. "What is it you understand? You were born in the woods, like I was."

"I understand humans are bad," Fox said.

"Because they put us in cages? Koba put Rocket and Maurice in a cage. He put humans in cages. How are humans bad and Koba good?"

"It's not like that," Fox said. "Not about bad and good. It's about survival."

"You're the one who used the word 'bad,'" Ray pointed out. "If the word doesn't mean anything, why use it at all?"

Fox looked angry, but like Ray, he was probably lonely. In the woods, apes were never far from other apes, always grooming or being groomed, talking, telling stories, drumming. Together.

"Never mind," he signed. "Forget it. No use in arguing. Let's get out of here. Then you can try to kill me."

Fox looked surprised—and at first, he even seemed angrier. Then he calmed down a little.

"How can we escape?" he asked. "I saw you try to break your cage. It didn't work. And they only seem to open from the outside."

"Then one of us must get outside," Ray said.

Fox made a dismissive sound.

"Did you hear what the humans said?" Ray asked. "The people on the ship—they have asked these humans for help. For some kind of weapon. If they come to fight Caesar also—"

"It doesn't matter what happens to Caesar," Fox said. "Apes will be safe."

Ray felt as if he had swallowed a cold lump of mud after mistaking it for an oyster.

"What?" he said.

But Fox now had a chagrined look on his face. What were Koba's followers planning? How many of them were there? A handful? Twenty? A hundred?

"Fox—"

He was interrupted by the door opening. The red-haired human stood there, staring at him with an expression that meant nothing on the face of an ape, but which clearly expressed something powerful. He changed his gaze to Fox, and then came back to him.

"You're using sign language," he said. "You're talking to each other."

Ray's first impulse was to wonder how they had been caught, how the man could know that. But he quickly realized it didn't matter. The only decision now was whether to keep silent or speak up, and the only reason to choose one or the other was if it increased his chances of escape.

And Fox was right—the only time the humans took them out of the cages, they were bound with chains or ropes. He suspected, too, that the other doors in the place were locked, so even if they managed to slip their bonds and subdue any humans in the room, they were still probably trapped. None of that was going to change unless something else did. Leaving the situation as it stood now, they had no chance of escape.

So he decided he would change things.

"Yes," he signed.

The eyes of the red-headed man opened wide.

"And you can understand what I say when I speak?"

"Some," Ray signed. "Some of your words I do not know."

He glanced at Fox. The chimp had his head down and his teeth showing. Ray decided to ignore the threat. He didn't care what Fox thought.

"Damn," the man muttered. "And I don't know the first thing about sign language. Naturally." He shook a finger at Ray. "Hang on. I'll be back."

He left, giving Ray a few moments to consider what had just happened. How had the man known he and Fox were talking? Obviously, he had some way to see them when they thought they were alone. A peephole or something. Were they always watched? It seemed likely. In all the time that they had been in the glass cages, this was the first occasion he and Fox had spoken, and they had been noticed immediately.

It was a while before the man returned, and he had a bag of things with him. The woman was also with him.

"I don't have the real stuff," he explained. "But this is some of my granddaughter's stuff. I picked it up yesterday. It ought to do."

He pulled out a box that had holes of different shapes, and then brightly colored pegs, also in different shapes.

"Can you put the right shapes in the right holes?" the man asked.

Ray looked the things over, wondering if there was some sort of trick involved. It was sort of a silly question. But as the two continued to watch him, he decided they were serious. So he took the square thing and put it in the square hole, and round in round, the one shaped like a starfish in the starfish hole, and on, until they were all accounted for.

"Okay," the man said.

"Couldn't any ape do that?" the woman said. "If your six-year-old granddaughter can do it—"

"Easy," Ray grunted.

Both humans went very still, and their faces made him want to laugh.

"Did you—did you say something?" the man finally asked.

"This easy," Ray told them. He pulled the pegs out and tried to put the one with three sides in the hole with four.

"Easy. Can see how fit."

He remembered something Koba told him once, evidence for how stupid humans were, at least from his point of view. How they thought a chimp's grin of terror was funny, how it made humans believe apes were laughing.

So he grinned like a scared chimp. In response, both humans made similar expressions in return. It was horrifying, but he knew it meant something different for them. And almost instantly, they seemed a little more relaxed.

But just a little.

"He's freaking talking," the man said.

"Yes," the woman replied. "I did gather that, even without a minor in anthropology. I take it that's unusual?"

"It's—ah—unprecedented. Maybe impossible."

"In which case I would have to say your definition of 'impossible' differs from mine," she said. Then she leaned toward Ray.

"What is your name?" she asked.

"Ray," he replied. "Your?"

"Jesus God," the man swore.

"My name is Messenger," she said. "Commander Abigail Messenger, if that means anything to you. This is

Doctor Horn. Can you tell us where you're from?"

"Forest," he said. "Big trees. Far away."

"Forest?" she said. "Have you heard of a place called San Francisco?"

"Human village," Ray said. He didn't think it would be wise to say that apes controlled it now, even though—from the conversation they'd had earlier—they probably knew that.

"Humans live there?" she said.

"Yes," he replied. It wasn't a lie, although there weren't many left and those that did remain had been fighting against Caesar the last he knew.

"And why have you come here?" she asked.

He searched for the right words.

"Truck?" he said, moving his hands like wheels. "Bring here."

"He's a smartass," Horn said.

"I mean before that," Messenger pressed. "Before the people from Esperanza found you. What were you doing?"

"Search," Ray said.

"Searching for what?" Messenger said.

He gave what he knew to be a human shrug. "Just search. Not know what."

He touched his throat. "Talk, hard," he said. He raised his hands. "Hand talk easy."

"Yes," Messenger said. "We'll try to find someone who knows sign language." She glanced over at Fox.

"He can talk, too? All of you can?"

"Yes," he said.

"I see," she said. She and Horn shared a glance that seemed to contain some sort of information, although it was still hard for Ray to understand human facial expressions.

"One more question, and then I'll let you rest," she said. "You apes. Your people. What do you want?"

"Survive," he said. "Peace."

* * *

The next time Horn and Messenger came, they had another person with them. He was male, tall, with silver hair worn in a braid. He was polite; he didn't try to make eye contact right away, and when he did, he didn't hold it for too long.

"Start with the orangutan," Messenger said.

"May I sit down?" the man said. "My old legs don't work so well, these days."

Messenger pulled a chair with wheels over, and the man settled into it. He still looked uncomfortable.

"Shouldn't we be wearing some kind of—ah—gear? I heard…"

"The lab area is perfectly safe," Horn said. "Lead shielding."

"Okay." The new man put his hands on his knees and faced Ray.

"How are you?" he signed.

Ray felt an unexpected burst of humor. He had never seen a human sign, and it looked weird, those stubby, hairless, alien-looking hands shaping the familiar words.

"In a cage," Ray said.

The man blinked, then took a long, slow breath.

"Okay," he said. "This is for real, huh?"

"Just talk to it," Messenger said. "Ask it about where it's from. How many of them there are."

"Just—do you mind if I just wrap my head around this first?"

"There's no hurry," Messenger said.

The man who could sign turned back to Ray.

"My name," he signed. Then he spoke out loud. "Armand."

"My name is Ray," Ray replied, both signing and grunting his name.

"Ray, like stream of light?" Armand asked.

"Yes."

"That's a good name," Armand said. "I like it."

"I like it too," Ray replied. "My father gave it to me."

"All the better," Armand said. "My father named me, too." He paused.

"What's been happening, Ray?"

"They've been asking me questions," Ray said.

"Have they hurt you?"

"Some," Ray said, warily.

"While asking you questions?"

"No," Ray said. "Before. Poked me with needle, shaved fur." He pointed to the bald spot on his head.

"Okay," Messenger interrupted. "Enough of that. From now on, I want to know what you're asking him and what his answers are."

Armand looked sideways at her, then back to Ray.

"Did you understand that?" he asked.

"Yes," Ray said.

"Good. Are there a lot of people like you where you're from?" He spoke the words as he signed them.

"A lot," Ray said. Armand repeated him aloud.

"Hundreds?"

"Many hundreds," Ray said.

"All orangutans?"

"Apes," Ray replied. "Orangutans, chimpanzees, bonobos, gorillas."

"Really?" Armand said. "That's wild."

"Like animal?" Ray asked, not certain what the man meant.

He laughed. "No. Wild can mean—amazing. You know amazing?"

"Yes," Ray said. "Human lights are amazing."

"That's funny," Armand said. He grinned again.

"What's funny?" Messenger demanded.

"Oh," Armand said. "He made the sign for 'human' and then 'light.' Makes me think of a human shining, you know, like a lightbulb. What he means are 'electric' lights as opposed to like, sunlight. He made up a sign. Probably means he never saw electric lights until recently."

"What's the sign for 'electric light'?" Messenger asked.

"It's just 'light,'" he said. "Or was, back in the day. What it means, though, is that he's not like a parrot, or whatever. He can make up new words—or signs—when he needs them."

He rotated back to face Ray and smiled again. It was a big smile, and would have been very alarming if it was the first human smile he had seen, if he didn't know what it meant.

He and Armand talked for a long time. Armand was slow at first, but he quickly picked up speed. Some of his signs were different, too, but he also adapted to that. He knew a lot of signs that Ray did not, mostly to do with human things.

Armand asked a lot of questions.

Many of the questions were about the apes and the battle between apes and humans. They seemed to know a good bit about what had happened, so Ray was careful not to actually lie about anything, while still holding back a lot of what he knew. They had moved Fox someplace else, probably so he and Fox couldn't talk to each other or know what the other was saying to them.

And Ray feared what Fox was saying to them, a great deal. Once the humans knew that the apes understood them, they had begun being very careful of what they spoke of. They no longer talked about the ship, or whether they were going to help them in their war against the apes, or about gas, whatever that was. But they did eventually ask Ray about the war.

Ray had been thinking a lot about what to tell them.

"We thought the humans were all gone," he said. "The elders watched them from a distance, fighting among themselves. After a while, we didn't see them at all. We almost forgot about them. I was born in the forest, and never saw a human. But then they came. They came to make the lights again."

"A hydroelectric generator, apparently," Messenger inserted, talking to a new person, a short male dressed in blue, somewhat as she was, except that his knees didn't show. "We got that much from them before we lost touch."

"And you tried to stop them from—turning the lights on?" the new man said.

"This is Admiral Edwards," Messenger said.

"No," Ray said. "We helped them turn on the lights."

"What happened, then?" Edwards asked. "Why did apes and humans fight?"

"Koba," Ray said. "A bonobo. He was poorly treated by humans, before. He didn't want to help humans, so he started a war. Apes and humans died. It was a mistake, and our leader killed Koba. Now we only want peace."

"And yet you attacked the ship from Base Lewis McChord."

"We were attacked first," Ray said. "Apes only want to be left alone."

"Really?" Edwards said. "Your friend tells a different story."

"Fox isn't my friend," Ray said. "Fox followed Koba. He still follows him. He doesn't speak for apes."

"I see," the admiral said. "He says the same thing about you."

Ray shrugged, as humanly as possible.

"You told Commander Messenger you were looking for something. What was it?"

"We just came to see what was here," Ray said.

"Really," the Admiral said. "You weren't aware of us? Of Diablo?"

"I don't know what you mean," Ray said.

Edwards stared intently at him for a long, terrible moment.

"Who is Caesar?" he asked, finally, in a soft voice.

Ray didn't answer.

"Okay," the Admiral said, after a few more heartbeats. "Prep him. Prep them both."

"What's going on?" Armand said, aloud.

"You are under contract," Edwards said. "Your job is to ask questions of them, not of me. Do your job."

18

Back in the forest, among trees so familiar they might almost count as family, Cornelia felt better.

But she did not feel as if she was home.

She could still remember home, although the years and the awakening had respectively dimmed and distorted her memories. She remembered the heat most of all, but also the territory around the river. In a lean season, she and her parents and a few others would travel in small bands, foraging day-to-day, often feeling the pangs of hunger. She remembered learning to crack panda and kola nuts with a stone, fish termites from a mound with a straw, identify the kinds of fig that were best to eat, that the leaves of certain plants were good for stomach ache. They built beds and slept in the strong-limbed trees with glossy clusters of leaves, pinkish-white blossoms and flat seed-pods when they could find them, in lesser trees if they could not. She still remembered the slight odor of the blossoms, unlike anything she had smelled since.

In good times, when food was plentiful, her family and the other dispersed bands all came together not far from the river. She only clearly remembered one such gathering, not long before the humans captured her and took her forever away from the land of her birth. It was a crazy time, with many other children to play with. The men blustered at one another, females left their bands to mate, elders renewed acquaintance. For her, it had been an exciting time, one of the best of her early life.

Life after the awakening had been like that all of the time. Caesar had resisted the tendency of apes to split up into smaller groups for survival. They had learned to hunt and forage for the strange foods of their new home; they had built not just beds, but a village where all were welcome, where every evening was like the great reunions of her youth. Except that it was in every way larger; the village was not merely a chimp gathering on a grand scale, but included bonobos, gorillas, and orangutans. Each kind of ape had its own instincts and customs—were in some ways quite alien to one another—and yet under her husband's leadership, the many had somehow become one.

And in that sense, the village had become both more and less than a home to her; it was, above all, where she belonged.

But now, thanks to Koba, all of that was gone. The village they had built together was burned to ruins, and the forest again seemed to her as foreboding as it was welcoming. Until they had a new place, erected a new village, she would never feel as if she truly belonged here. For her, home was no longer something she was born to, but which had to be created.

Since the war with humans began, she had felt a certain fear stir within her. She had not confided it to Caesar; he had far too much to worry about as it was. She had not, in fact, spoken of it to anyone. In the city, she had been too busy for her mind to seize exactly what was bothering her; there had been wounded to tend, then the move to another building, followed by trying to quell the terror after the human attack.

But now she began to see what it was. Caesar had always insisted that apes together were strong. It had been the basis of their society, the foundation upon which their village had been built. And for years they had been together, and they had been strong.

But not as strong as they had believed. Koba had split them with far less effort than she could have ever imagined. It was like when a tree suddenly fell; in reality, there must have been a weakness in its roots or a rotten place in its core all along. It seemed fine, until a long rain or a strong wind came.

The wind and the rain had come. Had the tree fallen or merely tilted? Could it be healed?

Her fear was that it could not be. That the divisions among them would become greater, not less.

She noticed Ajax edging closer again, trying to get her attention without being too obvious about it.

There were two things that set her experience with the apes apart from the times of gathering she had known as a child. The first was that she was now an adult. As a child, she hadn't been aware of the various dramas playing out around her—the rivalries, the misunderstandings, the imperfect, tangled webs of relationship that adults had to try and negotiate. After the awakening, the drama had only increased, and since Koba's betrayal it had become even worse. Koba had no mate or children, but Stone and many of the others who had followed him did.

The second was that she was not merely one of many apes trying to negotiate the social milieu—she was Caesar's mate. As such, she was expected to deal with all of it. She was in charge.

Which was why Ajax was stalking her, and not some other female.

"What is it?" she asked the gorilla.

"I wish you would consider riding," he said.

Horses were in short supply. The army back in the human city had most of them, and the best riding horses. Most of the mounts they had with them were pack animals.

"We have only a few good for riding," she told Ajax. "Rain is on one of them—she is pregnant, and very near her time. The others are for the wounded."

"You were ill, not so long ago. And you are queen."

The sign he used actually meant "crown," and originally referred to the strings of shell or flowers she wore to signify that she was the Alpha female. More and more, though, it referred not to the object, but to the wearer. Caesar remembered the word *queen* from some stories that Will once read to him, although that sign, he said, was different.

"I am no longer ill," she said. "And I am able to walk, so I will."

"We could carry you," Ajax said. "We could make a litter, and two gorillas could bear it."

"Am I game, to be brought home from the hunt?" she asked. "We move at the pace of our slowest member. I am not the slowest. When everyone who cannot match my pace has a mount, then I will take the one that is left."

"As you say," Ajax replied. He didn't look happy about it. He also didn't leave.

"Is there something else?"

"Our scouts have returned," he said. "I have recommendations for this afternoon's camp."

She hadn't been exaggerating about their speed as a group. After crossing the bridge in the dark, they had advanced only far enough to hide themselves in the trees. The next day hadn't taken them much farther. Today, she had hoped to at least move beyond the sight of the city. So far, the humans had not produced any of the flying machines they had deployed when Caesar had first led them into the forest; but descriptions of the thing that had struck the building near where she and the other women had been hidden sounded suspiciously like the machine that had set the woods ablaze and nearly killed her and many others. The farther they were from the humans— and the more quickly they got there—the better.

But setting up camp took time, with children and injured to care for, even with fire extending the time they could work beyond the sunset.

She listened to Ajax's recommendations and made her choice. When they reached the spot, she was pleasantly surprised to see that some of the gorillas had gone ahead and begun preparations. A fire had been started, albeit a small one, so that a beacon of smoke did not call attention to their location. Beds for her and her attendants had been woven and placed in the thick, twisting branches of a bay laurel near a stream. Once they arrived, the children and younger women scattered to forage. She saw Lake leading some of the young boys toward the stream, armed with barbed spears for fishing.

She was helping the other women prepare places for the wounded when Red—another member of the gorilla guard—arrived, signaling deferentially for her attention.

"What is it?"

"It's Rain," he said. "She insisted on helping to dig for roots."

He paused nervously, and she thought he looked a bit embarrassed. Males were often reluctant to discuss certain female issues.

"Has she gone into labor?"

Red looked at her blankly.

"Is she having the baby?" she said.

"Oh," Red said, signaling in the affirmative. "I think so."

"Alert the midwives," she said. "Where is she?"

"I can show you," Red said.

"Very well," Cornelia said. "Cornelius?"

Her son stirred sleepily from his perch in the branches, and let himself down into her arms.

"Show me the way," she told Red.

At first, Cornelia was impressed by how far Rain had managed to travel, given her condition. She also began to question the young chimp's judgment, as Red led her deeper into a redwood stand. If she was looking for edible roots, this was far from the best place to find them. Most grew on more open ground—in meadows, or near water. Why hadn't she gone to the creek? She wouldn't have had to travel so far, and would certainly have had more luck.

"Was she alone?" Cornelia asked Red.

"I think she was," Red replied.

Cornelia stopped and glared at the gorilla. "Didn't you see her?"

For a moment, Red said nothing. He looked almost as if he didn't know what to say.

"No," he said. "Primrose told me."

"So Primrose was with her?"

Red was acting peculiar, edging toward her. And she knew he was lying—she had seen Primrose going fishing with Lake.

Women did most of the gathering of plants. Rain would know better than to look for tubers here.

Red would not.

She looked past Red and pointed.

"Oh, I see her," she said. "There she is."

Red started to turn, looking puzzled, but seeing nothing he roared and leapt toward her.

But Cornelia was already scrambling up a tree, with Cornelius clinging to her back.

"Stop!" Red shouted.

Cornelia launched herself toward the next tree, reaching for the limb, almost misjudging. Months heavy with child, then a hard birth and the sickness that followed had taken their toll. Her body wasn't quite capable of what her mind thought it was.

She spared a quick look back as she swung behind the next tree. Red was racing along behind her, his rifle still slung on his back, so his plan wasn't to kill her. Or maybe it was, but he wanted to do so quietly, so the others wouldn't hear. Or maybe she was just losing her mind. Maybe—

From the edge of her vision, she saw someone swinging toward her from off to her right. She was at first relieved, but then she saw that it was Grey. Grey was supposed to be with Caesar, with the army, back in the city. Grey had been one of Koba's closest followers...

She wasn't losing her mind.

Cornelius squeaked in delight as she hurled herself the opposite direction, passing over Red, and headed toward the mountain that loomed in the distance. At the same time, she saw two more chimps, coming from the direction Red had been leading her.

No, unfortunately, she wasn't crazy. But now she was beginning to panic, a little. What were Red and Grey up to?

Red she didn't know that well. Grey she had known for a long time. After Caesar killed Koba, he had come back to Caesar and sworn his allegiance once again.

But maybe he hadn't meant it. In fact, it almost seemed certain that he hadn't.

She came to the edge of the redwoods and dropped down into an open meadow, sprinting across it on all fours. She could hear the chimps hooting, now, and knew they were hunting her like an animal, trying to drive her where they wanted her to go.

But she had surprised them. They hadn't believed they would need to hunt her at all, but that Red would simply lead her to them. But why? What did they want with her?

The last rays of the sun were slanting through the trees ahead as she made it across the field and leapt back into the lower-growing oaks and maples. She was starting to get a feel for climbing again; her lungs were beginning to burn, and the salt of sweat in her nose made her think of those first heady days of freedom, almost constantly running, rarely sleeping, carrying the wounded and never knowing what they would face next—but knowing at least that they would face it free.

But it had been humans chasing her then, not apes.

She stopped trying to think, then, and let ancient instincts take over. She was lighter than most of the males chasing her, even with Cornelius on her back, so she chose the narrower, fainter path through the trees in hopes that they would either have to take a longer way or fall. Soon it would be dark, too dark for any of them to see, and then it would be a new situation entirely.

She didn't see Pongo until he was right on her, swinging out of her right blind spot and grabbing for her wrist. She had a glimpse of his mouth, gaping with threat, and then something happened inside of her. It was as if the trees and mountains and sky all blew away, leaving nothing, nothing but her child on her back, and the predator trying to bite it. Heat seemed to shiver through her belly.

Cornelia had been upset before. She had been angry.

But she had never known *rage*. She swung her free hand around, grabbed Pongo's ear and dug her claws in. Then, as he screamed, she fastened her teeth on his face. He shrilled even louder, and she was vaguely aware that they were both falling. Cornelia landed on top of him on stony ground. She tasted blood, and the single thing going through her mind was to keep attacking him until he either left or stopped moving. Pongo continued shrieking, trying to pull away, beating at her chest, but one of her canines had cut through his lip and was stuck there, and he couldn't get free. Meanwhile, she yanked at his ear until it tore straight off.

He did break away then, her tooth ripping through his lip, and she was almost disappointed when he bolted, clutching the side of his head and weaving off through the trees.

Fury turned to desperation as she cast about looking for Cornelius, before realizing he had managed to cling to her back the entire time.

She spat blood from her mouth and ran toward the next tree, hearing the other chimps converging from what seemed like every direction.

19

Blue Eyes lay flat in the scrubby, spiky weeds at the top of the hill, staring down at the strange buildings on the rocky beach below. The restless sea was just beyond a small bay not quite enclosed by stony arms—and on that sea, an assortment of boats and ships floated.

At first he thought the largest was the ship from San Francisco, but it wasn't shaped quite the same and was not nearly as large. The others were smaller yet, some looking as if they were only able to carry three or four men or apes.

On the land side, a high fence surrounded everything, topped with coils of the wire with spikes all over it. Growing up, he had come across such wire now and then, in the former human lands along the edges of the forest, and had learned to avoid it.

In the center of everything were two weird, domed structures that reminded Blue Eyes a little of the ape sanctuary. These domes, however, were made of something more solid than glass. They butted against a long, low, boxlike building. A scattering of other low-built structures were crowded within the fence.

"This is where the lights come from?" he said. He

remembered the place in the forest his father had helped the humans repair. He'd gathered that falling water somehow made the lights there. Here he didn't see a river, however—only the ocean.

"It's a nuclear reactor," Feliz whispered. She looked at him as if she expected some response.

"You know, it makes power out of nuclear stuff," she said. "Radiation?"

"Not water?" Blue Eyes asked.

"No," she said. "Silly." Then her face turned a peculiar shade of pink.

"Okay, I don't understand it either. But I've heard if you work there too long, you get sick, because there's some kind of leak. And Jack said if it ever really messes up, the explosion will be so big we won't even hear it way over in Esperanza." She waited again, as if to make sure he understood.

"You know," she said, "because we'd all be dead before the sound got there."

Blue Eyes examined the thing with new respect. It didn't look all that dangerous. But the things humans built often were a lot more terrible than they appeared.

"So you believe Ray is down there," Blue Eyes said.

"Well if he's not," Feliz replied, "I don't know where he is."

When they first met, Blue Eyes had believed Feliz was taking him to her village, to be caged. Maybe she had been planning to—if so, she had changed her mind. Instead they had bypassed the village entirely, following an old road through the hills for several days before reaching the coast and following it down to this place.

Blue Eyes had never seen or imagined such an unwelcoming landscape.

His home was a land of mist and gentle rain. When the sun came, she was welcome, but she usually did not overstay that welcome. It was true that if one went too far from the sea, on the sunrise side of the mountains, the land became drier.

But not like this. The few trees that grew here looked as if they had been sculpted from bleached bone, and the brush—in some places as thick and intertwined as briars, in others just barely covering the soil—was brittle and dry. He had always thought of the sun as a bonfire in the sky, providing warmth to bask in, respite from the chill and damp. Here she was more like a wildfire, consuming or withering everything she touched. Indeed, they spent the better part of a day passing over ground that wasn't just dry, but blackened into charcoal. He thought it was the most terrible thing he had ever seen, and he at first believed that the land had somehow been killed, that it would never return to life.

But then he noticed small green sprouts, here and there, tiny seedlings pushing sunward through the ash. Even here, in this place of dust, life followed death.

But it did not comfort him much.

When they had first begun their journey, he had nursed a bit of optimism, hope that he would find another forest—a more remote, safer place for apes to live. And yet the farther he got from home, the more awful things became. The few stands of redwoods he'd seen further north had seemed promising, but they were surrounded by desolation—and humans. From what he had seen, the south was no place for apes.

The wild-born apes in the village—like his mother— spoke of fabulous forests of fruit, of welcoming trees whose branches spread one-to-another, where an ape could travel a lifetime without ever setting foot on the ground. And he believed them, although he thought perhaps they were exaggerating. But no one knew where those forests grew. What would happen if he kept traveling? Feliz said that if one continued toward sunrise, away from the coast, everything became even drier, so dry that almost nothing grew at all. But what lay beyond that? She didn't know, she said. Maybe Jack did. Maybe if one went far enough, to the very ends of the world, the paradises of legend would reveal themselves.

Or maybe they were across the sea, as Maurice once speculated.

Wherever they were must be far away, and the sparse countryside here left Blue Eyes feeling exposed; their only cover was the hill itself, for the vegetation here was too short to offer any protection. He saw humans everywhere, most of them with guns, and he felt a conviction growing in his belly.

Despite his own aspirations, he hadn't been sent on this journey to find a new home for apes—he'd been directed to search for any humans that might pose a threat to the troop. When he first saw Feliz's village, he hadn't been sure. When the lights came on, he had begun to worry.

But he was now without doubt—this was it. This was what his father had feared he would discover. Here were ships, and power, guns—everything that made humans dangerous.

"Go somewhere safer," he told Feliz. "Talk."

They retreated further into the hills. There were no remains of human houses anywhere near the place, as if even back in the days before the plague the area had been considered dangerous. But they did manage to find a line of trees and thorn bushes along the banks of a stream so shallow it hardly came to his knee at its deepest. Still, it was wet, and the sun was hidden a bit, and dragonflies hunted prey in the reeds. But even that accustomed sight had an alien touch in it. Rather than the shiny green or red dragonflies he was familiar with, these were drab and a little furry—they looked somehow more like moths, with dark bands on their lacy wings.

But he at least knew what they were.

He didn't know if he and Feliz *were* any safer here than under the open sky, but it felt that way.

"Tell me more about Diablo," Blue Eyes said.

"Most of what I know I got from Jack," Feliz said. "I was little when the Diablo people came. Esperanza was already a town, and we were trying to get along, but there was trouble from over in the big valley. Crazy people, you know? Jack says they would eat people sometimes. Now and then a few of them would show up, and we would give them food and stuff so they would go away. But Jack said he always worried that one day they would come and take everything, and kill us too, or worse. And then one day these people turn up from the other direction, from over by the sea. They said they were from the government, and they could protect us and give us electricity. And all we had to do was pick a few people every year to be in their army for a couple of years. Jack said it wasn't a good deal, but it was better than what the other guys were offering. My mom was one of the first ones volunteered to go."

"What happened?" he signed.

Feliz had been picking up the hand talk pretty quickly. She was smart like that.

"She got killed," she said. "Fighting down south."

"Father?" he croaked.

"Plague got him," she said. "I don't even remember my dad."

"Sorry," he said.

"It's okay," she said. "I've got Jack and Carla. And I know what you're thinking, won't they be worried, and yeah, but they know I can take care of myself."

"Why help me?"

"Well, I've been wondering that myself," she said. "I think it's because I'm sorry we caught your friend Ray in the first place. Jack's heart is in the right place when it comes to us—he takes care of us and all, and when I thought Ray was just an animal, or even a monster like Gram used to say, that was one thing. But I figure you guys are more like me. Like us. And you shouldn't be locked up or tied to a pole. Or whatever they're doing to him and that other one in Diablo, you know what I mean. It's like my Gram said, everything that's born will die, and the trick is to have the time in between not be purely terrible, or if it is terrible, at least let it be the terrible you choose. I just want poor Ray to be able to choose."

It was startling to hear Feliz say that. The words were different, but it was so like what so many of the elders said of their days in captivity. It also, without warning, prompted him to remember Ash, just before Koba killed him. He had spoken from his heart, said what so many were thinking— that what Koba was doing was wrong, that it went against everything they had grown up believing. Only Ash had had the courage to speak that to Koba. He might even have thought his words would soften Koba's heart.

Instead Koba had ended Ash's life as a warning to anyone who might speak against him. Blue Eyes knew Ash hadn't expected death—some form of punishment or rebuke, maybe, a show of dominance from Koba—but until that day, that very moment, the idea of ape killing ape was unthinkable.

But if Ash's words hadn't changed Koba's heart, they had changed Blue Eyes, and his death even more so. He had known he could no longer follow Koba, although he didn't have the courage to go against him, not directly. But when he could have captured Malcolm—or killed him— he did not, and that led to the discovery that his father was not dead, that everything Koba said was a lie. Ash had changed Blue Eyes' path in life by his death.

So, some good had come from Ash's death. But if Ash could talk, if Blue Eyes could dream like Ray and see his friend in the other place, would Ash feel it had been worth it? That his life and his death had had meaning? Or was that only for the living to decide?

"Hey, you still in there?" Feliz asked.

"Yes," Blue Eyes signed.

One thing he knew. He didn't want anyone else to die.

"You should go back home," he told Feliz.

"I should," she admitted. "But what're you going to do? How are you going to get them out?"

"I don't know. I'll think of something."

Her little eyebrows pinched together.

"Tell you what," she said. "I'll go down there and see what I can find out."

"No," Blue Eyes said. "Dangerous."

"To go into Diablo, yeah," Feliz said. "Or no, because they'd never let me in. But there's a little town just around the corner there, Avila Point. All those soldiers and scientists need people to cook and clean and paint their boats and— other stuff. One of my cousins got work here last year. That's all outside of the gate, and they don't watch all that closely who comes and goes. I'll just see if anybody's talking. I won't even have to lie—just tell 'em I'm from Esperanza, and curious about what happened to our monkeys."

Blue Eyes thought about the compound, the fence, all the humans with guns. Even if he got by all of that, would he have any idea where to find Ray?

He touched her lightly.

"Safe?" he said.

"I'll be safe," she said. "The worst that happens is someone will try to make me go home."

* * *

They took Ray from his cage, and they hurt him.

It was different from before; this time there was no injection, nothing to rob his senses of the full knowledge of what they were doing to him. They put clamps on him that at first were merely uncomfortable. They stuck something in his mouth. The room was darkened, so he couldn't see anyone, but a very bright light was shining on his face—only on his face.

And then every muscle in his body seemed to try to tear itself from his bones. It was like plunging into the coldest water imaginable, but whereas the shock there was quickly over, this went on and on.

When it stopped, Armand moved just into the light, enough for Ray to see the hand talk. And they began asking him questions. Who was Caesar? How many apes were there? How many guns did they have?

At first he tried not to answer, but soon he only wanted it to stop, so he said whatever he thought would make it end. Hundreds of apes? Yes. Thousands? Yes. Did Caesar plan to wipe out all of humanity? Yes, yes, that was his plan. Or no. Maybe no?

But no matter what he said, the torture did not stop. It just kept going and going, until he couldn't make his fingers do the signs anymore, until he couldn't see, and their words became like the distant cries of mockingbirds in the night.

Then they finally put him back in his cage, for a while. They gave him fruit and water, and he thought they were done.

They weren't done, though. They came for him again.

This time he tried to fight, but he was too weak, and it all happened again. He tried to leave, to vanish into dream, vacate his body and forget what was happening to it—and for a little while, he managed it. But then his blood and bone called him back, back to the fear and agony—and the questions. He could not see Messenger or Edwards, but Armand hovered at the edge of his vision, pale, like a reflection in a moonlit pool. His eyes seemed like dark holes, and at times Ray thought he saw water running down his cheeks.

Finally, the questions ended, although the pain lingered, eating deep into his bones. His vision began to fade, and he felt as if a heavy weight had been placed on his head.

As the light faded, he saw Armand's fingers were still moving.

Lord, make me an instrument of your peace... Armand signed.

Then what remained of the light went away.

20

Caesar had known Maurice long enough to recognize by his body language that the orangutan brought bad news.

"What is it?" he asked.

"Grey," Maurice said. "Some of the others. We can't find them."

Caesar chewed on that a moment as he surveyed the human positions from where he stood atop the Golden Gate Bridge.

"Koba supporters?" he finally asked.

"Mostly," Maurice replied.

"No one knows where they went?"

"There was one report they were seen heading east," Maurice said. "Spear said he thought he heard one of them say something like that. He thought they were just looking for supplies at the time."

"They might have let Spear hear them," Caesar said. "They could have gone anywhere. Pick some scouts…"

He was interrupted by the brilliant light of an explosion on the south end of the bridge.

He wasn't surprised—in fact, he was almost relieved. The humans had been working their way up the beach for days, getting closer and closer, until they were near enough to charge. The strain of waiting, of trying to stay ready, was beginning to wear all of them thin. Now that they were finally launching their attack, the anticipation at least was over.

"Never mind," he told Maurice. "I will deal with them later. I can't spare anyone right now."

They were near the middle of the bridge, at the top of one of the huge pylons that supported the structure. From there he could see the blossom of fire against their barricades. The armed trucks were moving up the beach, followed by hordes of humans on foot.

A quick look around showed him it wasn't the ship firing on them; it was still far out at sea, although it did seem to now be in motion. Instead, the humans seemed to be using shoulder-launched weapons like those his apes had used against the ship.

Well, they still had a few of those.

"Shoot our missiles at the trucks," he said. "Then abandon the pylons. When we fire, the ship will see us, and we will only be targets up here."

That said, he and Maurice began descending. A moment later, he heard the first whoosh of rockets roaring down toward the human army. He had the satisfaction of seeing several of the vehicles engulfed in flame and smoke.

But that was the end of their rockets. From now on, all of their fighting would be done with guns and spears.

"Are we ready?" Maurice asked, as they reached the street level of the bridge.

"To retreat into the forest?" Caesar said. "It would have been better if they had waited another few days. If we can hold on here for a little longer, make them think our plan is to win the war in the city—"

He was cut off by a deafening series of thuds from

above, followed by the more distant reports of the ship's guns. Caesar hoped the pylons were all cleared, as planned. The fewer losses here, the better. If the humans pursued them into the woods, the war could stretch out for a very long time, and they would need every ape they had.

Sparks and ash began raining all around them as he and Maurice raced toward their forward position.

McCullough watched with a certain amount of cold satisfaction as ape-launched rockets destroyed his first wave of armored vehicles. None of them were manned, and the weapons on them weren't real, but besides enticing the kongs to waste ammunition, they now provided cover for his soldiers to move up behind. The apes had their own wall, a mass of old trucks, SUVs, buses and even one old streetcar.

He had guessed they would have a few men on top of the nearest pylons; now he knew. What he didn't know was whether they had more rockets. As the Bofors guns out on the ship began to speak, he knew it didn't matter. He hadn't been willing to waste shells when he wasn't certain they were necessary, but now the apes would either die or abandon their high ground.

He sent the real armored cars up next, and then more troops to support them. He watched as his men lobbed improvised napalm bombs over the barrier with what amounted to arbalests made with tire rubber. That would push the apes back from their barrier and give his soldiers space and time to storm the wall without meeting hairy monsters on the other side. Once they had control of that—

The ground beneath his feet shifted, and for a heartbeat he thought it was an earthquake. But then he felt the heat on his back and a concussion wave that knocked him half off of his feet.

He stumbled around and saw smoke boiling in a solid line from the hillside to the beach. Earth, asphalt, and sand had collapsed to form a ditch that began at a hole in the hills and went all the way to the water.

From the tunnel in the hillside, dark figures emerged, and although McCullough could not hear through the din, he saw the muzzle flash of rifles winking at him.

The storm drains, he realized. He had been so busy thinking about rooftops and buildings, about apes swinging over and underneath things, he hadn't given much consideration to what might be under the ground. Now his forward operation was cut off from the bulk of his army, and him with it.

"Right here!" he started yelling. "Bring that vehicle around, here—"

A bullet spanged against the truck he was standing by, and he saw the bugger, a chimpanzee that had broken from the cover of the drain and was charging across the field toward him. He took careful aim, following it until it leapt into the air and no longer had any control over its momentum, and then shot. It slammed into the truck and tried to rise, but he put two more bullets into it to hurry it on back to hell.

A quick glance showed him at least four of his people were down, but the rest had now formed up, some taking positions to fire directly at the apes and others working around to flank them. He felt a white-hot pride flash through him; his soldiers knew their jobs. The ape charging him might just as well have been a blue-painted Celt howling his way toward a Roman legion.

Still, Roman legions had been overwhelmed—and now he saw apes coming over their own wall, despite the fire raging on the other side, using the cables on the margins to get around the blaze. He had been prepared for that before, but now everyone had shifted to encounter the new threat, and there wasn't adequate cover to prevent them doing it.

He glanced at the smoking ditch and saw it wasn't that wide. The apes had stuffed what was probably a twenty-four inch pipe with some kind of explosive and then set it off with something simple, like a stick of dynamite or a grenade. It wasn't barrier enough to keep him from retreating.

"Fall back," he shouted. Herrera lay a few yards away, and he no longer had need of his rifle. McCullough picked it up and began laying down covering fire as his soldiers retreated to their last fortified position, about twenty yards back.

Tricky as always, Caesar, he thought.

It was a setback, not a disaster. This was far from over.

Caesar watched with gratification as the humans retreated, and the flames on and behind his wall began to burn lower. The stink of chemicals was thick in the air, making it hard to breathe, but soon the wind from the sea picked up and began to disperse the worst of it.

"Well, that was a good trick," Maurice observed.

"Worked better than I thought it would," Caesar said. "But that's my last trick. Next time they come, we'll have to fight retreat. Maybe they won't try again until tomorrow."

"Why don't we just leave now?" Maurice asked. "With all this smoke, they may not even notice."

"The women will not be moving quickly," Caesar replied. "I want to give them all the time we can."

He saw Luca approaching. Something about the set of his shoulders told Caesar all was not well.

"What is it?" he asked.

"Humans," he said. "On the other side of the bridge."

"What?" Caesar looked off across the water, at the ship. It had never been out of sight, even at night. There was no opportunity for it to transport soldiers to the other side of the bridge. How had they done it?

But at the moment, that was not the most important question.

"What are they doing?" he asked.

"Building a wall," Luca replied.

Generals and military leaders of many nations and ages had tried to eliminate luck from the waging of war. When they could not eliminate it, they often discounted it by claiming there was no such thing, that what seemed lucky was merely good preparation and unluckiness resulted from poor planning, training, and equipment.

What John's father said about luck was a sort of synthesis of the two; that luck was invoked to account for the expression of all factors that were unidentified. Whether they were unknown due to lack of proper diligence or whether they were essentially unknowable didn't make any practical difference, but could be used to assign blame later, which was—for his father—a useless exercise. You tightened the screws on luck as much as you could in the time you had and given the resources available, you went for it, you didn't look back, only forward, to the next engagement.

Luck, in John's mind, had more to do with probability and the intelligence informing probability. Without satellites, current maps or advance, on-the-ground recon, for instance, there had been no way of knowing for sure that the highway that crossed the San Francisco Bay from Richmond to San Quentin was still intact enough to get a vehicle across—the locals hadn't been that way in years, and in fact very little was known about the eastern side of the bay. But in earthquake-prone California, things were built to last, so the chances were good the long way around to the Muir Woods still existed. Of course, they did encounter many roadblocks, some more-or-less natural—the result of vehicle pile-ups—and others the deliberately built artifacts of earlier combat in the area. If those blockages had been worse, it might have taken them far too long to clear the way, and his mission would have failed. But—as "luck" would have it—they had risked the odds and come out on the plus side of the column.

It was also lucky that the apes hadn't been ready for them to take that route, in the sense that they didn't know what the apes were and weren't aware of when it came to the layout of the greater San Francisco Bay. The Colonel had figured, given what they knew about the apes, that they might not know about the long way around—or if they did, wouldn't consider it a major priority to guard.

In any event, John and his squad had made the arduous trek east, northwest, and then back south to the north side of the Golden Gate without any major hazard, loss of life, or equipment.

But now that they were there, the threat level had changed, significantly. The apes hadn't been stupid enough to leave the north end entirely unwatched. As their trucks pulled up, they came under fire almost immediately. He called it in as the M60s they had mounted on two of the trucks joined the conversation, and got Forest in forward command.

"We're here," he told her.

"Good," she said. "We've just started the assault on our end. Can you secure it?"

"We'll do our best."

It wasn't enough to blockade their end of the bridge, of course—the kongs could just come swinging along below it or drop into the water and swim—assuming the apes could swim. He wasn't sure about that, but he had decided to presume that they were regular Olympians—even his father had underestimated them, and he didn't plan to do the same.

That meant deploying his M60s to cover either side of the bridge, along with barricading the end of it.

They drew up four of their vehicles to block the streets, then got behind them and started a steady stream of fire as the M60s moved to flanking positions.

The apes had skittered back, up and into cover at the first rounds from the large-caliber weapons, but now they were coming back, and John saw plenty more moving forward from further up. He felt the hackles on his neck rise. There seemed to be thousands of them; he had thirty soldiers. He started to wonder about their luck again.

The apes didn't like getting shot any more than most people did; they were uncanny in their speed and agility and their ability to fire while moving. He was never sure if his own bullets were finding their marks, although he saw a few of the enemy fall.

And then, despite the flanking fire, the apes were suddenly all over the place. He finished off a clip on a monstrous beast that came hurtling from behind a cable, bounding toward them, spraying fire as he came. Four more dropped or came up from beneath as John struggled to reload. By the time he looked back up, those were down, but now there were too many to easily count, coming at them from everywhere.

"Hang in there, everybody," he shouted. "It shouldn't be long now."

"It's too long already," Peters said, switching to his sidearm. "Goddamn it, how many of these things are there?"

Gunfire was a constant roar, now. Some of the apes

swarmed up the cables, shooting down at them. He saw Richards pitch back, clawing at his throat. Eltringham screamed as if hit, but kept shooting.

"Come on, come on," he snarled, under his breath.

He watched in horrified astonishment as a gorilla took three hits but came on, grabbing the truck he was behind and tossing it over like it didn't weigh anything. He rolled to the side, saw it coming at him, huge fists pumping at the ground. John tried to get back to his feet, but the creature was too fast. He managed to claw his pistol out and get a shot off. The gorilla reared up—and everything went white, then orange, as the first rounds from the ship slammed into the bridge ten yards up.

When the smoke cleared, there were several more ape bodies piled around their barricade, including the gorilla. The rest had retreated, back toward the middle of the bridge.

"That was timely," Peters said.

"They couldn't move into position until we were here," John said. "Otherwise they would have probably figured out what we were up to." He rose and took quick stock. Eltringham was unconscious now, and Richards was dead. He still had twenty-eight soldiers.

"Start moving some of those cars up," he said. "We need to close this off, while they're still freaking out about the ship."

When the world came back, Ray was still strapped to the board. It remained dark in most of the room, although the bright light still glared in his eyes, so he only slitted them open. He closed them firmly again when he heard the humans were speaking. At first it just sounded like nothing, like babies making noises, but gradually it began to sort into sense.

"... agree with this man—what's his name?"

"McCullough," someone answered. "Colonel McCullough." He couldn't see her, but Ray recognized Messenger by her voice.

"You agree that they're a threat?" she said.

"Yes." That was the Admiral, Edwards.

"Why?" Horn said. "Until now they've shown no inclination to expand their range."

"They didn't have guns, either," the Admiral said. "Or rocket launchers, and probably very little concept of warfare. But that's over now. If we just leave them alone, what will they be like in another ten years? Fifty? You've seen how smart these two are. Given time with our technology, what might they be capable of?"

"Admiral—"

"And that's not even the most immediate danger," Edwards continued. "All of this we've built. Do you know how fragile it all is? We had to fight like hell to get this far. Things are just starting to look up. You and I know the apes pose no danger as far as the Simian Flu goes, but most people aren't aware of that. What if we see a return to the hysteria of a few years ago? There are at least ten different bosses in the lower central valley, and thankfully they're mostly fighting it out with one another, because there isn't anything left to unify them. What held them together before was their conviction that the disease was some kind of message sent by God. Now no one gets sick, and God isn't talking to them anymore. But what if they find out about the apes? They might start hearing the voices again. One of them could pull the rest together, like Genghis Khan did the Mongols. But if we help this McCullough in good faith, form an alliance with him and his superiors—"

"It would be nice if we could actually talk to his superiors," Messenger said. "If he actually has any."

"We're working on that," the Admiral said. "Radio communications are still problematic. But I'm willing to take a chance on this. Give him what he wants."

"And if it's all a trick, and he uses it against us?"

"It's not a trick. He really is fighting apes. I think we've determined that pretty substantially. And if McCullough decides he would rather fight us than the apes—well, he'll discover we have a lot more of what we're sending him than he might want to deal with."

"Do we tell him about these two?" Horn asked.

"I think we've learned everything we can from them," the Admiral said. "McCullough may have a more... focused set of questions to ask."

"We're sending them to him?" Messenger said.

"Sure," the Admiral replied. "It will show a further measure of our goodwill and at the same time leave him wondering exactly how much we do and don't know. It will give us a better bargaining position. He'll hear the rumors eventually, anyway, if things go the way we hope. It's not like we can shut everyone in Esperanza up, or our people here, for that matter. We could kill the two of them, I suppose, and make the bodies public, but that wouldn't quell worries that more of them might wander down. Better that everyone think we're on the situation, working with other *sane* survivors to make the world a better place, and so on."

"In other words, we tell the truth," Messenger said.

"Much of what we have is built on trust," Edwards told her. "Survivors are an independent lot. Government is a thing they are naturally suspicious of—and not without reason. We offer them electricity and protection against bandits and each other. If we start lying to them about things we don't absolutely have to, it will eventually be found out, and that already delicate trust falls apart. Some will decide the power isn't worth it. Make no mistake, we need the settlements as much—maybe more—than they need us. This can be a big win for us—a successful war against the 'evil' apes that costs nothing on our end. No taxes, no new conscriptions, no one already serving as a soldier put at risk. We send a minimum crew with the weapons, they deliver them and the apes, they come back. We demonstrate to the people that we have their best interests at heart, and we reinforce the fact that a central authority is useful when it comes to negotiations like this."

Ray grasped at each word, but he did not understand all of them. But two things were clear. He and Fox were going home—not home to freedom, but to more torture, followed by death.

And that death was coming for all apes.

Winter woke in the early dawn. He wasn't quite sure what was wrong at first but then he realized the gun he'd gone to sleep cradling was gone. He sat up from his makeshift bed of branches. He had taken the early watch, just after sundown, and been relieved by Oak. Then he had taken his rest. But the gun had been with him, he was sure of that.

"Move slowly," someone said.

He looked over and saw that it was Red, who had both his own gun and Winter's.

"I thought I lost that," he told Red, relieved.

"Sit back down," Red said.

He did so, puzzled by Red's tone.

But then he started realizing something was wrong. Across the camp, the women and children had been crowded together in a rough circle. They were surrounded by several apes with guns, mostly chimpanzees. One of them was Grey. But Grey and the others were supposed to be with the army. With Caesar.

Separate from the women and children, three members of the gorilla guard sat on the ground. All had their hands tied with rope. They, too, were closely guarded by Oak and several chimpanzees.

"What's going on?" he asked.

"Caesar has been defeated," Red told him. "All of our brothers who remained in the city are dead."

Winter saw the signs forming, but they hardly seemed to make sense. The entire army, dead? How could it be?

But then he remembered the weapon that he saw strike near their refuge, and realized that it was more than possible.

But why were the gorillas under guard?

Red anticipated the question.

"Ajax betrayed us," he said. "Ajax, and at least half of the gorilla guard."

"I don't understand."

"When Grey brought the news, they tried to take over," Red said. "Ajax kidnapped the queen and the young prince. He's hoping the women will obey him if he has her."

"I don't understand," Winter said. "Luca put Ajax in charge."

"Luca is dead," Red told him. "And if we don't move, we will be, too, and soon. The humans won't wait long to come after us."

Winter felt dizzy at how fast everything was changing. Since they'd found the humans still existed it had been like slipping down a steep, muddy slope. Now and then, a foot nearly seemed to find purchase, but then the slide continued. And no one knew what was at the bottom.

"Where are we going?" Winter asked.

"I'm not sure," Red said. "Grey is our leader now. Do you understand?"

"I understand," Winter said. He reached his arms out to take his gun.

Red didn't move to give it to him.

"I wish I could be sure about you, Winter," he said. "But we don't know how many of the gorillas were with Ajax." He gestured at the four captives. "These four fought. Ursus fought, too. He fought too hard."

"Ursus is dead?" Winter said.

"We had no choice," Red said.

"Well, I'm no traitor," Winter said.

"I hope not," Red said. "Prove yourself. Prove we can trust you, and you can have your gun back."

21

The next morning, they moved out immediately, with the rising sun to their right. Grey remembered a trip he and Koba had taken, years ago, before elk had become so plentiful near the village and had to be found further away. They had been searching for hunting territory, but also looking for new lands to settle. Koba had always believed they needed to move farther from the city and the stain of human presence in the world. And although no direction they explored was without the evidence of human occupation, they had discovered other enclaves of the redwood forest. On that trip, however—their longest—he and Koba had traveled outward for several days, and there discovered a forest that dwarfed their own—at least in area. The trees were different—not as tall—and the land was more mountainous. But there were rivers and lakes in plenty, and elk roamed there in vast herds. All sorts of other game was plentiful.

When they returned to Caesar with the news, he had at least pretended to consider moving the troop, but had many arguments against it; it was too far, it wasn't near the sea and its many resources, it was by Koba's own report colder. Added to the fact that humans seemed on the verge of killing one another off, he hadn't thought the long trek worthwhile.

Koba had managed to hide his disappointment from most, but not from Grey. Koba believed that Caesar couldn't bear to move away from sight of the human city; his tender feelings for humans wouldn't let him.

Grey remembered that trip fondly. It wasn't easy to get to know Koba. Bonobos in general were the most social of all apes, sometimes to the point of being annoying. Not Koba. He kept mostly to himself. He had never formed a mating bond or fathered children.

But on the journey north, a mountain lion surprised them while they were drinking. Unable to retrieve their spears before being forced to flee they had spent two days in a tree, outwaiting the carnivore, finally slipping off in the night when they heard her attack something else nearby. Then, together, they had built a fire, and with their torches and spears, chased the big cat away from her kill—an antelope—and eaten their fill before moving on. They had spent a long day resting on an island in a lake. Coming across a house humans had once lived in, they had broken it to pieces and set fire to it, warming themselves and calling out like wild apes while it burned.

And when they returned, they were—if not friends— then at least trusted companions.

Now it was easy to see that Koba had been right then, as he had been right about so many things. If Caesar had followed Koba's suggestion and moved the village to the north, they would never have encountered the humans from the city. There would have been no split between Caesar and Koba, no war, nothing for Grey to be confused about.

And none of this would be happening.

But it was happening, and he was taking the women

north, to that place he and Koba had discovered, and maybe farther.

Red came alongside his horse and paced it, walking on all fours.

Grey glanced around, to make sure they were far enough ahead no one could hear him.

"Have you found Cornelia yet?" he asked Red.

"No. It may be that she is trying to return to the city, to tell Caesar. I've sent Olo and Sampson to cut her off."

"And Ajax?"

"No. But he was wounded. He may be dead. I sent Flint and Shell to track him."

"This isn't going the way we planned," Grey said. He almost said, the way *you* planned, since Red had proposed all of it, but Grey was Alpha now. Even though he and Red both knew whose idea it had been, it was not something to say aloud, even between the two of them. Because the day might come—might come soon—when he had to put Red in his place. Physically, that would be difficult, so he needed to keep dominance in other ways.

"Cornelia surprised us," Red said. "She was weak, and I thought she would be easily made captive. With her and her son as our hostages, we could have easily disarmed the loyal gorillas and asserted dominance. So we changed the plan. It seems to be working."

"Unless Cornelia returns," Grey said. "Or Ajax, for that matter."

Red seemed to shrink a bit, showing submission.

"What?" Grey demanded. "What have you done?"

"I anticipated your desire," Red said.

"What desire?"

"As you say, if Cornelia or Ajax return, it could ruin everything. We've already lost Ursus—another fight among us could be disastrous."

"You've given out that they should be killed?" Grey said.

"I assumed it was what you would want," Red said. "It is unfortunate, but..."

"Ape not kill ape," Grey said.

"That was Caesar's law," Red said. "Caesar himself broke it."

"Koba broke it first."

"True," Red said. "Does that matter?"

Grey thought about it.

"No."

"Should I rescind the order?" Red asked.

"No," Grey said, reluctantly. "But you should know something."

"What is that?" Red asked.

"If Caesar loses his battle with the humans, if he dies, the humans may follow us where we're going. Or they may not, if we go far enough. They might lose interest. But if Caesar wins, and comes to find us—there is only one end to that. Nothing will stop him. We will spend the rest of our lives running. When he catches us—and he *will* eventually catch us—then we will die. From here on there is no turning back."

When Feliz didn't return that evening, Blue Eyes wandered restlessly up and down the stream for a while, but as the first stars appeared, he left the little valley and started up into the hills. Even as the seaward sky faded to rust, the eerie glow of human light crept from behind the hills. When he was able, he stayed in underbrush, but soon, again, it was only the folds of the land he could hide in, and he was acutely aware that sharp eyes could see him from many spear throws in any direction.

He paused briefly to stare down at the twin domes, the

place where humans kept lightning in a cage, where Ray was also captive. He felt a little less exposed looking down, knowing that humans, like apes, could more easily look into a light place from a dark one than the other way around.

If anything, there were more guards at night, and the fences seemed more forbidding than ever. What would his father do? He had stormed buildings and cages all over the human city during the awakening.

Of course, Caesar hadn't done it alone. His rallying call had always been "apes together strong." But Blue Eyes was alone. Many apes could accomplish a lot. But just one? Just him? He didn't feel very powerful at all.

He continued past the power plant, paralleling the coast in the direction Feliz had gone. He was nearing the ridge when he heard a sharp, metallic sound.

"Hold it there!" someone said.

The voice was human, of course, and not one he knew. Blue Eyes stood very tall, but otherwise did not move. Maybe if the man didn't get too close, he would think Blue Eyes was human, too.

The man rose out of what Blue Eyes had first taken for a copse of bushes or small trees. He now saw the brush hid a structure of some kind, like the blinds of branches and leaves apes made sometimes when hunting alone.

The man came closer, his gun held in a ready position.

"Who is that?" the man asked. He pulled something from his side, and then a bright light was suddenly in Blue Eyes' face. So much, he thought, for passing as human.

"Jesus!" the man gasped.

Blue Eyes dropped to all fours and charged, knowing it was futile, that he would be shot long before he reached the man. The light swung crazily, trying to follow him as he hurled himself forward, expecting at any instant to feel the bullet take his life.

But the gun never fired; he misjudged his leap, thinking the man was farther away than he was, and thus hit him so hard it knocked the breath out of both of them.

But Blue Eyes was the first to recover. He wrenched the rifle from the man's hands and then bore him back to the ground. He hit him as he would another ape, but humans were less sturdy, and this time when the man struck the earth, with Blue Eyes' weight behind him, he lay quietly, without moving.

Blue Eyes thought at first he had killed the man, but then he saw his nostrils flare, subside, flare again.

"Hey, you."

He looked up to see two more silhouettes, at least one armed. This time, the humans were too far away to hope to rush in time. His only choice was to run.

"Blue Eyes?" one of the shadows said.

He paused, his breathing whistling a little.

"Feliz?"

"What are you doing down there? Sounded like a fight."

"Fight," he confirmed.

"Oh, crap," she said. "I mean, oh man. Did you kill him?"

"No."

As she drew near, he saw there was a male with her. He was bearded, with a good deal of gray, his hair pulled back behind his head. An elder.

"Got someone who wants to meet you," she said.

The elder human smelled bad, like rotten fruit. He walked a bit erratically, and had a little trouble with his words.

"He's drunk off his ass," the girl told him. "I mean butt—uh, booty. I found him in a bar. He's been talking a whole lot, I guess, which is what led me to him."

She glanced down at the unconscious man.

"We probably ought to do something about him," she said.

They tore the man's clothing into strips, bound and gagged him, then carried him a decent distance from the site of the fight.

Only then did Feliz introduce the elder.

"This is Armand," she said.

Armand looked at him through squinted eyes. Then he raised his hands.

"I'm sorry," he said, using the hand talk.

At first, Blue Eyes was so shocked he didn't respond.

"Sorry for what?" he finally asked.

"They brought me in to translate for your friends," he said. "Both of my parents were deaf, so I learned this growing up. I didn't know what was going to happen, I swear."

That didn't sound good at all, Blue Eyes thought. He felt his pulse quicken.

"What happened?" Blue Eyes asked. "How is he?"

Armand's eyes unfocused a little. He looked away, then turned back.

"Which one?" he asked.

"Ray," Blue Eyes said. "The orangutan."

The man sighed. "Not good," he said. "They hurt him. They hurt him a lot, and I was there, and I didn't –" He stopped, as if to gather his breath after a hard sprint. "They wanted him to tell them secrets about your..." He seemed to search for a sign, then shrugged.

"People," he finished.

Blue Eyes felt a chill that had nothing to do with the nocturnal breeze.

"How badly was he hurt?" he signed.

"I'm not a doctor," Armand said. "I can't be sure. But I don't think they did anything permanent." Again, he had trouble meeting Blue Eyes' gaze. "Not yet, anyway," he finished, softly.

The "yet" hung in the air between them, like the darkness between stars.

"And the other one?" Blue Eyes asked. "Fox?"

"He fought harder," Armand said. "They hurt him more. But he's still alive."

"Why are you telling me this?" Blue Eyes asked.

The man pulled something from his jacket, a bottle of liquid, and took a long drink of it. Then he whispered aloud, something Blue Eyes didn't catch. His breath smelled, more than ever, of decay.

Then he wagged a finger at the two of them.

"If you have men who will exclude any of God's creatures from the shelter of compassion and pity," Armand said, "you will have men who will deal likewise with their fellow men."

He stared at Blue Eyes for a moment, this time meeting his gaze directly. Then he looked at Feliz.

"No?" he said.

"Is that from the Bible?" Feliz asked.

Armand shook his head. "St. Francis," he murmured. His lids drooped, as if he was very tired. But then he sat back, and his eyes seemed to blaze open, shining in the light of the new-risen moon.

"Why am I telling you all this?" he snapped. "'Cause I'm drunk. And I'm mad. I didn't want to be dragged into this. Wanted nothing to do with it. I came from down in L.A. The things I saw there, the things people do…" He trailed off. "We did this to ourselves, you know that, right? They called it the Simian Flu, and people are stupid, so they thought the apes caused it, but they didn't. Men made that virus. Men who couldn't leave freaking well enough alone. Genetic engineering—how does that even sound like a good idea? It's our sin, not theirs. Ours."

Armand put his hand to his face, and Blue Eyes realized the elder was crying.

"They hurt them," he said. "They hurt them so much. And I didn't do anything, just what they told me to do. Just my job. Because I've got no goddamn soul, you know? And now I have to go with them, because no one up there knows sign, either, and watch it all happen again." He took another drink and looked squarely at Blue Eyes.

"Or not," he said, softly.

"Go where?" Blue Eyes asked. "Where are Ray and Fox going?"

"Back up to San Francisco," he said. "Tomorrow. By boat."

Blue Eyes sat back, thinking, trying to picture the place in his mind, where the power plant was, where the ships were.

"They will take him outside of the fence?" Blue Eyes said.

Armand took another drink from his bottle.

"You plan to rescue them, I take it," Armand said.

"Rescue Ray," Blue Eyes said.

Armand scrunched his forehead and leaned close, as if searching for something very small in Blue Eyes' face.

"I translated for both of them, you know," he said. "Fox, too. I know something about what went down between you guys. The ape civil war, and everything. I don't pretend to understand all of it. But when I was talking to your friend Ray, I noticed something. He talks about all of you apes as if you are one species. But you aren't. I know I don't look like much now, but there was a time I… knew things. Chimpanzees and orangutans are pretty different. You can't interbreed, right? Make children together. As a chimp, you are more different from an orangutan than I am from any human on Earth. Humans are one species. And yet we still managed to carve each other into groups of hatred and mutual exclusion based on skin tone, whether our hair is frizzy or straight, what we eat and don't eat, how we dress. We made slaves of one another and fought terrible wars over that stuff because for us, even the fact that we're all the same species wasn't enough to create solidarity. Because something in our heads is better at dividing things up than putting them together. I used to believe we could change that—really believe it.

"But you guys, you had a different start. You're new. You don't have to go down the path we did. And from what I can see, you were doing okay until a few months ago. Until you met us again. And I think you've stumbled. You've discovered vengeance and retribution, and those are easy things to like. They call to your nature, just as they call to mine. Because we're cousins, man. We came out of the same place, way back when. But that's the wrong road to go down."

"What else is there?" Blue Eyes asked. "When someone kills your friends, when someone tries to kill you, what else can you do?"

"You can forgive them," he said.

Blue Eyes couldn't find words, but a grunt of disgust escaped more-or-less without his permission.

"Yeah," Armand said. "I know it's hard. A lot harder than hatred. Look, Fox is hurting. He once understood his world, and now he doesn't. He needed some answers, and he took the first ones someone offered him. But he loves your people, you apes, as much as anyone. You and him, you have that in common. And a lot more, I'll bet."

"I don't want to understand what Koba was feeling when he killed Ash," Blue Eyes snapped. "It doesn't matter. What he *did* is the only thing that matters!"

"Who are Koba and Ash?" Armand asked. "I was talking about Fox."

Blue Eyes was already starting to sign another angry response, but Armand's words stopped him. He realized he hadn't been picturing Fox in the cage, but Koba. He had twisted them together in his mind.

"I agree with one thing you said," Armand told him, when he didn't answer. "What we do—or don't do—are the only things that really matter. And I'm tired of not doing. So if you want me to help rescue your fellow apes, I will do what I can. But we have to act soon."

"You're drunk as sh—ah, stinking drunk," Feliz said.

"Sister," Armand said, "I can't think of a better condition to be in."

McCullough listened to John detail his end of the situation. He didn't interrupt or interject, but waited until he was sure the lieutenant was finished.

"That all sounds good," he said. "I'm sorry you lost Richards."

"So am I, sir," John replied. "What's happening on that end, if I may ask."

McCullough briefly laid out the assault, the attack from the sewer drains, the retreat. John listened as he had, without comment.

"I'm sending you some reinforcements," McCullough then said.

"Are we going to push soon, sir?"

McCullough paused.

"No," he said. "Not yet. I'll let you know. In the meantime, I want you to thoroughly fortify your position. Check your back. They might have reserves in the woods— the last thing we want is for you to get boxed in the way they are."

"Yes, sir. I've set up watch posts, but we'll reinforce our rear. How many reinforcements can I expect?"

"I'm sparing another twenty," he said.

"Very well," John said. "I'll be ready for them."

"John?" he said.

There was a long pause on the other end of the line.

"Sir?"

"Your great-grandfather was in the Battle of Hürtgen Forest. You remember that?"

"Yes, sir," John replied. "Kept a bunch of Panzers from crossing the Maas."

"With half a squad," McCullough said. "He got the Silver Star for that—one of two."

"Yes, sir. I've always been proud of that, sir."

"You should be," McCullough said. "I always have been. If he—" his throat caught, slightly, as he remembered the old man. He had been quiet about his service, never brought up the Silver Stars a single time that McCullough could remember. He had carried his accomplishments with immense dignity and humility.

"John," he said, "no word ever spoken by another man ever made me feel as humble and as honored as the day your great-grandfather told me he was proud of me. It was after that thing overseas."

"Yes, sir," John answered.

"I wish he could have known you, John," McCullough said. "I wish he could know you right now."

"Thank you, sir."

"I'll be back in touch."

He handed the microphone to Forest.

She followed him with her gaze. He knew what she was avoiding saying, out loud, anyway.

"Speak, Forest," he said.

"What are you waiting for, sir?" she asked. "You have the kongs where you want them. If you give them time, they might wriggle out of the trap."

"I know," he said. "It's just—I keep running it through my head. We can take the bridge. We can. But it's going to

252

be a bloodbath. Our casualties will be—very high."

"That's the way I figure it, too, sir," Forest said.

"There are no women or children on that bridge," McCullough said. "I think he's already sent them back into the woods. He's trying to hold us back until he thinks they're safe."

"That's—possible, sir," Forest said. "Or the rest could still be in the city, someplace."

"I don't think so," McCullough said. "No, he's trying to delay us. Who knows? He might be willing to sacrifice every last ape up on that bridge if it means his children live—his legacy continues. It's what I would do. But his supply line has been cut now. Every day he stays up there makes him weaker. But he'll stay until he has no choice— then he'll try to get out."

"And it will still be a bloodbath," Forest said. "And if I were the apes, I would go north. It's the weaker position, and it's also where his escape route is."

He knew that. John was sitting on the meatgrinder. He could pull him back, put someone else in charge, but that could create some morale problems, which he absolutely did not need right now.

"We have at least until morning," he said. "Get some rest, Forest."

McCullough drifted toward the indistinct boundary between waking and sleep, but could never quite seem to arrive. When he'd been younger, he'd been able to drop off in an instant—sitting upright on a train, lying on cold concrete, in a hammock swarmed by mosquitos— whatever the situation required. A soldier needed to sleep or he got sloppy, and so a good soldier learned how to get it. But now, sometimes, he felt like Moses. He could see the border, the promised land beyond—but not quite reach it.

Tonight, the border seemed like a dark river; he could walk up to it, wade in its shallows, feel the tug of the current that wanted to take him across. And yet he couldn't quite surrender to it. But although deep sleep and full dreams eluded him, his thoughts became loose, fuzzy at the edges. Images flashed through his mind, trying to organize themselves into something meaningful, but in the end only becoming more difficult to pin down.

It had its pleasures, the borders of sleep. He was at least somewhat in control; now and then he had real moments of insight. More often he came out of it feeling disappointed, as if something important had just slipped by him, taken off by the river but leaving him behind.

He thought again of his grandfather, with his high, balding forehead, strong jaw, and crow's feet. And his father, with that shock of auburn hair and eyebrows that always made him look a little surprised. He recalled the photograph of his great-grandfather as a young man, clean-shaven, in his doughboy uniform, looking very serious. And his great-great-grandfather, his picture taken years after his service in the Civil War, with a long barb of a beard and curly hair down to his ears. There was even a painting of *his* grandfather, John Bishop McCullough, who fought in the war of 1812. McCullough had seen it in a museum in Virginia and taken a photograph of it for his wall. But as he lined up his ancestors there on the banks of the river, he realized he couldn't quite remember the face in the painting; it had become indistinct, as if seen through thick, flawed glass. With the faint emotion of the almost-asleep, he realized his great-grandfather's face had also become blurred, and his grandfather's—and even that of his father. Blurred and dim, so their eyes seemed sunken in, their features broader and simpler, their noses mere smudges.

In fact, he realized they looked like apes.

It wasn't quite a dream, but he suddenly apprehended that he was halfway across the river, starting to sink, and he no longer wanted to go that way, for that way lay nightmares.

He opened his eyes and lay there for a while, now very much awake. Tomorrow, or the next day, there was going to be blood. A lot of it. And it felt to him like everything he knew, and loved, and hoped for, was at risk. He had felt that way before, but not in a great while. For years, he had just been—cold.

He wasn't sure how long he had been lying there when someone rapped on his door.

It was Forest, of course.

"Sorry to disturb you, sir," she said. "But someone is on the radio for you."

"I thought I told you to get some sleep," he admonished.

"I'm planning on it, sir," she said.

"Yeah," he said. He rose and went into the radio room.

When he came out, a few moments later, he must have been smiling, because Forest all but did a double-take.

"Good news, sir?"

"Yes, Forest," he said. "Good news. The best goddamn news I've had in a while. Now get some rest. That's an order."

He went back to bed himself, and this time sleep came swiftly, with neither memory nor pain to deter it.

22

Ray woke when the humans came into the room, but he didn't have any fight in him. He watched listlessly as they stuck another needle in his arm, and once more the world of light and thought faded away.

The next time he woke, it was to unfamiliar motion; it somewhat resembled riding a horse, but the rhythm was much slower. He felt sick, on the verge of vomiting, and realized by the mess that he had already done so at least once. Whimpering, he pulled himself up, trying to figure out where he was and what was happening.

He was no longer in the glass cage, but in another built of wire. The cage was in a gray-green room lit by glowing tubes on a very low ceiling.

"Yeah, me too," a human voice said. He dragged his head up and saw the translator, Armand, talking to him.

"I'm not too fond of the sea even when I'm not hung over," Armand confided.

Ray didn't know what the last two words meant together. Armand was signing as well, and the sign he used was to point to his head and make a weird face.

Ray found he didn't care enough to ask for clarification.

"Where am I?" Ray asked, instead. That he *would* like to know.

"We're on a boat," Armand signed. He wasn't speaking sound words anymore. "Don't speak with your mouth, okay? Just sign."

"Okay," Ray said.

He noticed then that Fox was in a cage right next to him, albeit crouched on the far side of it. But if Fox got close enough, Ray would be able to reach him, maybe strangle him.

Armand seemed to notice the look.

"No," he signed. "Play nice, you two."

"Go away," Fox signed. "Human, go away."

Armand sat back. He wiped a sleeve across his forehead, which was sweating profusely.

"Look," he said. "Both of you. I wouldn't trust me, either, if I were an ape. But you need to listen to me. What they did to you, the pain, the questions? It's going to happen again. Unless you let me help you."

Fox made an angry noise and retreated to the back of the cage.

But Ray knew Armand was telling the truth.

"Go on," Ray said, after a few heartbeats.

"I met your friend, Blue Eyes," Armand said. "We've got a plan to get you out of here. But I can't have you two fighting each other. Do you understand?"

"Blue Eyes?" Ray signed. "What about Rocket?"

Armand shook his head. "He said to tell you Rocket went back to warn your boss about something. Blue Eyes was with a human girl—your friend Feliz."

Ray mulled that over for moment. How had Feliz and Blue Eyes met? Most of the possibilities didn't seem promising. Had Blue Eyes tried to rescue him, and failed?

"Is Blue Eyes captive?" he asked.

"No," Armand said. "He's fine. Just pay attention. There was no way to get you out of Diablo. Everything was too well watched, too many soldiers. But this ship must stop to pick up fuel in another hour or so—the big depot is up the shore, on the northern border. That's when it will happen. So you need to be ready."

"Can you get us out of the cages?" Ray asked.

"I don't have the key yet," Armand replied. "But by the time it all goes down, I will. It's just hanging on a hook—it's not like they expect me to spring you. When they go out to refuel, I'll get it."

"I don't trust you," Fox signed.

"I know," Armand said. "I'm sorry for what happened to you. At the time, I thought there was nothing I could do. If I had refused to translate, I'm not sure what they would have done, but they wouldn't have stopped, I know that. This way, at least, I'm still here. Still with you. Able to make amends."

The fog came heavy that night, and in the morning lay thick among the trees. Cornelia rose as soon as she could see, after a long and sleepless night.

Cornelius protested a bit when she began to move. She soothed him.

"The fog is our friend," she told him, even though she knew he didn't understand her yet. But he liked to watch her hands move, and now and then he imitated her.

The fog had always been a friend to the apes. It had been their ally when Caesar led them across the bridge. It had hidden them when the flying machines came to kill them.

And now it concealed her from other apes. She was now in territory she knew so well, she had no need of landmarks to navigate. Nor was she traveling randomly—she had a destination in mind. Before the village had been built, there was the land itself. Even after the humans ceased hunting them, life was very close to the bone; foraging had occupied much of her time, even after Blue Eyes began to grow inside of her.

By mid-morning, she had found it; along a creek on the moss-covered south side of a canyon wall, screened by ferns and a tangle of bushes, a place where an older, larger stream had eaten away at the stone and left a rock shelter behind. It was just high enough at its tallest point to stand in. It did not go very deeply into the canyon wall, but there was plenty of dry space.

She approached cautiously; it had been years since she was here, and it was possible some animal had made a home of it.

And as she paused, she heard a faint and familiar noise inside. She crept a little closer, and pushed aside the vegetation.

Someone hooted, softly, a stifled fear-response, a hushed warning.

She saw it was Tinker, Rocket's wife. And with her, crouched a little further back, Maple and Fisher.

"Cornelia," Tinker gasped, as she came to embrace her. "I hoped you would come here."

When Blue Eyes was born, the village had only just begun. He was not born in it, as Cornelius had been, but here, in a place only the women knew. Why they chose it, why they kept it secret, had never been discussed. Many of those born in the first years had been born here; it was here the midwives had first made their veils and taught the rituals of birth.

After the village was built, it was safer to give birth there, and in the ethos of the village, where all apes worked together, the women felt pressure to bring their new ways within the walls that enclosed them all. And so they had.

But they hadn't forgotten this place, where so many of their sons and daughters had first drawn breath. And as far as Cornelia knew, it was still a secret to the men.

"What has happened?" she asked them.

"Grey has taken over the troop," Tinker said. "He told us Caesar was dead, and that Ajax had taken you away. But I saw you leave with Red, in the afternoon. I knew they were lying. And Ajax—I don't know where he is, but there was a trail of blood. Someone tried to cover it up, but I found it."

Cornelius clambered over to play with Maple; Tinker produced some dried meat and fruit, and they ate together as they tried to work out what was going on.

"I think they meant to capture you," Tinker told Cornelia. "I think they meant to force you to tell us to cooperate with them."

"That makes sense," Cornelia said. "Then the gorilla guard might have surrendered without a fight."

"Most of them didn't fight anyway," Tinker said. "Red, Oak, and Olo were already with Grey. The others were disarmed while they slept. Ajax and Ursus fought—they killed Ursus."

Cornelia absorbed that silently for a moment.

"Could it be true?" she finally asked. "Is Caesar dead?"

"We thought Caesar was dead once when he was not," Tinker said. "And many of the apes who came with Grey were strong with Koba; not one of Caesar's commanders is said to have survived. Most of the women don't believe what Grey says, or at least they doubt it. But they go along with Grey for fear of their children." She looked to Cornelia with trepidation.

"Grey has declared his wife, Cedar, as queen. She wears your crown."

Cornelia nodded. She knew Cedar well; she liked to be

the center of attention, and usually thought she was being slighted, that she was never quite treated as well as she should be.

But as problems went, Cedar was not an important one, right now.

"We must tell Caesar," Maple said.

"No," Cornelia signed. "They will be watching for that. The way back to the city is too narrow, too easy to watch. No, right now we must find Ajax."

"What about the troop?" Tinker said. "Grey is moving them north."

"They will be easy to follow," Cornelia said. "We don't need a tracker to follow a group that size. We must find Ajax, and we must stay alive. And we must escape or stop those who are hunting us."

"Maybe they've given up," Maple said.

"No," Tinker said. "They can't allow Cornelia to go free. Or any of us for that matter. Someone will be hunting us."

"How long have you been here?" Cornelia asked.

"We arrived only shortly before you did," Tinker replied.

"If Tinker is right," Cornelia said, "they will find this place soon. Maybe very soon. Fisher, you're the quickest. Go downstream to the sea. Leave a trail, then turn back north and cover your tracks. Can you do that?"

"Yes," Fisher said.

"The rest of us will go to find Ajax. He almost certainly will try to reach Caesar."

"I brought this," Tinker said. She picked up a spear and offered it to Cornelia.

"It belonged to Ash," she said.

"You keep it," Cornelia said. She stroked her friend on the arm. "Use it if you have to," she said. "We must survive. For Caesar. For the children. And for ourselves."

They were hardly a stone's throw from the cave when

Cornelia cautioned them to a halt, as she heard something moving through the trees. The three of them huddled on the south side of an immense redwood, waiting.

A moment later they came into view, an orangutan and a chimp. Cornelia didn't have a good enough view to see who it was, but they were moving slowly down the gorge, searching.

Then she didn't see anything; the forest was deathly silent. Cornelius started trying to play again, and she was terrified he would make a noise; she folded him against her chest, to try and keep him silent.

She heard Tinker's breath quicken, and followed her gaze. At first she saw nothing, but then she noticed the arm of a chimp, coming around a redwood trunk three trees away. He was moving slowly, deliberately. He hadn't seen them yet; he was looking the wrong direction. But if he turned his head halfway, and looked just a little down...

From the direction of the cave, someone called, the short call of an orangutan. The chimp—she could now see it was Pongo, with a still-raw lip—stopped and looked back in that direction.

She saw him touch his face and scowl. Then he suddenly leapt, crossing the distance between him and the next tree and gripping a branch to swing from.

Going away from them, back down into the gorge. They had found Fisher's trail.

When she was sure he was out of sight, she signaled for them to begin moving again, quickly.

Blue Eyes was reluctantly climbing into the car when he felt, rather than saw, something rushing toward him. He tried to pivot away from whatever-it-was that now loomed in his peripheral vision, but it was too late. The blow landed on his shoulder, sending spears of pain down his neck and back, hurling him across the vehicle past Feliz's surprised face. He hit the ground roughly, but managed to roll and regain his feet.

The car screeched a metallic protest as Aghoo leapt up on it, bending the hood beneath his weight. Feliz yelped and scrambled out her still-open door as the huge gorilla raised up in a raw display of anger.

Aghoo was even more massive than Blue Eyes remembered. He would break Blue Eyes in half if he got his hands on him.

"Where is Fox?" Aghoo demanded, bunching his shoulders and scowling in obvious threat. Involuntarily, Blue Eyes felt himself shrinking back, and had to force himself to stand up to the other ape.

"Captive of the humans," Blue Eyes signed. "In a cage." He gestured at Feliz. "We're going to get him loose."

"You're working with human?" Aghoo grunted, baring his teeth at Feliz, who was still backing away. Blue Eyes noticed that her gun, like his, was in the car. Aghoo had his slung on his back, and although he made no move to use it, Stripe stood a stone's throw away, holding his at the ready.

"Yes, she's helping," Blue Eyes said. "We have to hurry, though—we don't have much time."

"Son of Caesar," Aghoo spat. "Son of nothing." He took off his gun and tossed it to Stripe. "Caesar killed my king," he said. "Aghoo will kill Caesar's son. Blue Eyes will never be king."

"Listen to me," Blue Eyes said. "There is a boat—another boat. Fox and Ray are on it—they are going to be hurt, badly, and then they will die. There is also a weapon on the ship, a weapon the humans will use to kill all of the apes in the city."

Aghoo paused, but not for long. He hooted in derision, and it seemed to Blue Eyes that he had said perhaps exactly the *wrong* thing.

"By now," Aghoo said, "only the army is in the city. Only the army loyal to Caesar. The women and children will be back in the forest. With our people, the army of Koba. It is good if Caesar and his army dies. It will make it easier for us to rule."

He jumped down from the car and raised up on his hind legs. "Will the son of Caesar fight, or die like helpless prey?"

Blue Eyes barked and raised up to his full height, too, roaring a challenge in Aghoo's face.

Then he ran.

Armand had given them the key to the car, which was at the edge of the human town, just where the hills met the beach. The plan was simple; Blue Eyes and Feliz would drive up the coast before the ship left the harbor and wait at the place where it would take on fuel. Then, with Armand's help they would take over the ship, free the apes, and dump the ship's cargo of deadly gas into the ocean.

But none of that would happen if they didn't reach the refueling depot before the ship, and the ship was about to leave, which meant he and Feliz should already be driving north in the car.

Instead he was scrambling up the side of the hill, trying to stay out of reach of a gorilla who meant to twist his neck off.

He should be able to outrun the bigger ape; his biggest fear was that Stripe would shoot at him, because even if the other chimpanzee missed, the sound was sure to wake the village and the soldiers that guarded it. But Stripe and Aghoo, whatever other failings they had, were not purely stupid. They didn't want a hundred humans swarming around them any more than Blue Eyes did. Besides that, Aghoo clearly wanted to personally beat him to a pulp. That wouldn't be hard if the gorilla could catch him; Aghoo was probably twice his weight, and what little of that weight wasn't muscle was bone.

Stripe was *fast*. Even with two guns slung on his back, he quickly started gaining on Blue Eyes' left flank. Aghoo was on his right, going a bit slower, but if Blue Eyes tried to turn that way, he would be going right into the gorilla's path. They were herding him like game, and he began to reluctantly concede that as things stood, they would eventually catch him. His goal was to make it to the top of the ridge before that happened. After that he might have more ways to break, and hopefully manage to double back and return to the car. He tried to sprint faster, and for a few dozen yards he did, but then he started to flag. He had hoped the others would tire, as well, but Aghoo—unbelievably— seemed to be picking up speed, and Stripe was easily keeping abreast of him. He wasn't going to make it.

If he had to go through one of them, it would have to be Stripe, and better sooner than later, when he was exhausted. So he suddenly veered that way. Stripe seemed like he had been half-expecting that; he dropped his guns and charged to meet Blue Eyes.

At the last instant before they collided, Blue Eyes leapt into the air, putting one hand on Stripe's head as he vaulted over the chimp. His heart soared as he almost seemed to take wing, feeling like a bird of the air, free, and in a minute, gone…

Then Stripe's fingers closed around his ankle. His flight ended with him face-down in the chaparral, tasting his own blood.

He kicked free and rolled back up, head ringing. Stripe came at him, and everything seemed to slow.

Then everything went sort of red. With a screech, he knotted his fists together and clubbed Stripe on the side of the mouth. The hit was so solid, the shock of it lodged in his own chest. Stripe screamed and flew aside. That might have been a good time to run, but Blue Eyes was tired of running. Instead he went after Stripe, boxing him on his ears, kicking him in the chest, then snapping at his enemy's throat.

Then something like an ocean wave took hold of him and he was suddenly flying again, his stomach tickling as his weight went away. Before, once again, he met the hard, dry dirt of the hill.

Aghoo loomed over him.

"Coward," the gorilla muttered. He started forward, a giant stooping on an insect, but then suddenly he stumbled forward, out of control. At first Blue Eyes couldn't see why; but then he realized another ape had leapt upon the gorilla's back. Aghoo landed on his knuckles and jerked around in a semicircle, as the chimp that had attacked him hung on, as if he had mounted an ungentled horse...

"Rocket!" Blue Eyes said, recognizing the late arrival.

Rocket couldn't respond; Aghoo had managed to get one huge hand behind him, slinging Rocket over his head to somersault downslope.

Blue Eyes backed up to join him, and the two chimps came together, waiting for Aghoo's next charge.

The gorilla lurched toward them, but then—instead of attacking—he picked up one of the guns Stripe had dropped.

"Run down the hill," Rocket told Blue Eyes. Then he charged the gorilla.

Aghoo aimed at Rocket, but then he suddenly stood straighter, the whites of his eyes huge in the moonlight. He dropped the gun, and clapped a hand to his throat.

A faint report sounded below.

Aghoo collapsed without a further sound. Stripe, just regaining his feet, screeched in terror and ran back over the hill, away from shore.

Blue Eyes grabbed Rocket by the hand.

"Come on," he said. "We have to hurry."

Feliz was in the car, with the engine running.

"Hurry," she said. "Someone was bound to have heard that." She still had her gun in her lap.

"Is this one friendly?" she asked, of Rocket, as the two of them leapt into the car.

"Friend," Blue Eyes grunted. He looked up the slope, where Aghoo lay in a heap.

"He was so far away," he said. "And almost dark. How did you do that?"

"Yeah," she said, sadly. "I'm not as good a shot as you think. I wasn't trying to kill him, just hurt him. I screwed up. Let's go!"

Blue Eyes heard shouts of alarm from the direction of the village.

He and Rocket were barely in the car when it seemed to leap forward, so quickly that Blue Eyes nearly fell out the back, and if he hadn't had a bar to grab onto he probably would have. Then they were flying down the road, swerving madly from side to side.

"You know how?" Blue Eyes asked, watching Feliz yank wildly on the round thing in front of her.

"Seen it done plenty of times," she said. "I'm getting the hang of it."

The glass wall in the front of the car suddenly cracked. It looked like a spider web.

"Jeez," Feliz said, ducking her head as low as she could and still see. "Talk about shootin' without asking questions. How the hell—*heck* do they know we're up to no good? This could all be perfectly innocent!"

They went around a curve so fast that Blue Eyes feared the entire vehicle would turn over. He was sure that apes were never meant to travel at such speeds, and his confidence in that belief became firmer with each passing heartbeat.

The gunfire faded behind them, and after a moment,

the only sound was the roar of the strange machine they sat in, the rush of wind, and an odd almost-whistle where the bullet had pierced the glass.

Blue Eyes finally had time to turn to Rocket.

"Did you return to the troop?" he asked.

"No," Rocket replied. "I didn't get far before I ran into Aghoo and Stripe. I managed to get away, but only by coming back south. And after that they picked up your trail. I thought you would need help."

"I told you to warn Caesar," Blue Eyes said.

"If I had, you might be dead," Rocket said. He raised his head up so the wind was blowing on his face.

"Aren't you going to introduce me?" Feliz demanded.

Blue Eyes wasn't quite sure what she meant.

She turned around, which seemed bad, as she could no longer see where she was driving the car. "My name is Feliz," she told Rocket.

"Rocket," the older chimp answered, as Blue Eyes pulled on her arm, pointing forward.

"Yeah," she said. "I've heard about you."

"Where are we going?" Rocket asked.

As Blue Eyes explained, the car sped along the road, scaring up clouds of gulls from the black stuff it was built of. The sea was calmer than he had seen it in the last few days. Pelicans flew low above the waves, hunting their morning meals. Farther out, he saw dolphins, four or five of them.

"The weapon on the ship," Rocket said. "Is it some kind of gun?"

"Gas," Blue Eyes said. He didn't know the sign.

"What is gas?" Rocket asked, aloud.

"I don't know," Blue Eyes replied.

"I do," Feliz said. Her voice was oddly flat, and her face, normally expressive, now seemed almost devoid of emotion.

"There's different kinds," she said. "Some of it makes

you puke up your lungs. Literally. There's another kind that sort of gives you the shakes, and you don't stop until you're dead. Jack says nobody is supposed to use it, but they used it anyway."

"Who?"

"Diablo," she said. "They used it over in the east, and down south. I mean, the people they used it on were bad, really bad. And there were too many of them to fight them any other way. So, Diablo used gas. Problem is, gas doesn't always go where it's supposed to go. It's just like air, you know, except it kills you. Sometimes the wind shifts."

Blue Eyes noticed she was crying. She wasn't making any of the sounds humans usually did, but water was coming out of her eyes.

"Your mother die from gas?" he asked.

"Yeah," she said, nodding. "She just happened to be in the wrong place at the wrong time when the wind changed."

"I'm sorry."

"It's okay," she said. "She's in a better place."

"What do you mean?" Blue Eyes asked. "A better place?"

"You know," she said. "Heaven, with the angels and all? Pearly gates, streets of gold? You've never heard of that?"

"No," Blue Eyes said. "Not like that, anyway."

She smiled. "Maybe ape heaven is paved with bananas," she said. "I don't know all about that pearl and gold stuff. All I know is, if I could see my mom again—that would be the only heaven I cared about."

Blue Eyes watched an eagle turn, high above, trying to keep from looking how fast the road was coming at them.

"That I understand," he said.

For a while, Feliz said nothing.

"I'm worried," she finally told him.

"What about?" he asked.

"All that fuss with the other apes," she said. "We got a

late start. I thought we would see the ship out there, and pass it. But I'm afraid we're late."

"How long will it take for them to get fuel?"

"I don't know," she said. "I've never seen anyone fuel a boat before. But it might not take long."

23

Winter lowered his pack to the ground, exhausted. Grey had set a staggering pace through unforgiving terrain, and the pack Winter had been asked to carry was easily twice as heavy as any he had ever put on. With most of the horses gone, Ursus dead, Ajax fled, and Oak out hunting for him, there were fewer gorillas than ever to do the heavy carrying.

Winter still wasn't quite sure where he stood. He hadn't been hobbled like the four captive gorillas—the ones Grey didn't trust—and his pack wasn't as massive as those they carried. But Red—who didn't wear a pack at all—never let him far from his sight.

At least, not until now. The gorilla had gone off to meet with Grey and Sampson, leaving him to unload and help the women set up camp.

What Winter really wanted to do was rest, but he knew things were better for him than they could be; he needed to show Grey and Red he could be trusted. While the remaining members of the guard set up their perimeter, Winter went out to bring in wood for the fire.

He brought one load of branches in and then went back

out, looking for lighter knot, which would make the fire easier to get going. Digging into a half-rotten log looking for some, he came across a few grubs and popped them in his mouth.

He had been trying not to think about Luca, to wonder how he had died. Had he even had a chance to fight, or had he been incinerated by one of the human weapons from so far away he'd never seen it coming? He hated to think of Luca dying at all, much less like that.

And how far could the human weapons reach? Could they find Winter in the forest? He remembered stories of the awakening, about a silver thing that flew through the air and rained fire down upon the apes.

Everything was wrong; all was unsettled. It seemed incredible. The entire army, gone—half of everyone he knew, alive one day, dead the next. They had no village to return to, and even if they found a place far away enough from the humans to be safe, how long would it take to build a new village? How many days or years before things returned to normal?

But then, things could never be normal again, not if Caesar and Luca and more than half the troop were dead.

He looked up from his task and found Red was watching him through the trees.

"I'm looking for lighter knot," Winter signed.

Red nodded approvingly. "Is something wrong?" he asked.

"Everything," Winter said. "Luca told me that gorillas were the walls of the village, even when there is no village. But if Ajax has turned against us, and the others—"

"The others will come around," Red said. "What Luca told you was true. We must be the wall; we must shield the women and children from harm, even if that harm is traitors from our own people."

He reached around and pulled off the rifle he wore by a strap. Winter stiffened with fear.

"Take this," Red said. "We're short-handed as it is. I told Grey you could be trusted. Don't prove me wrong."

Winter took the weapon gingerly.

"I won't disappoint you," he said.

"If the traitors return, will you be able to shoot him?"

"Ajax?"

"Ajax," Red said. "And there are others. Some of the women sneaked away in the night."

"Why?" Winter asked.

"At first we believed Ajax kidnapped Cornelia so the women would do what he said. That he was trying to make himself Alpha. But now Grey believes something else happened; that it was Cornelia who poisoned the mind of Ajax. And now some of her closest supporters—like Tinker—have gone to her as well."

"I don't understand."

"With Caesar dead, Cornelia is no longer queen. No longer the female Alpha. Blue Eyes is gone, probably dead too, so he will not return to take his father's place. Without them, Cornelia is nothing. She knew that, and that Grey's mate Cedar would replace her. So Cornelia acted to keep her position. She may try to return and reclaim it."

"I must shoot the queen?" Winter said.

"She is no longer the queen," he said. "She hurt Pongo, badly. Did you know that? And she schemes against us. Some say she would rather lead the humans to us than lose her status."

It didn't seem possible. Winter had known the queen his entire life.

Red gripped his arm, gently.

"I'm trying to help you, Winter," he said. "We need you with us."

Winter wished Luca was around to talk to, but he wasn't. Luca should have been with them, with the gorilla guard, rather than fighting an impossible battle with Caesar. It was Luca's fault Winter was even in this situation.

But he would nevertheless honor Luca's wish.

"I am in the gorilla guard," Winter said. "I am the wall against our enemies. I will do whatever I must to keep the troop safe."

"I knew I could count on you," Red told him.

Ray thought he felt a change in the way the boat was moving, as if it was slowing down.

"Fox," he said.

Fox looked at him. His eyes seemed dull.

"We shouldn't be enemies, Fox. Not when the troop is at risk."

Fox's eyebrows lowered, and he turned slightly to the side.

"I'm tired of cages," he said. "Sick of being captive."

"Yes," Ray replied. "And now we have a chance to escape. But we have to work together."

"You trust the human?" Fox asked.

"Yes," Ray said. "But even if I didn't—what other hope do we have?"

Fox didn't answer, so Ray kept going.

"You asked me if I understood, now. Koba, the elders, all of it. I don't know. You and I, we've only been in cages for a few days. Koba was born in one. I think I understand why Koba hated humans so much. But I also understand why Caesar cares for them. But what I understand most of all is that apes must never be in cages again. We must be free. Caesar led us to freedom once—he can do it again."

Ray wouldn't meet his eyes. "You don't know," Fox

signed. "You don't know everything we planned."

"Well, I know you were planning on killing me—and Blue Eyes, and Rocket. And Caesar, I guess."

"Not Caesar," Fox said. "We didn't plan to kill Caesar. We were going to let humans do that."

"Oh," Ray said. "And then you were going to steal the women and run off into the forest, is that it?"

Fox looked a little surprised. "Did someone tell you?"

Ray snorted. "It's obvious. And it's a stupid plan. First of all, the women would fight you. But more than that— do you really think after they've killed Caesar and his whole army, the humans won't come after you? They want to kill us *all*, Fox."

Fox looked ashamed.

"We were going to hide from the humans," he said. "We followed you not just to kill you, but to look for possible hiding places. More forests. Safer forests."

"And did you find any?" Ray asked.

"No," Fox admitted.

"No," Ray said. "So your brilliant plan is to get most of our warriors slaughtered and then go hide—who would be in charge? Grey?"

Fox backed up a little. "Someone *did* tell you," he said.

"Fox, it won't work. We have to get free—and we must help Caesar. Help him win."

"How?" Fox asked. "Even if I agree—how?"

Ray was wondering if he ought to answer that when the ship suddenly pulled like it was in honey instead of water, and then bumped into something. A moment later the door opened. A furtive-looking Armand appeared. He came over to the cage and pushed something into the lock.

"Okay," he said. "I'm letting you out. Things should start pretty soon."

The instant the door opened, Ray bounced out of it,

feeling suddenly stronger than he thought possible. How many days had he been in one cage or another? He stretched everything, enjoying the luxury of complete motion.

Fox came out more slowly.

"Must we fight?" Ray asked the chimp.

"No," Fox said. "We will finish this here—escape together. Then we will each go our own way. You will tell Blue Eyes?"

Ray held his gaze for a moment. Then he nodded.

"I can't speak for Blue Eyes," he said. "But I will tell him what I agreed."

"Great," Armand said. "Now pay attention. We're on a ship called the *Naglfar*, parked on the side of a big rock. If everything went as planned, your friends got here early; they should be up on top of the rock, above us. Besides me, there are only six men on board. And listen, this is important—I don't want them killed, not if there is any other way. Your friends are going to distract them, and we'll come at them from behind. But no killing. Please."

"I don't want to kill," Ray said.

"Good," Armand replied. "That's the spirit."

"So we go, now?"

"No," Armand said. "We wait."

"No, I don't think we will," a voice said behind him.

Behind Armand's shoulder, Ray saw Messenger's familiar face appear in the doorway.

Fox hooted and leapt toward her, but there was a soldier there, as well, and he hit Fox with something, a long black club that made a weird snapping noise and left a faint smell of scorched fur and—something else—in the air. Fox collapsed to the deck, whimpering.

"Armand, you turn around and back up," Messenger said. "Get out of the way."

"What's going on?" Armand asked.

"You didn't think we would check you out?" she asked. "I had my doubts about you, but you were all we had. Still are, so you're safe, for now, although there will be a trial when we return. If you do your part from now on, it might not go that badly for you."

Armand didn't move. "What you're planning is genocide," he said. "I can't be a part of it."

"Genocide?" Messenger said. "Genocide can only be waged against a human ethnic group. That's the definition. They aren't human."

"They're intelligent," he said. "They have souls. You're quibbling."

"Souls?" she said. "That's a bold statement, for someone with your background."

"It's an inevitable statement for someone with my background," Armand retorted.

Messenger shrugged. "You can believe whatever mumbo-jumbo you wish. Makes no difference to me, or to this mission. And for the record, I'm not 'planning' genocide or anything else—I'm following orders, delivering a cargo to an ally. What he does with the cargo is his business."

"You're trying to talk your way around this," Armand said. "You can't. It's not right, and you know it."

"What's not right is fighting for ten years to reestablish civilization and then see it slip from our fingers," Messenger said. "I don't have time for this. Evans."

The soldier who had hit Fox suddenly stepped forward and struck Armand, too. Ray dove at the soldier, reaching for his arm, but the man was quick, stepping back and bringing the baton down on Ray. He felt the same sort of jolt he had when they had been asking him questions; everything behind his eyes went white, and he smelled his own pelt burning as he fell to the floor, convulsing.

In a fog of pain, Ray was aware of several more men

entering the room. They put loops around his and Fox's necks and pulled them tight. The loops were on the ends of rigid poles, putting the humans out of arm's reach, even if Ray's muscles would obey his commands—which they wouldn't.

"We decided we could spare a camera in here," Messenger told Armand, who, gasping, had dragged himself against the wall. "I don't know sign language, but it was obvious you were planning something. Who is outside?"

"No one," Armand said.

"I'm willing to bet that's not true," she said. "But we'll find out. We're going to walk these two out the front. They may not shoot if they're there. Even though I doubt very much that any collaborators of yours get this far; local security has been alerted. Anyone who doesn't belong here will be detained or eliminated before they reach the dock."

"That's the place, I guess," Feliz said, pointing to what looked like a small mountain ahead. It lay beyond a long, narrow strip of beach, and was shaped like a dome. The road, however, turned away, headed inland to what appeared to be either a human village or the ruins of one.

"There!" she shouted.

Blue Eyes saw; something was just vanishing behind the rocky upthrust.

"Hang on," Feliz said.

Rocket yelped as the human girl suddenly turned the car off of the road. They bumped across a rocky divide and then onto the sand. She gunned it, frightening yet more sea birds and a few sleepy seals.

As they neared the rock, another spider web of cracks appeared in the windshield. Feliz yanked the wheel, slewing the car sideways. Two more bullets spanged into the metal doors as they all scrambled out.

"I see them," Feliz said. "On the rock."

Blue Eyes gauged the distance. They were close, but there was nothing but open ground between them and the shooters.

"You guys go ahead," Feliz said, working the bolt action on her rifle. "Run fast. I think I can keep them busy until you get close."

Blue Eyes touched her lightly on the shoulder.

"Are you sure?"

"Yep," she said. "Just—try not to kill them, okay?"

"Okay," Blue Eyes said. "Thank you. Thank you for everything."

"Sure," she said. Then she raised to a crouch behind the car and aimed her rifle.

"On three, okay? One, two…"

At three he and Rocket were in motion. The sand in front of him jumped, and then he heard the loud crack of Feliz's rifle. He tried to focus on running, but everything in him was screaming for him to go the other way. Would he feel the bullet? Would he know the moment when he died? And would anyone even know what happened to him?

Another bullet whined by his ear. Behind him, Feliz was still shooting.

He knew what he was fighting for. He knew why he should be fearless.

But he wasn't.

Rocket, despite his advancing years, had picked up a big lead on him. Their antagonists were visible now, three of them. He saw one of them lean out, line up his rifle toward him. Blue Eyes knew he should try to dodge to the side, but his legs kept carrying him forward.

No, the voice inside of him said. *No!*

Then the man jerked back, dropping his rifle as he did so. Rocket unlimbered his rifle and sprayed bullets at the men on the rock, then hurled himself at the sea-pocked surface.

Blue Eyes covered the last few yards and scrambled up the stone as well, wincing at the sharp bite of barnacles on the palms of his hands.

Another man appeared, aiming at him, but now Blue Eyes had gone strangely quiet inside. He saw the stone near the man's face suddenly shatter, saw him duck back behind his cover.

Then he was there, right on top of the man. The gun wasn't quite pointed at him. With one hand, he grabbed the barrel, pushing it away. He heard the report as it went off, watched the man's terrified face as Blue Eyes' other arm swung down like a club. The sniper dropped like a sack of tubers, and Blue Eyes hurled the rifle into the sea, only just beginning to comprehend that he had burned his palm on the hot barrel.

He looked up, panting. Rocket had taken out one of the others. The third they found with a bullet wound in his shoulder. When he saw them, he weakly pleaded for his life. Blue Eyes took his weapon, hoping it had ammunition.

More bullets slapped into the rocks. A quick look showed several soldiers on the beach. One lay on his back; three more were charging toward the car, which was now in motion, with Feliz behind the wheel. Blue Eyes aimed at the men shooting at her and fired a few rounds, at which point they all turned back toward him and Rocket. At least four more humans were coming around the rock.

"Up!" he told Rocket.

The two of them scrambled on the stone face, trying to ignore the shots impacting all around them. But after a few moments, they were high enough that the curve of the huge rock hid them from their attackers.

The ship was below, near a series of white tanks, but it was already beginning to move away from the dock.

Several soldiers stood guard, but none were looking up at them.

One of them turned at the last moment, but it was far too late, and in a few heartbeats, he and Rocket had subdued them. Then they could only stare at the boat as it moved away from them across the water. It was already too far away—and moving far too quickly—to even consider swimming after it, even if Blue Eyes had been a good swimmer—which he was not.

He felt suddenly drained; the fire that had seemed to drive him forward was gone, an emptiness formed, like the hollow place in a sick tree.

He looked over at Rocket, who had a curiously determined look in his eye.

"What?" he asked.

For answer, Rocket bounded forward, around one of the fuel tanks. Blue Eyes noticed something he hadn't before; a small boat, not much longer than a big car.

Rocket leapt onto the boat, reached under a tarp, and pulled out a struggling human by the arm.

"Oh, God," the human shouted. "Please, I didn't do anything. I'm not even with these guys—"

Blue Eyes stood over him. He gestured at the boat.

"You can drive this?" he demanded.

"Oh, holy crap," the man said. He was a thin, wiry fellow with black hair worn to his shoulders. "You're talking. You're talking, aren't you? What the hell is happening?"

Blue Eyes came nearer, until their faces were almost touching. He spoke each word separately, trying to make each as clear as possible.

"Can. You. Drive. The. Boat?"

The man didn't say anything at first; but he started nodding his head up-and-down so hard it seemed like he was trying to shake something off it.

"Sure," he said finally. "Yeah, I'm a good—boat driver. Just don't hurt me, okay?"

"Drive the boat, now!" Rocket exploded.

"Oh, God!"

Blue Eyes put his hand on Rocket's shoulder.

"Do it," he told the man. "And we won't hurt you."

The man started the boat much as Feliz had started the car, and like the car, the boat had a wheel that changed its direction.

"Just—can you untie that?" the man asked, pointing at a rope lashed around a metal thing on the dock. To Blue Eyes, it resembled the head of a cow, complete with horns.

Blue Eyes unraveled the rope, and they started pulling away. Not much after that, gunfire started up again, as the men from the other side of the rock made it around.

"Wow," the man said. "I'm gonna die. It's not fair."

Despite his worries, however, they were soon far enough out at sea that his prediction did not seem in immediate danger of coming true. The other boat—the one with Ray and Fox on it—was no longer in sight.

"I saw those other monkeys on the Diablo ship," the man said. "Friends of yours, I guess."

"Yes," Blue Eyes said.

"Cool," he said. "I always liked monkeys. And red. My grandmother used to say something about monkeys. I don't remember what, exactly, but probably something good."

Blue Eyes couldn't find anything in all of that to respond to, so he didn't reply.

The man cleared his throat.

"So—uh—where should I drop you guys off?" he asked.

"Follow the other ship," Blue Eyes said.

"Yeah," the man sighed. "That's what I figured. You

know the odds of catching them aren't real good, right? That's a real ocean-going boat. This little thing, I just use it for fishing along the coast. It's not—"

"Catch them," Blue Eyes said.

"Sure, right," the man said. "I get that, and all. But if we do catch them, they'll—you know—shoot us out of the water."

Rocket moved a little closer and vented loud a threat-hoot.

"Catch 'em," the man said. "Aye aye."

24

Caesar met with Luca and Maurice halfway up the pylon on the north end of the bridge. Together they considered the human camps on either side of the great structure.

"They're waiting on something," Caesar said.

"Waiting for us to starve," Maurice said. "Or more likely, run out of water."

"Maybe," Caesar said. They had water and food, both for themselves and the horses, to last for at least another week—he had spent the days before the ship arrived making certain they had supplies. But the humans might not know that.

But he also didn't think that was it.

"They fought hard," Caesar said. "Very hard, as if determined to destroy us in one big fight. They have us in a bad position. With their weapons, they could beat us, now—why wait?"

"They could beat us," Maurice said. "But any of them would die. Maybe their leader is not one to waste life."

"Then he is waiting on something," Caesar said. "More humans, a new weapon—something. So, we can't wait."

"What then?" Luca said. The gorilla sounded eager. He

had been of the opinion they should go on the offensive for days.

"We go against the northern camp, where the forest is," Caesar said. "All of us, all at once."

Maurice sighed. "So many will die," he said. "If we succeed at all, most of us will die."

"But some of us might survive," Caesar said. "That is better than none of us. I fear if we wait until the humans have what they want—whatever they're waiting for—none of us will ever see the women and children again."

"It is better if we have a chance," Luca said.

"Maurice?"

The orangutan nodded. "It is the sensible thing to do," he admitted, reluctantly. "If anything in war can ever be called sensible."

Caesar looked from one to the other.

"Very well," he said. "Let them all know. Get them ready."

None of them were hunters, but any ape from the old days knew something about tracking, and neither the trail Ajax left nor that of the apes following him was subtle. Cornelia and others picked it up in late afternoon and followed it until dark.

Ajax was either lost or not trying to return to Caesar; his blood led through territory that became more and more familiar as they went along, but it did not lead south. Cornelia had a feeling she knew, then, what the gorilla's destination was. A gentle rain began as they approached it.

It still smelled like smoke, despite the passage of time, despite the rain. She was surprised at how much of it was still standing; the biggest timbers were scorched to charcoal on the outside, but the fire had burned out before reaching the heartwood. Most of the wall could still be traced, and even the spiral pattern of what had once been her dwelling retained a semblance of its shape.

In his pain, perhaps delirious, Ajax had returned home. To the place he had pledged to defend with his life. To the Ape Village, which Koba had burned.

Cornelia could not enter it at first. In some way the burning of the village was a greater sin than Koba's attempt to murder Caesar. To destroy this place that all apes had built together, their haven, their shared hearth…

It should have been unthinkable, even for Koba. Maybe especially for Koba.

But anger was the emotion that twisted, that seemed to make all wrongs right. It made the senseless seem sensible, if only for a short time. But a short time was all that was needed to light a fire or shoot a bullet.

She took a deep breath of the smoke-perfumed air, and passed through the blackened gates.

They found the body of a chimpanzee just around the first bend of the entrance, where the gorillas usually placed the first of their guardians. His head looked like it had been struck by something heavy and blunt. Maple looked away, but Cornelia couldn't. Even in his mutilated state, she recognized Flint, the son of Cleo and Rafael.

She had been there when Flint was born; it had been a hard birth for his mother. There had been a twin, stillborn, but Flint was healthy. He was almost exactly the same age as Blue Eyes, the same age Ash had been. His father had been one of the first apes to teach the others how to hunt and had died in Koba's assault on the human city.

Now Flint was dead, too. Like Ash. And Blue Eyes…?

For an instant, she was paralyzed by the memory of her son, his birth, his childhood, all those years moving by like so much water in a mountain stream. Now he was gone, who knew where.

But at least he wasn't here. At least Blue Eyes hadn't had to choose between his own life and taking Flint's.

After a moment, they quietly moved on, further into the village.

They found Ajax slumped against the wall in Maurice's school area. Cornelia knew the moment she saw him that it was too late; his eyes were like glass, fixed on nothing; his fur was matted with blood, and blood had pooled on the ground next to him.

Not far away lay Shell. Shell was still alive, but probably not for long. A spear had been driven through his belly and split the beaded bones of his spine. He could still move his arms, and as they approached, he managed to point the rifle in his hand at Cornelia.

"Shell," she said. "Put that down."

"He killed me," Shell said. "Ajax killed me."

Cornelia drew herself to her full height.

"I am Cornelia," she said. "Wife of Caesar. Your queen."

"Wife of Caesar," he said. "Caesar killed Koba."

"Koba killed my son!" Tinker signed, then barked at him. "Koba deserved to die."

"Koba was strong," Shell said.

Cornelia took a step, and another, until she was too close for Shell to miss, even in his condition.

"Shell," she said, softly but sternly. "Put your weapon down."

"There's nothing you can do for me," Shell said. "I know that."

"You're wrong," Cornelia said. Then she crouched beside him. He turned the gun to follow her, but she ignored it and began to brush his forehead and pick the twigs from his fur.

First he just gaped at her, and then, slowly, he let the weapon sag to the ground.

She took Shell's head in her lap.

Shell looked up at Tinker.

"I… sorry about Ash," he croaked. Blood came to his lips when he spoke.

He turned to look up at Cornelia. His eyes were wet.

"I remember when you were all little, Shell," she said. "You, Ash, my Blue Eyes. The day with the butterflies. Do you remember that?"

His eyes widened a little.

"We never saw that kind before," he said. "There were so many, so pretty…"

"You all hopped and turned about," she said. "Trying to catch them. It was funny to watch. It made me happy."

Shell reached up and touched her arm.

"I… scared," he whispered.

"We only saw those butterflies once," Cornelia said. "They went away, and they never returned. But we never forgot them, did we?"

"No," he said.

"We won't forget you either, Shell," she said. "I won't."

"I… so sorry…" he murmured. His eyes had begun moving restlessly, as if he was asleep and dreaming.

"Don't think of that," she said. "That's all done. Think of the butterflies."

He made the sign, weakly, both hands crossed at the wrists on his chest, flapping. Then he looked up at the sky, where blue streaks were breaking in the clouds.

A few moments later, his hands stopped moving, and his breathing stilled.

"Cornelia," Tinker said, aloud.

Cornelia turned to where Tinker was staring. There, perched on one of the blackened walls, sat Oak, one of the gorilla guard. He held a rifle in his hand. She locked gazes with him, and for a moment, he didn't flinch. Then he held the weapon out by the barrel and dropped it to the ground.

"Ape not kill ape," he said. Then he climbed down and crouched in obeisance.

"We'll make beds for Shell and Ajax in the trees," she said, after a moment. "Flint, too."

"What then?" Tinker asked.

"Then I'm going home," she replied.

Blue Eyes had never imagined the sea like this, rising and falling in gigantic swells, the horizon vanishing for small eternities, reappearing as if seen from the top of a mountain, only to vanish into another watery gorge. The sky was a pearly muddle, rent intermittently by rays of pure gold and rifts of turquoise blue.

When they were balanced on the tops of the tallest waves, the ship they were chasing could just be seen. It was the closest they had gotten in the more than a day they had been following it.

Blue Eyes spent most of that time sick. Rocket fared a little better, which was good, because if not Captain Kim—what the human called himself—might have been rid of them simply by pushing them overboard.

As the weather got rougher, and Kim grew more used to their presence, he talked even more than initially, often in a language that Blue Eyes did not understand.

"We're never gonna catch that boat," he said that afternoon, as the sky darkened. "This little boat, man— it's just not designed for this. It's a miracle we're not already on the bottom, see."

Usually it was just enough to wave the gun at him to get him to quiet down or at least change the subject. Once, when he started steering the boat toward shore, Rocket went so far as to fire a warning shot, wasting another round of their precious ammunition.

A few hours after sundown, the winds died down a little, and stars were visible through fitful fissures in the clouds. The other ship was just a tiny pair of lights flickering in and out of view on the horizon.

"You're sure they're going to San Francisco?" Kim asked. "I didn't think there was anyone up there. I mean, that's where it started, right? Where it was worst."

"I don't know," Blue Eyes said. "I wasn't born yet."

"Damn," Kim said. "You're less than ten years old?"

"Ten," Blue Eyes confirmed.

"You guys grow up quick," he said. "Ten is just a kid for us humans. Of course, I guess that depends. My grandpa was into some pretty awful stuff by that age, back in Laos. Not his choice." He eyed Blue Eyes' gun. "Like you, maybe."

Blue Eyes didn't answer. He was still sick, and he was tired of having to use his throat. The hand language was so much more natural, effortless, but of course Kim didn't know it.

He wondered what had happened on the other ship. Kim had described seeing the two apes in some sort of choking devices, pushed onto the outside of the boat. That and the fact that soldiers seemed to have been expecting them made Blue Eyes suspicious that their plans had been discovered. Or—possibly—Armand had betrayed them. Blue Eyes somehow doubted the last—it seemed more likely that Armand might have slipped up by accident, especially if he was drinking the sharp-smelling drink.

Did they know they were being followed? Kim's boat hadn't been able to get very near, and it was so little. Blue Eyes figured that only someone very diligently searching would notice them.

Either way—it didn't matter. They had to keep after them, no matter what.

Kim cleared his throat, as he often did before saying something he thought they weren't going to like.

"Look, man," he said. "I've got something to tell you. I didn't bring it up already because I was afraid you would—you know—shoot me. But we have a problem. I've never been to San Francisco—I've never been further north than San Simeon. But with a full tank, this little bucket has a range of maybe two hundred miles. If we're going further than that, we're dead in the water, unless you know a place we can stop for fuel."

"No," Blue Eyes said. "I don't know anything about that."

"It also sort of makes me wonder how I'm gettin' home," Kim said.

"Walk," Blue Eyes said.

"Yeah," Kim said. "Sure, why didn't I think of that? But look, there is one possibility. A buddy of mine once went as far up as Monterey. He said the place was a ghost town, but he did find some fuel left in the tanks on the docks. He siphoned off as much as he could use, but he said there was plenty left. It might still be there."

"The other ship? Will it need fuel?"

"Bigger ship," Kim said. "More fuel. But this will hardly take us off course. If we go dead out here—forget catching them. We won't even make it back to shore."

Blue Eyes glanced at Rocket, who just gave him a little shrug.

Blue Eyes knew many human machines had something like a fire inside of them—that much you could smell, if you were around them. And both Feliz and Armand had talked about fuel as something that had to be renewed, and was in short supply. But that was all he knew.

"Let me show you," Kim said. He beckoned Blue Eyes toward the console. "See this needle?" he said. "When it was way up here, we were full. You see where it is now.

When it gets to here, we're done for. Get it?"

Blue Eyes stared at the gauge. It made sense. Maybe. It was frustrating how little he knew of these things. It was hard to make the right decision.

"Take us there," he said. "We will see if there is fuel. But if not, we will go on anyway."

"Cool," Kim said. "You won't regret this, man."

The morning brought heavy fog, and hard buffets of wind. The other ship was nowhere to be seen. By the time the mist began to burn off, Blue Eyes could make out the contours of the shore, off to their right.

"Just a little further, I think," Kim said.

Blue Eyes turned to Rocket.

"Get some rope," he signed. "We'll tie him to the boat."

Rocket nodded and started toward a coil of rope near the stern of the boat.

When he turned back to Kim, the human was watching Rocket.

"Damn," Kim said.

Blue Eyes sprang toward him, but he was still having trouble with the way the boat rolled in the water, and he misstepped. He probably wouldn't have made it anyway— Kim was already diving over the rail. He hit the water and vanished beneath it, then came up half a stone's throw away, his arms cutting the water in a peculiar fashion. Blue Eyes was surprised at how fast he moved.

He leapt in after him.

The first shock was how cold the water was; for a moment, all of his limbs seemed paralyzed, and the water closed over his head. Then, as he realized he couldn't breathe, he started thrashing toward the surface. He felt heavy, very heavy, and the harder he flailed with his arms and legs, the less he seemed to move. He and Ash had gone into the river, many times, even into the deep parts. They had learned to swim, or at least so he thought. But against this monster, against the frigid waves of the sea, he felt helpless.

Something hit his head, and he grabbed for it instinctively, even as black spots began to dance in front of his eyes. His hand closed on something wet and rough, and he got his other hand on it, and then his feet, and pulled himself out of the water.

Rocket stood in the boat, paying the rope out to him.

"Nice try," Rocket said, as Blue Eyes pulled himself into the boat, teeth chattering.

Rocket brought the blankets they had been sleeping on, and he wrapped up. The sun was shining now, and he could see the shore, but of Kim there was no sign.

"We can bring the boat to land," Rocket said. "Try to walk the rest of the way."

"That will be too slow," Blue Eyes said. "We'll never make it in time."

"What then?" Rocket asked.

Blue Eyes took a deep breath and let it out. Then he went to the console.

"I've been watching him," he told Rocket. "I think I can drive the boat."

The problem, Blue Eyes realized, was not just in operating the boat—it was in getting where they were going. He knew how to make the boat go and how to turn it; but without having the ship in sight, he wasn't sure which direction to turn it in. But what he could not afford to do was lose any more time than Kim's ruse had already cost them.

San Francisco was on the coast. So was Diablo. He and Ray and Rocket had followed the shore south before going off-track trying to lose Aghoo and the others. Although Blue Eyes had heard a bit of confusing talk of other oceans in other places, everything he knew seemed to suggest that, so far as he was concerned, there was only one coast, and if he kept it in sight, and kept it on his right, he would eventually end up in San Francisco.

Once the fog was gone, that didn't create a huge problem, and so for the rest of the day they churned north, following the beach.

But then, toward the end of the day, the wind picked up, and kept picking up. When the swells started rising, one crashed into the side of the boat, and it nearly tipped over. Blue Eyes yanked on the wheel, remembering how Kim tried to keep the sharp end of the boat pointed into the waves, like a spear. A spear that hit a tree with its point wasn't likely to break. But swing a spear at a tree, and it might snap in the middle.

So he fought to keep his face pointed into the rise and fall of the sea.

When he was a young chimp, they had visited the shore at least once a year, and in some years many times, especially if game was scarce. The coast had food, some of which—oysters, fish, crab, kelp—could be found year around. He had always liked those trips, the smell of the air, the restless water that yet somehow produced restful sounds as it met the shore.

This, this heaving, terrible thing, he had never imagined. But even as it terrified him, he began to realize it was also beautiful. It wasn't that the ocean was trying to drown a pair of impudent apes who dared to sail upon his back—the sea did not notice them at all, or care whether they lived or died. Blue Eyes had always thought of the forest as eternal, as something that had been there since the beginning of time and eternally would be; even if one tree died, another sprouted to replace it.

But now it seemed to him that the sea was somehow older than even the forest, or maybe land itself, as deep and seemingly infinite as the sky it mirrored.

He wondered what Ray would say about it. The sea had figured in Ray's dreams about the dead. Blue Eyes had not dreamed of such things, although he wished to. He had not seen Ash in anything other than his waking memory. But Ray, if he yet lived, was on these waters, too. Perhaps they were speaking to him, as well.

25

In the gray light of morning, Cornelia woke to find Tinker curled against her. She put her arm around the other chimp, who stirred toward wakefulness.

"I dreamed of Rocket and Blue Eyes," Tinker murmured, once her eyes were open.

"You did?" Cornelia asked. She and the other women had long discussed the nature of dreams, and whether they meant anything or not. They weren't real, she believed, like a cutting stone or a root was real, but neither was thought real, in that sense, or a feeling like happiness. None of that was something you could grasp in your hand, but it was still important.

"I don't remember the details," Tinker said. "But I was afraid for them."

"I'm afraid for them awake and asleep," Cornelia said. "But I would fear more for them if they were here."

"Rocket would be with Caesar, if not with Blue Eyes," Tinker said.

"I know," Cornelia said. She hesitated. "I am glad Rocket is with Blue Eyes," she said. "Being the son of Caesar—is not easy for him. So much is expected of him—by Caesar and the others, but by himself most of all. Rocket is—easier. Caesar knows more—but Rocket understands more."

Tinker laid her head on Cornelia's chest.

"Do you remember when Caesar first came to us, to the sanctuary?" she asked.

"He was wearing a shirt," Cornelia remembered. "A human shirt."

"He knew very little about being an ape," Tinker said. "He was puzzling to us all, that much I remember. And Rocket treated him—"

"As any Alpha would treat an intruding male," Cornelia said. "I remember that as well."

"But Caesar learned so fast," Tinker said, "and his ways were not our ways. He used Buck, a gorilla, to dominate Rocket. What chimpanzee would have ever thought of that?"

"Caesar," Cornelia replied.

"Yes, only Caesar. And Rocket was humbled. And I assumed..." She broke off, obviously embarrassed.

"What?" Cornelia asked.

"I assumed I would be Caesar's, then. All the other females thought so, too. It was the way things were done, back then."

"You wanted him?" Cornelia asked.

"I knew I was supposed to," Tinker said. "He was so smart, so strong, so different. It was like he was a light, outshining all others."

Cornelia made a knowing sound.

"That I remember," she said. "I was so young, but I knew even then that he and... but I never knew you—"

"But I didn't," Tinker said. "That's what was so strange. Rocket was less. He was no longer Alpha, and I felt... sorry for him. But still it was Rocket I wanted, not Caesar. Caesar was blinding, like the sun. I could not bear it. Rocket was—Rocket. My mate. I didn't want to give him up. And then—thankfully—Caesar didn't ask me to."

"He probably didn't even know he had the right," Cornelia said.

"Maybe not—but he would not have anyway. Caesar was always thinking about us, not himself. What was best for us. He made alliance with Rocket, even though he could have continued to shame him and keep him in submission. He took our old ways and made something new out of them, something wonderful. I love him for that. But never the way I love Rocket."

Cornelia was a little startled at Tinker's use of the sign for love. Caesar used it only when they were alone, and sparingly. She didn't know any of the other apes even knew the sign.

Apparently, she didn't know everything.

"I'm glad Blue Eyes is with Rocket, too," Tinker said. "Ash is gone. Probably, we will never have another son. Blue Eyes is all of Ash that Rocket has left."

Cornelia embraced her friend, and for a while, neither signed, but then the true light of day began spilling through the burned village, and it was time for her to go.

"I leave Cornelius with you, Tinker," she said. "I cannot take him with me. If I do not return, find Caesar. Take him his son. Can you do that?"

"Yes," Tinker said.

Cornelia pushed her sleeping child into Tinker's arms and nuzzled her face against him—softly, so as not to wake him. Then she rose, and gathered her things.

Oak was waiting for her, and so was Maple.

"We wish to go with you, queen," Oak said. She saw he had retrieved his weapon.

"You may go with me," she replied. "But if you do, you will leave that gun here."

Without the slightest hesitation, Oak dropped the weapon on the ground.

"I have come to hate those things," he said.

Blue Eyes' fingers were so numb with cold, he could no longer feel the wheel. He was soaked to the bone, and the boat was half-full of water. The sea raised them up and hurled them down, and it was all a jumble, as if he was falling from a high treetop, grasping for branches, but each time his fingers closed on something it was only a twig, which snapped off without slowing his fall. Rocket crouched next to him, trying to help, keeping him awake with his presence. They could see nothing, no light of any kind. And finally, Blue Eyes knew despair. He had believed he had known it before, but this was more crushing than anything he had ever experienced. Even when the sea began to relent, and the wind died back, he felt no better. The boat was still, the engine silent, its fuel all spent.

He did not so much sleep as pass out.

And in the dark, on the silent sea, he dreamed.

He was by the river, fishing, feeling lonely. At first he wasn't sure why, or who he was missing, but then he remembered.

Ash. Ash wasn't with him.

But he realized that he knew he was dreaming. And if that was so, then in his dream he should be able to have what he wanted.

And what he wanted was Ash.

He heard footsteps, and a moment later, Ash crouched down beside him. He grinned at Blue Eyes and began tightening the binding on his fishing spear.

"I'll catch so many more fish than you, today," he said.

"Not today," Blue Eyes retorted, playing along for the moment. But he couldn't help looking at his friend, wondering if he would see something different about him, some signifier that he was no longer alive. But he was just the same as Blue Eyes remembered.

"Ash?" he said.

"Yes?"

"I'm sorry, Ash. I failed you. I just let Koba…" He couldn't finish.

"It's okay," Ash said. "What could you have done?"

"I could have had your courage. I could have stood with you against Koba. Then, maybe others would have resisted him, too."

Ash finished messing with his spear and stood up, approaching the water.

"Death doesn't go backwards," he said. "No more than you can go back and do things you didn't."

"But I failed you," he said. "And now I've failed Ray, I've failed my father—I've failed all of our people."

Ash looked up from the stream.

"Blue Eyes, you have done things no ape has done," he said. "You have tried. Caesar would be proud."

Ash's words lodged in him, and he acknowledged them without feeling any joy. Maybe his father would be proud that he tried. Or maybe he would be angry that Blue Eyes had not returned immediately to warn him of the humans to the south. Probably he would be both, if he knew what Blue Eyes had done, seen, and been through. But he did not know, and never would know. When Caesar and the rest of the troop were dying from the gas the humans brought with them, what would his last thought be? Would he wonder, then, if his son had failed him?

"I think I will die soon, too," Blue Eyes told Ash.

"Are you still afraid of it?"

"A little," he admitted. "Not as much. What is it like?"

Ash wrinkled his brow and squatted back down.

"I don't know," he said. "I'm not totally dead."

"What do you mean?"

"Well—*you* aren't dead. My father isn't dead, or my mother. So I am not. I don't know if what Ray saw is true—if there is another place we go when our hearts stop beating. But I do know the place I came from, where you still are. And there, the only thing that lives on is memory. But that is a lot, I think."

"But is it real?"

"Is anger real, or pain, or joy? If any of those things are real, so am I."

"What if there is no one left who remembers you?"

Ash leapt up, stabbed his spear into the water, and came up with a fish.

"Look at that!" he said. "I told you I would catch more fish than you."

He didn't ask Ash the question again; he knew the answer. After all, it was his dream.

Ash knew they were done, as well.

"Time to wake up," Ash said. "You have things to do."

And so Blue Eyes woke, still wet, still freezing, with Rocket lying against him.

It was light, but he still couldn't see much in the dense fog that shrouded everything.

But he did see something, the vaguest of shadows in the mist.

Rocket stirred, shivered, and shook himself. Then he looked where Blue Eyes was looking. His eyebrows arched up.

"The boat," he signed. "You found it."

"Lieutenant."

John looked up from the maps he had spread on his makeshift field table, the hood of a battered old Camaro.

The lull in combat had given him time to think, and even spare a couple of scouts to explore the nearby redwoods. There they found plenty of evidence of the apes, some of it pretty recent—it appeared that a large number of them had gone back into the woods only a few days before the siege began. But it did not seem as if they were still there; rather, it looked as if they were moving away from San Francisco as quickly as they could. He had suggested to his father that it might be worth sending a detail after them. It seemed likely that the apes in the wood were mostly noncoms—females, children, the elderly. If they were under threat, the apes on the bridge might be forced to negotiate.

The Colonel had dismissed the suggestion for two reasons, one that made good sense and another that was more—philosophical in nature.

The sensible objection was that their forces were already split on to two fronts, so to speak. Sending soldiers into the woods to search for a third front which didn't appear to exist yet could strain them to the breaking point, especially if John was wrong and they found more than they bargained for.

The other reason was that the Colonel had no interest in negotiating with the apes on the bridge; he wanted to annihilate them. After that, there would always be time to hunt down those who had fled into the woods and finish them off.

John, wanting something useful to do during the lull in combat, had been trying to work out where the other kongs might be going, to minimize the effort of finding them later. He did so a bit half-heartedly. He could not quite see the apes as the monsters his father did; it seemed to him, piecing together bits from the stories of the Sanfrans, that the humans had been spoiling for a fight as much as the apes, but the apes had jumped first, from self-defense. It might have been worth the effort to at least try to talk to their leader. If nothing else, it could have been really fascinating. But that wasn't how his father wanted it, so it wasn't how things were going to be.

"What is it, Private Selig?" he asked.

"Something is happening on the bridge," Selig said. "I think you should come see, sir."

John rolled up the maps, slipped a rubber band around them and replaced them in their cardboard cylinder before following the private up to the bridge.

The sun was just starting to brighten the fog, and at first he wasn't sure what he was seeing. He took some field glasses and strained for a better look.

"They're on their horses."

"Yes, sir," Selig said.

"Get the Colonel on the line."

Reconnaissance from the *Daedalus* confirmed his sense from the end of the span; the apes were massing about a quarter of a mile way, just at the furthest edge of visibility in the fog.

"Might be a feint," he told his father. "Showing us a charge here, but really preparing something on your side."

The Colonel didn't speak for a moment, although John could hear his breath as he worked at his cigar.

"Lieutenant," he said, "you may be right. But my gut says they're going to try and come right through you. You can't let that happen; you have to hold them there. The boat from down south is literally minutes away, do you understand? If you can keep them back for just a little while, we can gas the whole lot of them while we have them in one place. If they escape into the woods, this operation could take years."

He sounded cold, colder than John had ever heard him before, and John realized something he had been refusing to acknowledge, even privately.

The Colonel would do anything to win this war. If that included sacrificing his own son and everyone on this side of the bridge, he was prepared to do it. In fact, that was probably why he had been chosen. John wasn't the highest-ranking officer or the best qualified for the position, but if casualties were high on this side, no one would complain that the Colonel was playing favorites; if he put his own son on the line, everyone else would be willing to go along.

And the gas? Was there any way of knowing where it would go once it was used? Presumably it would be launched onto the bridge in grenade form, but the slightest vagaries of the wind could bring it down on them, too.

And none of that mattered. He knew his father loved him, as difficult as it was for him to show it at times. But for his father, the mission—as *he* defined it—was more important than *anything*. When you were the son and namesake of John McCullough, that was something you had to make your peace with, and he believed he was there. His father had to know he could count on him, no matter what he asked. And by that, he would know how much John loved *him*.

But his men were another matter. If the wind shifted, if the gas came for them, he wanted to make sure they were mobile, ready to go.

He slid the headset onto his neck and began getting his people ready for the assault.

They took Kim's boat as near to the other as they could, but it sank before they reached it.

Blue Eyes thought he had been cold before, but fully submerged in the ocean, what was left of the heat in him seemed to dissipate instantly. If it weren't for the orange floats they'd put on, he knew he would have sunken beneath the waves before swimming three strokes. Even with that help, the boat was unattainably far away, though on land it would have taken only a few long strides to reach it.

It was Rocket who dragged him through the sea and found the chain by which he dragged the both of them from the water onto the deck of the vessel. Blue Eyes tried to keep quiet, but the chattering of his teeth sounded like sticks breaking to his own ears.

He could only see one human on watch, near the back of the boat, armed with a rifle. He began creeping toward him, but Rocket touched him on the shoulder and signaled that he would do it.

The man must have heard something in the last second, because he started to turn. Rocket danced around him with surprising speed, so when the fellow turned, he saw nothing. As he turned back, Rocket clubbed him with both fists. The man fell heavily to the deck, and Rocket took his weapon.

In the raised center part of the ship they found a door. Rocket went through, sniffing. When they came to a stairwell, he stopped.

"Down there," he signed. "I smell them."

They had just started down when they heard a dull thud, carried across the waves. Blue Eyes jerked his head around to look, and saw a yellow glow appear in the fog, and then another. The mist was starting to lift, and through it he now saw the outline of the great bridge—and toward the north end of it, the big ship. It was the ship's guns they had heard firing, and the explosion at the end of the bridge they were now seeing.

Suddenly, the boat's engines began to growl, and it slowly started moving, picking up speed, headed toward the other ship.

Blue Eyes wasn't sure what was happening, but he felt all the way to his core that there was no time to waste.

He went down the steps in a single jump.

And came nearly face-to-face with a human.

Before Blue Eyes could react, the man pulled a sidearm; in the enclosed space, the report was deafening. Blue Eyes blinked, realized he hadn't been hit, and then slammed into the man. The human crashed to the deck.

"Keep him down," Blue Eyes told Rocket.

When the door first opened, Ray thought he might be dreaming again. But even in his dreams he was pretty sure that Blue Eyes could not have been more bedraggled, wet, and miserable looking.

Fox sat up in his cage with an audible gasp.

Blue Eyes made the sign for quiet and approached the cage.

Ray indicated the lock, and the need for a key. Blue Eyes pulled on the cage before he understood.

"Where is the key?" he signed.

Ray gestured toward Armand, who was handcuffed to a pipe on the wall, asleep. Blue Eyes went over to the drowsing man and covered his mouth.

Armand woke with a start, but quickly seemed to understand the situation.

"There is a man in the hold," he said. "He should have a key."

Blue Eyes raced back to the other room, searched the unconscious man, and returned a moment later with a chain of jingling keys.

He took them back to Armand, who first unlocked himself and then Ray and Fox. Blue Eyes regarded the other chimp warily.

"Fox will help us," Ray said.

"Will he?" Blue Eyes asked.

"I will," Fox said. "Ray and I agreed."

Blue Eyes studied Fox for a moment.

"Come on, then," he said.

In the hold, Ray was pleasantly surprised to see Rocket, but didn't think it was the time to ask for explanations.

When they emerged on deck, Armand signed desperately for their attention.

"The gas," he said. "I heard them talking, before they chained me up. They're taking the gas to the other ship, where they have the means to launch it."

"Launch it?" Blue Eyes said.

Armand gazed up at the Golden Gate Bridge. On either end of it, they could see the occasional sparks of muzzle flashes.

"Your people are on the bridge, right?" Armand said. "The big ship has something that can throw the gas up there, spread it around in the air. It could kill all of them. Easily."

"Where is the gas?" Blue Eyes asked.

"In the aft compartment," Armand said. "But there isn't any easy way to offload it without being noticed. What we really need to do is take control of the ship." He pointed upwards.

"Show us," Blue Eyes said.

When they reached the upper deck, however, they found themselves staring down the barrels of several guns, wielded by Commander Messenger and two soldiers.

"More apes," Messenger said. "I guess I shouldn't be surprised. Ray, drop the gun to the deck. You too, whoever you are." She nodded at Rocket.

Ray looked at Blue Eyes for guidance, and realized his friend was tensing to leap at the humans.

Fox beat Blue Eyes to it. He sprang low and hard, hitting one of the soldiers at the knees, lifting him and smashing him to the deck. Ray watched the other soldier take aim at Fox. He started forward, knowing he would never make it in time.

But then Armand was there, lurching between Fox and the soldier. The gun went off, and Armand stumbled, wide-eyed.

"Huh?" he said.

Blue Eyes and Rocket hadn't been idle. In a flurry of blows, they took down Messenger and the second soldier; then Rocket and Blue Eyes charged into the cabin, to where the man driving the boat was.

Armand was still alive, but he didn't look good. His face was drained of color, and blood soaked his shirt. Fox crouched next to him, signing something Ray couldn't make out.

Armand looked up from Fox and began talking.

"Remember our deal," he said, weakly. "You aren't to kill them. There are two inflatable rafts. They have drawings on them that show what to do. Put Messenger and the soldiers in one. You take the other."

"What about you?" Ray said.

"I have something to do," Armand said. He stumbled into the pilot's cabin and got behind the wheel.

They found the life rafts; Ray leapt back in surprise and a little delight as they inflated. Sometimes the things humans made were just fantastic.

By the time the rafts were ready, the other humans were beginning to come around. Blue Eyes and Rocket disarmed them and forced them into one of the water craft at gunpoint. Once Messenger and the others were afloat, they started occupying the other raft.

Ray hung back as the others got in.

"Ray?" Blue Eyes said.

"Go on," Ray said. "Armand may not be able to do this alone."

"Ray," Blue Eyes said. "Get in the raft."

"He's dying," Ray said. "He needs my help. We can't risk the chance that he might fail."

Blue Eyes unlatched his life jacket and threw it up to Ray.

"Wear this," he said. "It will help you float."

"Thanks," Ray said. "Tell Caesar I did my best."

"You tell him," Blue Eyes said.

Ray nodded, then, as the raft started to drift away, clambered up the rungs toward the pilot's cabin, pulling the vest on as he did so.

Armand favored him with a glance as he came in.

"You should go, my friend," he said.

"The rafts are already gone," Ray said. "I'm here to stay. What are you doing?"

"The chemical agents on this boat," Armand said. "They're too dangerous. I'm taking them as far out to sea as I can. Then I'll blow a hole in the ship with a grenade or something. Sink it. Probably not good for the ocean, but sometimes you must make choices, y'know?"

Ray looked at the pool of blood accumulating on the floor.

"You're not going to make it, Armand," he said.

"I have to try," Armand said. "I can't be responsible—can't let it happen."

"Then let me help you," Ray said. "Show me how to drive the boat."

Armand took a slow breath, shaking.

"You're probably right," he said. "Come here. It isn't too difficult." He smiled. "A monkey could do it."

Ray sat behind the controls, listening intently to Armand's instructions. He began to turn the boat.

"I'm glad to have your company," Armand said.

"Are you afraid?" Ray asked.

Armand coughed. "Yes," he said. "And no. What do you know about death?"

"I've been thinking about it," Ray said. "I have had dreams."

"Would you tell me?"

Ray told him then, about the underground of trees, the stars beneath the world, seeing the shadows of his father and Ash.

When he was finished, Armand had a faint smile on his face.

"Your people deserve their chance," he said "Their time. Their ways. Without us." He looked up. "I hope you do better than we did."

He let out a long breath, wincing as he did so.

"Am I afraid, you ask," he said. "You know, as a young man—a very young man—I took an oath. I pledged myself to God. I lived in poverty and contemplation, and I thought I had it all figured out. But none of this is simple. Creation isn't simple. But there is more to all of this than we see, Ray, and it is worth paying attention to your dreams. And yes, I am scared—but I'm also excited. To find out what does lie beyond. And I'm so very honored to have your company."

Ray had the boat turned now.

"Is this good enough?" he asked.

"Yes," Armand said. "Straight out to sea."

Ray began to accelerate. He turned to ask Armand how he would know they had gone far enough, and saw that Armand's eyes had gone empty, like Ash's had been.

"Farewell, Armand," he said.

26

Caesar stared down the span as the fog began to thin, surveying the soldiers and weapons arrayed against them. The horses, restless, were having a hard time standing still.

"We stay together to the bottom," he told the other mounted apes. "Then we split left and right. The right follows me, the left, Luca. Our targets are the mounted guns. If we reach those, that will clear the way for the unmounted."

What he didn't say was that he figured more than half of them would die before reaching the guns.

He stood as tall as he could in the saddle.

"Apes! Together! Strong!" he bellowed.

Behind him, the rest of his army repeated the words. They rang out as if from a single throat, piercing the mist and echoing over the waters far below.

And they began their charge.

When Winter saw Oak approaching with Cornelia and Maple, he assumed that the two women were prisoners of the gorilla. But something seemed strange about the situation. It was only when they were much closer, just a few arm lengths away, that he realized what was bothering him.

Oak didn't have a gun.

Winter lifted his own still-unfamiliar weapon, not sure who to point it at. He settled on Cornelia, since he had been ordered to shoot her on sight.

"Winter," Cornelia said. "What are you doing?"

"I'm the wall," Winter said. "I protect the village. You have betrayed us."

"Who told you that?" Cornelia asked.

"Red," Winter said. Then he thought maybe he shouldn't have.

"Winter," Oak said. "The queen is not your betrayer. Red is. Grey is. I am."

"What do you mean?"

"Winter," Cornelia said. "Lower your weapon."

He had imagined this moment ever since he and Red had discussed the possibility. But he had not imagined it like this, with the queen coming unarmed, being so calm. He had envisioned a fight, the queen and her followers trying to kill him.

This didn't make as much sense.

"I'm supposed to shoot you," Winter said. "I'm supposed to keep you out."

Oak took a step, placing himself between Cornelia and Winter's gun. That was even more confusing—Oak was supposed to be on his side. Red said so.

"You will not shoot the queen, Winter," Oak said.

Winter backed up a pace and shook the gun at the other gorilla. "She isn't the queen, any longer," he said. "Stay back, Oak. You aren't going to confuse me."

"It's okay, Oak," Cornelia said, stepping around him. "Winter, I am not the enemy. But if you think I am, then shoot me."

"Queen—" Oak grunted.

"Stay there," Cornelia said.

Winter stared at her, trying to understand.

"Where is Luca?" he asked.

"With Caesar," Cornelia said. "With the army."

"Is he dead?"

"I don't know," Cornelia replied. "He may be. He may not be. But Red lied to you."

She took a step toward him.

"Stop!" he said.

But she kept coming. Her hands were open at her sides. Winter closed his eyes and tried to squeeze the trigger. But he couldn't.

Cornelia touched his shoulder as she went by. Maple followed her, and then Oak, who gave him a fierce look but said nothing further.

Panting, Winter sat down, placing the gun in front of him, and folded his arms over his head. He didn't know the truth, or what was really going on. All he knew was that Red had trusted him, and he had failed.

He remembered Luca saying that the enemy would always seek the weakest part of the wall to cross, and he understood why Cornelia had come through his checkpoint rather than another. She knew he was weak.

And she was right.

The camp was on a hillside just inside of the trees; beyond lay a brambled landscape of succession forest patiently swallowing up old human habitations and roads.

The women were gathered together in a cluster of trees near a stream. As they saw Cornelia approach, they began chattering among themselves, some calling out to her, others shrinking from her sight, afraid to confront her.

She saw the midwives gathered around a bed constructed just above the ground, using fallen logs as supports.

When she reached the gathering, everyone fell silent.

"Is it Rain?" Cornelia asked. "Is she having her child?"

One of the midwives, Tall, nodded.

Cornelia pushed her way through, until she could see Rain. The young chimp was panting, loudly, obviously in pain, but when she saw Cornelia, she tried to sit up.

"No, Rain," she said. "This is your time."

She crouched down next to Rain. One of the midwives offered her a veil, and she slipped it on.

A few moments later, she heard hoarse calls in the distance. Then Cedar arrived, wearing the crown of beads and strands.

"It's time to break camp," Cedar said. "Grey commands that we should begin the day's march."

"We cannot," Cornelia said. "As you can see, Rain is in labor."

Cedar blinked.

"Cornelia?" she said.

"Cedar."

"You should not be here, Cornelia," she said. "Our king has called for your death."

"Do you mean Grey?" Cornelia asked.

Cedar straightened up defiantly. "Yes," she said. "Caesar is dead. Grey is king now."

"And you are queen," Cornelia replied. "And you should know what that means. It means you go tell your husband that the women will not move until the birth is done and mother and child are ready to move."

Cedar's brow knitted.

"I need only call the guard," she said.

"Cornelia is right," someone said, aloud. Cornelia saw that it was Redbird, Cedar's mother's sister's child.

The others began to murmur assent. Cedar looked around, confused, and then vented a sharp pant-hoot.

"I am queen," she said. "I will tell him."

"And I will be here," Cornelia said. "With Rain."

Red saw Winter approaching, everything about him screaming shame and submission. He listened with growing impatience as the young gorilla explained what had happened.

"Give me your gun," Red said, when Winter was finished.

"I'm sorry," Winter said.

"And I'm disappointed," Red replied. He checked the weapon to make certain it was loaded, then slung it on his back.

"Red—" Winter began.

"No," Red snapped. "I trusted you. Go away. I have no time for you now."

Then he started toward where the women were camped.

He stopped short when he realized a birth was going on. He also saw that Grey was there, watching.

"Cornelia—" he began.

"I know," Grey said. "Cedar told me. She is with Rain. With the women."

"I will go get her," Red said.

"You won't," Grey replied. "Not during the birth. It would be breaking custom."

Red snorted. "Then I will break custom." He unlimbered his rifle and started toward the women.

The fog was thinner, and Blue Eyes strained to make out what was going on, as they rowed toward the bridge. And then he heard a distant shout—not one ape, but many.

Then the big ship suddenly began firing, the shells impacting the side of the bridge in brilliant explosions—

and now he saw them, apes on horseback charging along the span, rifles spitting yellow-orange. He watched, transfixed, feeling helpless.

Ray turned his gaze from Armand toward the open ocean. He didn't need to know how far to go, he decided—he would just keep going, until he came to the end of the world or the boat ran out of fuel. What would happen then, he did not know—but in a way, it did not matter.

Then something hit him in the back of the head, hard. His knees went funny as he tried to turn around. He was still awake, but everything was spinning. Someone grabbed him under the arms and began dragging him.

They were all the way down the ladder before he was able to struggle, and see that his attacker was Fox. The chimp was soaking wet. What had happened? He must have leapt from the raft at the last moment, and then the boat left the others behind...

"It's okay, Ray," Fox croaked. "I watched you. Listened to Armand. I know what to do."

Ray tried to spin around and hit him, but he turned in empty air, and then Fox pushed him, hard, and he fell.

Not far. The cold belly of the sea took him in.

"Fox!" he shouted. But his mouth filled with salty water.

He saw the dark shape scramble up the side of the ship, vanish, then reappear in the lighted pilot's cabin.

The vest Blue Eyes had given him buoyed him up, and he swam desperately toward the boat, but it was outpacing him at a rate he could never hope to overtake.

"Fox!" he croaked once more.

And then, the boat began to turn again. For a brief moment, he thought Fox had changed his mind, and was coming back for him.

But then he understood. Fox was no longer taking the boat out to sea; he was aiming it at the larger ship near the end of the bridge.

Already Ray's arms and legs were starting to numb, but the jacket kept him afloat, as Blue Eyes said it would. He watched, helplessly, as the boat raced toward the ship.

As the apes began their charge, John remembered his father's talk of Beowulf and Grendel, of warriors and monsters from legend, and he felt as if he was frozen in such a moment. He was watching cavalry charging at him, horses ridden by something like men but not men, emerging from the mist as if from another time, another world even. At that moment, he understood that he stood in the same sacred place as a warrior in ancient Denmark, a Spartan at Thermopylae, a soldier of Elam, watching the Sumerian army marching toward him.

Soldiers were mortal. War was not.

The first shells from the Bofors struck the bridge, and the charge stumbled, lost momentum. A few soldiers squeezed off a few panicked rounds.

"No!" John shouted. "Not yet. They aren't close enough."

But as the horse-riders regrouped and started forward once again, he knew they soon would be. And the cost of stopping them was going to be very high.

But if his father was willing to pay it, so was he.

After a moment, Ray heard a human voice. It had to be incredibly loud, amplified by some sort of human machine, for him to hear it at this distance.

"*Naglfar*, this is the USS *Daedalus*. You're coming in too hot. Take it down."

Ray wasn't sure if Fox made the boat go faster, but he certainly did not slow it down.

"*Naglfar*," the voice came, a few moments later. "Change course or prepare to be fired upon."

The boat seemed small now, far away. He pictured Fox at the wheel, Armand slumped by his side.

Smoke suddenly puffed from the big ship—once, twice. As the sound reached him, the boat with Fox on it was suddenly engulfed in flame and smoke.

But then it emerged from the cloud, fire blazing on its deck, but still running strong. It slammed into the hull of the larger ship. The sound, a moment later, was horrific.

Several of the women looked up as Red arrived. He pushed his way through the first few, until he saw Cornelia crouching next to Rain.

"Cornelia," he grunted, and gestured with the gun.

"You will wait," Cornelia signed. "When the birth is over, I will come with you."

Then she turned back to Rain.

"Cornelia!" he shouted. "Come!"

But she ignored him.

That angered him more than anything she could have said. Snarling, he cocked the weapon.

But before he could point it, Oak stepped in front of him.

"Stop, Red," the other gorilla said.

"Move," Red said. "Or I shoot."

But even as he said it, Pearl, one of the gorilla females, pushed her way through to join Oak. All of the other women stood, and moved to block his sight of Cornelia and Rain.

"Move, all of you!" he bellowed. "I will shoot you!"

One chimp pushed her way through to the front. He recognized Cedar, wearing the queen's diadem.

"Tell them to move, Cedar," he said. "You are queen now."

"I am," she said. "And I tell you, Red, move back."

Red couldn't take it anymore. He slapped Cedar with the back of his hand.

She stumbled back, yelping in agony, her hands flying to her face. He saw blood on her teeth. The other women caught her, but none of them backed off, indeed, several took a step forward.

He raised the gun.

Then someone hit him from behind.

He lost the gun as he went sprawling. Shaking his head, he came up onto all fours and found himself facing Grey, who was standing at his full height.

"Grey!" he snarled.

"I was stupid to listen to you," Grey said. "Go."

"You are stupid," Red signed. "That much is true."

Then he charged.

Red was head-and-shoulders taller than Grey, and weighed as much as two chimps. But Grey was faster. He let Red commit to the charge, then dodged to the side, boxing the gorilla in the ear and then grabbing onto his pelt and swinging up onto his back. There he wrapped both arms around the massive neck, braced his feet, and pulled. He felt Red's massive muscles ripple beneath him as he tried to hold on, and for a moment it seemed possible. The gorilla staggered forward, then turned and slammed his back— and Grey—into a tree. Grey hung on, grimly, but when Red repeated the tactic a second time, his arms loosened and he fell off.

Red turned quickly and punched down at him with both massive arms; Grey managed to roll away from the attack, dancing back from the maddened ape.

Red came at him again, a little more cautiously.

"What do you hope to gain?" Red said. "Caesar will never forgive you now. You have betrayed him twice. Our only hope is to work together."

"Look at them," Grey snapped. "Do you think they will do anything for you? For me? It's over, Red. We've lost."

"No!" Red roared.

Grey realized he'd let the gorilla get too close; Red leapt into the air, flailing down at his head with his gigantic arms. Grey did the only thing he could; ran straight into the attack, putting his shoulders beneath Red while he was off the ground, and heaving him over. Red landed heavily, and Grey scrambled onto his back again, renewing his chokehold.

Red fought to get back up, and finally managed to get to all fours. He attempted to stand and slam Grey into a tree again, but this time he was already too weak from lack of air. Grey tightened his hold further using both arms and legs.

Finally, Red collapsed. Grey held him a few more moments, until he was sure, and then released him.

He climbed, breathless, to his feet.

"No one is to harm Cornelia," he signed. "Oak, release the other gorillas."

He leaned against a tree, hurting in every joint. He had just won the fight of his life, but in his belly he knew he had lost. Red was right. When Caesar returned…

But he would not wait for that. He would gather any who might still follow him and return to Caesar—fight if the king would let him and accept what punishment Caesar gave him.

"Grey?"

He turned at Red's voice, but he wasn't fully facing him when the gun chattered and the bullets struck him. Everything seemed to go white, and he understood that he was sitting down, and tried to get up again. Then Red was right in front of him, the gun pointed straight at his face.

Red shot Grey in the face; the chimp jerked and then lay back on the forest floor. Red raised the gun and fired in the air, howling, rushing toward the women and Oak.

He pointed the gun at Oak and pulled the trigger. Nothing happened.

For about five heartbeats, no one moved. Then Cedar screamed at the top of her lungs and leapt at him. He was so surprised that at first he didn't respond. Then he lifted his arm to knock her off and found another of the women had jumped on that, and two more were prying the gun from his hands. Someone bit his ear, and he yelped, as fists beat every part of his body, and the women shouted at him. After what seemed like a long time, he scrambled free, backing away from the mob, but they followed him, throwing clods of dirt, sticks, rocks, anything they could get their hands on.

He felt all his anger wick away, all of his bravado, replaced by shame and fear. The very earth seemed to be falling out from under his feet and the sky upon his head.

With a hoarse cry of surrender, he ran into the forest. He did not stop until well after nightfall.

McCullough heard the collision at the same instant it happened, through Captain Hayes's radio. It sounded like two tractor trailers crashing together, or five thousand piles of scrap metal dropped from ten stories up.

"Hayes?" he snapped. "Hayes?"

He heard the Captain's heavy breathing.

"Jesus," Hayes said. "I don't know if we're breached. The impact—"

"Hayes," McCullough shouted over the transmitter. "Listen to me. The gas. That boat was supposed to have gas on board."

"I know, I know," Hayes said. "I can't see. Too much smoke."

For a long moment, McCullough heard only silence.

"Hayes?" he said.

"Oh, God," Hayes gasped.

And then, nothing.

McCullough continued staring at the collided ships. The smoke from the fire was slowly drifting northeast, toward the bridge. The gas was probably invisible, but would move as the smoke did. All John needed was to keep the apes there, on his end of the bridge, for another few minutes, and it would be over.

He remembered the boy, in Seattle, puzzling over his own death. He remembered the young man he'd killed escaping the Apostles, how much he had looked like John.

He remembered John, a little thing in his mother's arms.

"Sir!" Forest said, behind him.

He switched channels. "John," he said.

"Sir," his son replied. "They're hitting us with everything they've got. But I think we can stop them."

McCullough paused for an instant, watching the smoke continue to drift.

He shook his head, as if waking from a bad dream.

"Get out of there now, John," he said. "Leave the guns. Leave everything. Just get the hell out of there. There's been a gas breach, do you understand? Your whole detachment is in danger. Go."

"But, sir," John said. "The apes…"

"We'll get them later," he said. "Today isn't the day. Go."

McCullough watched the smoke creep inland, praying there would be enough time.

One moment, they were charging into a hail of bullets; apes and horses were stumbling and falling all around him. The next moment, the humans were fleeing, leaping into their vehicles or running like mad. At first Caesar thought it was his charge that had broken them, as unlikely as it seemed. But then he noticed a lot of them were gesturing out to sea.

He saw a cloud of smoke drifting toward them. Was that what they were afraid of? Was it some sort of weapon? He remembered the fire, all those years ago, but the smoke, too—many apes had died from suffocation, with no burns on them at all.

He saw no point in taking chances. The way was clear.

"Into the forest," he shouted. "No stopping, no slowing."

And in a matter of minutes, the survivors were back beneath the trees, where they belonged, leaving more than he could easily count still and lifeless behind them.

John called a halt when they were midway across the bay. From there he could see the wind had changed direction and the toxic cloud was now moving away from them, out to sea. They had wounded that wouldn't make it any further without at least minimal attention, and those who weren't injured were exhausted, so he decided to extend the stop for an hour.

He reached for the radio, and after a moment had his father on the line. Or thought he did, because at first there was only silence after the radio operator told him to hold on.

"John?" his father finally said.

"Yes sir," he said. "We're on the 580. The apes crossed into the forest." He paused. "I think most of them made it, sir. They managed to stay ahead of the gas."

"That's okay," his father said. "Do what you need to do, get back here, and we'll figure out what to do next."

"Yes, sir."

"John?"

John looked off across the water, past the bridge. He couldn't see his father, of course, but he nevertheless somehow felt they were almost face-to-face.

"Sir?"

"I'm very proud of you."

The birth was a hard one, but Rain survived, and the children were twins, both girls, a very rare and portentous thing.

When it was over, she went to Cedar, who lay curled next to Grey's body.

Cedar lifted her head, but every muscle in her body showed submission and fear.

"I am sorry," she said, pulling the crown from her head. "I am nothing."

"You are not," Cornelia said, taking her in her arms. "You are never nothing. You are one of us. Always."

"But Grey," she said. "Caesar—"

"Caesar will know of your courage, that is all. And how well Grey fought."

Cedar closed her eyes, and stroked Grey's fur. Her hands, Cornelia noticed, were bloody.

"Thank you, my queen," Cedar whispered.

EPILOGUE

Once more, Ray emerged into the dark place, climbing his way up roots that spread toward the bright stars. The shadows watched him, silently. Except for their eyes, they were faceless, but he thought he knew them. They seemed to welcome him and urge him on.

On impulse, he climbed higher than before, wondering how far the roots went, how deep—or how high—they dug. And as he climbed, he noticed something odd.

His fur fell off first, and then his skin, and finally his muscles and organs, until he was just a skeleton, reaching one white-boned arm in front of another. It didn't hurt, and he wasn't afraid. In fact, almost the only thing he did feel was curiosity.

Higher he went, as the roots thinned to tendrils and then wisps of thread, but he no longer weighed anything, and above the lights of the stars grew ever brighter.

But he began to see something else was there, as well, something dark that blotted out the stars, and finally he did know fear. And he was cold; a wind was blowing, first this way, then that, causing the roots to sway back and forth. He began to get a little dizzy. He remembered the monster in his dream of the sea, for it seemed it was coming for him.

But then, on the wind, he thought he heard a voice, a human voice. He couldn't understand what it was saying, but it comforted him, especially when it began singing a long, slow melody. He began trying to hum along with it, and although his voice could not find the melody exactly, he realized that he had found, at last, a strange and beautiful harmony to accompany the song.

And as he sang, he began to grow heavy, so that the fine hairs of the roots no longer supported him; they bent with his weight, and he began to fall, grasping for handholds, but unable to find them. As he fell, he saw his organs and muscles coming back, and then his skin, his fur, and then he struck something cold, and wet.

Ray woke on a beach, so cold he almost couldn't move. Shivering, he uncurled and crawled away from the water, into the edge of a forest.

At first he thought he was still dreaming; but then he saw the burning boats, and the bridge in the distance. It was night, and he was on the northern shore of the bridge.

In the moonlight, he managed to pick his way through the woods until he found one of the old human roads.

The next morning, he found signs of apes passing, many of them, some on horseback, others on foot.

For three days, he followed, brachiating through the trees when he could, walking when he had to until, just at the edge of night, he smelled smoke, and heard apes.

He paused on the trunk of a redwood, watching them around the fire. He saw Caesar, and Cornelia, Maurice, Blue Eyes and Rocket. Rain had not one baby, but two. All together, around the fire, without a village, without drums, without anything they had built. He could see Blue Eyes and Rocket telling the story of the journey, the little ones watching with wide eyes, and Caesar, more serious, cautioning that it wasn't over, that hard times lay ahead, but that they could face it together.

Together. Strong.

And as he began to go down to them, Ray realized something.

He didn't belong there. Not yet. Blue Eyes and Rocket had finished their journey, but he had not finished his.

Something Armand had said stuck with him. About solitude and meditation, about wisdom.

And there was something else Armand had taught him. Humans had been killing each other for millennia, getting better at it with each passing year, it seemed. And now apes had started down that road, as well. Armand had begged him to find another way, a path for apes to follow that humans had never found.

For the moment, Caesar and the rest were at peace. But for how long? If he rejoined them, he would have to fight—and possibly kill. He knew now that he could not do that, could never take another ape or human life. Their path was not his, at least not at the moment. He felt there was something he might discover, something that might benefit all apes. But he would only find it alone.

So after a little while, he turned from the fire, from his friends and family and everything he had ever known, and went to find it.

McCullough finished his pushups and then went to the window, wiping sweat from his face. He picked up the stub of his cigar, slipped it into the corner of his mouth and stared out over the godforsaken city that stretched before him. He remembered his conversation with John—it seemed a very long time ago—when the boy had asked him if he still felt like Beowulf. He had answered that he felt more like Agamemnon. It was supposed to have been a joke.

What few people seemed to understand about the *Iliad*, about the Trojan War, was that when the poem opened, Agamemnon and Achilles had been on the beach before Troy for almost ten years. Ten years of war, far from home and family. It wasn't a story about young men in brief but glorious combat, but about old men growing older and harder, staring at the same sand, buildings, sky. Waiting. Fighting. Waiting some more.

He was very goddamn tired of waiting. He hadn't been in Seattle for ten years, but it was long enough, months too long. He should have been able to finish this in days.

He holstered his gun and went over to the radio cabin. Forest was long gone, evacuated to Seattle when an infection in her leg became too much for his people to deal with. Gomez was there, but left when McCullough ordered him out.

He sat there, looking at the machine, trying to order his thoughts, trying to figure out how he could say it differently this time. Make them understand.

But then, he came to a sort of understanding of his own.

He took his pistol out and shot the radio, three times. Then he left, as a wide-eyed Gomez watched him go.

Back in his office, a few hours later, a tap came at the door, and Corporal Stringer came in when he gave permission.

"Sir," Stringer said. "We've got someone here who wants to speak to you."

"Oh, yeah?" he said. "And who might that be?"

"An ape sympathizer, sir. He says he wants to help you make peace with them."

"He does, does he? And where has he been for the past few months?"

"Down south, I guess," Stringer said. "Apparently, he left about the time we got here."

"But he's come back," McCullough said. "To help us out."

"I guess so, sir," Stringer said.

"Well," McCullough said, laying his sidearm on his desk. "Show the man in."

ACKNOWLEDGEMENTS

Thanks to Cat Camacho for editing and Steve Saffel for suggesting this project. Appreciations to Steve Gove for copy-editing, Cameron Cornelius and Ali Scrivens for design. Thanks to Nicole Spiegel and Carol Roeder at Fox. Finally, thanks once again to Rick Jaffa, Amanda Silver, Matt Reeves, Mark Bomback and all the way back the beginning—Pierre Boulle, Franklin J. Schaffner, Michael Wilson, Rod Serling, Arthur P. Jacobs and everyone else who brought us to this point in this storied franchise.

ABOUT THE AUTHOR

New York Times bestselling author **John Gregory Keyes** was born in 1963, in Meridian, Mississippi. When he was seven, his family spent a year living in Many Farms, Arizona, on the Navajo Reservation, where many of the ideas and interests which led Greg to become a writer and informed his work were formed. His first published novel was *The Waterborn*, which was followed by a string of licensed books, including *Dawn of the Planet of the Apes: Firestorm, Interstellar: The Official Movie Novelization, Independence Day: Crucible,* the *Star Wars: New Jedi Order* novels *Edge of Victory I: Conquest, Edge of Victory II: Rebirth,* and *The Final Prophecy,* as well as tie-ins to the popular *Elder Scrolls* video game franchise. His original novels include *The Blackgod* and *The Age of Unreason* tetralogy. He has a BA and Masters in Anthropology and lives in Savannah, Georgia with his wife, Nell, and two children, Archer and Nellah. He enjoys writing, cooking, fencing, and raising his children.